Catching Toads

To Jayden
Enjoy!

Susan B

Catching Toads

by

Susan Brown

Yellow Farmhouse Publications

Catching Toads
ISBN Print Edition: 978-1-950402-07-6

Yellow Farmhouse Publications, Lake Stevens, WA, USA
Copyright © 2022
Publication Date: October 1, 2022
www.susanbrownwrites.com

Excerpt from *Twelve*
ISBN Print Edition: 978-1-950402-02-1
Copyright © Susan Brown 2021

Excerpt from *Not Yet Summer*
ISBN Print Edition: 978-1544984223
ISBN eBook Edition: 978-1544984227
Copyright © Susan Brown 1980 and 2017

Cover and Interior Design: Heather McIntyre
Cover&Layout, www.coverandlayout.com

Cover Photography: Beach © Helen Filatova; Boy © Simone Van Den Berg; Girl © Irina Bg

This book is dedicated both to the memories that make us who we are, and to my family before, during, and after. I am grateful for all your love and encouragement.

Books by Susan Brown
www.susanbrownwrites.com

Fantasy:

Twelve

The Nightmare and the Unicorn

Dragons of Earth, Sea, Fire, and Air series:

>Dragons of Frost and Fire
>
>Dragons of Desert and Dust
>
>Dragons of Wind and Waves
>
>A Thunder of Dragons
>
>* New! Boxed Set includes *Dragons of Frost and Fire, Dragons of Desert and Dust, Dragons of Wind and Waves, A Thunder of Dragons* – Find it on Amazon!

3 Witches series, **written with Linda Jordan and Susan Old**

>Witch Magic: *Blight of Blood*
>
>Witch Fire: *Wicked Winds*
>
>Witch Tree: *Poison Plum*
>
>Witch Stone: *Celtic Crossed*
>
>Witch Blood: *Blood's Birth*

The Adventure Books:

Hey, Chicken Man!

Pirates, Prowlers, and Cherry Pie

Sammy and the Devil Dog

Not Yet Summer

The Amber and Elliot Mysteries **with Anne Stephenson:**
Something's Fishy at Ash Lake
The Mad Hacker
The Secret of Ash Manor

Written with Anne Stephenson as Stephanie Browning:
Outbid by the Star
Undone by the Boss
Making Up is Hard to Do
The Boy She Left Behind, *An All American Boy Romance*

Short Story Collections:
Holiday Cheers: *Stories to Celebrate Your Year*
Romance in Pajama Pants: *Stories to Celebrate Your Happily Ever After*
Romance Sweet and Dark: *The Patchwork of Love*
Last Dance at the Polka Dot Restaurant: *And Other Travels Through Life*
Fantasy Shorts: *Stories to Tickle Your Wonder*

Catching Toads

Contents

Chapter 1

I let the screen door slam, hoping it would make my mother jump and hit a wrong key as she typed her story. But the rhythmic *clickety-click* of the typewriter never faltered. I wanted to slam the door again to get a reaction – any reaction – from my mother, but gave up. The freedom of the beach called me.

The brown-painted boards of the verandah were cold under my bare feet, and here and there puddles from the previous night's rain reflected little pieces of the sky. Everything was cold and wet and bleak, yet it was more inviting than the overheated summer house. Inside, with staccato talk radio murmuring behind her, my mother crouched over a new electric typewriter, cigarette burning unheeded beside her, trying to make something out of herself.

I despised her efforts. She had no right to drag me along in her quest for independence.

But Long Point Beach had always felt more like home to me than the city houses my parents had moved through during the upward campaign of my father's career. Those houses were a series of *Better Homes and Gardens* backdrops where, in my allotted bedrooms, I scribbled stories and sketched pictures in lieu of playing with the friends I always had to move away from. A dull, mildly lonely time without definition.

At the summer house, though, my memories crystallized into polaroid snapshots and tingling impressions. I'd spent every summer I could remember racing through drifts of white sand under a cobalt blue sky. Hot winds licked around my browned skin and tousled my flying hair. Shrieks of laughter, smells of coco butter lotion, and tastes of smoky juice from bonfire-roasted hot dogs seasoned my life. And I had friends who waited for me year after year when I emerged from the dull chrysalis of the winter months.

And here I was again, but not in summer. I looked this way and that through the trees that clustered around the long row of cottages.

Silent.

Empty.

All wrong.

Sand oozed grit between my toes as I stood undecided. The breeze carried the same indefinable water and green smells as other years, and overhead birds arrowed between the trees in nesting frenzies. It was so different. I waited for something, *anything* to feel normal.

The shudder in my world began at Easter when I came home from boarding school to the newest Toronto house. It was like a scene from an old Saturday afternoon movie. My father crossed his arms and stared out the bay window in statuesque outrage. My mother hovered beside the grand piano and nervously rubbed her finger along its graceful edge. She was like the piano – beautiful, satin finished, expecting someone to play on her.

"I don't believe it," I accused them.

"Believe it, Dream Girl," my father said. "The papers were signed yesterday. Your mother, my dear Sandy, says she wants her own life. It's all the fashion, I believe."

"Bryce!" my mother cried. Her voice was no longer musical or modulated. "No more! Don't you dare!"

Once again they began to overwhelm me, to melt my cocoon of emotional fog. I didn't know what I should say or do, or even what I should feel.

"No!" I shouted. "You can't do this to me!"

They stared at me. My father shrugged. As I ran crying from the room, my mother slammed shut the piano cover. The chords jangled through and through the house, out of tune.

For the rest of the long weekend, I begged and pleaded, stormed and sulked, but the divorce papers were signed. My family was dissolved. Everything had been decided and divided. My father got the city house with the attic studio, the new furniture, and the grand piano he didn't know how to play. My mother got the car, the summer house, all the old furniture it contained, and me.

Three days later she carried me off to the summer house, the few possessions she considered her own crammed into boxes and bags and suitcases, filling the trunk, towering in the back seat, overflowing onto me. I sat silently, watching the muddy tobacco fields stringing endlessly in front, beside, and behind as we sped past. I hated the way they looked so empty and forgotten.

"This is it at last, Sandy," my mother exclaimed suddenly. "The day we begin our new life."

"I don't want to live with you," I said.

"What did you say?"

"I don't want to live with you!" I shouted. "You did this! I want to stay with Daddy. It's your fault! You can't take me away. I won't live with you!"

"My fault," she repeated. "Of course."

I waited, needing more words from her, but she offered me none. And now, how I hated her. My father would never have turned silently from me.

"I won't give in," I told her at last as I stepped out of the car into the cold, wet sand by the beach house.

She looked across the hood of the car at me, still and challenging.

And so we began.

*   *   *

I had never been at the summer house in spring before, and despite myself and my rage, I liked it. The whole beloved landscape turned into a quilt that I could pull over my soul. There was a sense of comfort in the isolation, a sensation of being the only one alive. As I walked, my toes crumbled the crust of damp sand. Except for the gravel road into the cottages and the highway that skirted them, there was sand as far as I could walk or see – fine white sand that blew fiercely in autumn and spring storms and shimmered white-hot under summer sun.

As long as I could remember, we had spent every summer in our house on Long Point.

Most of the cottages were rough, unheated places without hot water or appliances. But my father had insisted on a show place of sorts. Year by year, our cottage had been transformed into a house – brown shingled, two stories high, with hot water, a stove, refrigerator, washer and drier inside, and, facing the water, a verandah with expensive redwood furniture. There was even a cinder-block garage with a guest house overtop that Dad had built when my older sister, Joanie, had gotten married six years before. She and her husband had moved to a different city and never used it.

Like all the other cottages, our summer house faced the beach, skirted and backed by pine and poplar trees and some fairly thick undergrowth, sheered off suddenly by the back road. On the far side of the road, the undergrowth straggled under pines so tall and dense it was like a woods closing around a second row of cottages. Those cottages were mostly rented by the week or month rather than occupied by the same people every year. We didn't think much of the people in the second row; none of the regular summer folks bothered with them.

As I rambled, dreaming about the summers I had played here as a child, the sun sailed free from the clouds, sprinkling through the boughs of the trees and down over the sand and undergrowth. A smile struggled up and at last escaped across my face. I lifted my skinny arms to the sun and, once again, I was my Daddy's Dream Girl.

How had he caught me so on his canvas as I lay dreaming in the sun? The snake grass and small plants waved about me and the sunlight glinted and shimmered over the little dune where I sprawled. That painting had been the first that really caught the eyes of the critics in New York. There had been many others in the nine years since then, but the painting of his Dream Girl had been the first.

When the art journals and then the popular magazines joined the growing pilgrimage to our house, I was always included in at least one of the photos. I was the Dream Girl.

My vicarious celebrity had disappeared by the time I was nine and *Bryce Welsham, Artistic Genius*, was the subject of a photo shoot from *Life* magazine. The photographer and the journalist came daily; I hung around, eager to be noticed by the strangers – by my busy father. Cameras, umbrella lights, intense young photography assistants with pounds of black equipment slung around their necks, filled the studio and select sections of the house. But the photographer was not interested in me – I was too old. My face and form had lost the fawnlike innocence of the Dream Girl. I, however, didn't see how they could feature my father without me.

"I'm the Dream Girl," I told the photographer.

He brushed past me to pose my father amid finished and unfinished canvases. I stared at the dust motes that floated in their own bright world of sunbeams streaming through the arched windows. I held out my hands to catch them, but they seemed to drift through my fingers as if I were a ghost.

"I am the Dream Girl," I whispered.

An assistant grunted at me as he frantically loaded cameras.

"I...am...the...*Dream...Girl!*" I grabbed film casings in each fist, whirled and ran, screaming and streaming raw film behind me. I bumped into tables, knocked aside equipment, and spewed paintbrush missiles and turpentine waves. My father roared. The photographer yelled. The stretched canvases clattered to the ground. I raced in weaving circles through the attic, shrieking destruction. My mother scurried from below stairs and swept me away to my room.

Shaking, she grabbed my arms and tried to pull me close to her. I smelled her sweat and perfume. "Sandy, how could you?"

I twisted away from her and flung myself backward onto the bed. "*I* am the Dream Girl," I panted. "I have to be there! Why won't they let me be in the photos?"

My mother's mouth straightened into a tight line and she left the room. The shadows shifted. I huddled on my bed, sick with despair over what I had done. Distantly, I heard my mother and father, their voices unusually hard and sharp, adding to my fear. But finally their words stopped and still no footsteps came to my door. I edged my way back into the heart of the house. From the second floor landing, I could just see my mother sitting by the living room window, drinking coffee. Above me, my father's footsteps moved across his studio floor.

The strangers were gone. I was not surprised. They had exploded into the house like angry genies thunderbolted from Aladdin's lamp and then disappeared in silent smoke. It was all part of the enchanted world my father inhabited. He was the wizard whose powers pulled people into the magic or shut them out.

I inched my way up to my father's studio. He stood before a half-finished canvas, brushes held at the ready in his splayed hand as he studied his work.

"Daddy?" I whispered.

He turned his head. I ran to him and wrapped my arms around his middle, sobbing into his old shirt. My nose filled with the sweet acridity of linseed oil, turpentine and beneath it all, my father. Above me, I felt his arms move and heard the soft rasp of a brush swept quickly over canvas. I turned my head to look at the painting; one of his forearms rested lightly on my head. He painted and I held onto him. We stayed that way until my mother called us away to dinner.

At the end of that summer I was sent to the boarding school. East Lakes Academy is a beautiful place, nestled by a small lake, rich and savory with old traditions and old trees. At the welcoming, settling-in day, my father was in his glory; my mother was silent. I was bewildered, not understanding the careful questions, answers and explanations. I whimpered like a much younger child, not caring that other indifferent kids and parents saw me.

"Sandy, Dream Girl," Daddy whispered into my straw-colored hair, "you'll be home in six weeks, for Thanksgiving."

"But I want to go home now."

"You know your mother can't stand the noise," he murmured regretfully. "And she...

we both...want you to have the very best education. You know that now I'm doing so well, you deserve to go to a school like this, with all the other kids of successful men."

And so I stayed at the boarding school. For almost five months I wrote only to my father, bitterly hoping that my mother would relent because of it and let me come home. She looked glad to see me, and sad when I left again, but I always left. I could not forgive her for sending me away, even after I learned to love my school.

But there were always the summers! The sun would be hot and every day the sand danced with fairies or hid glorious adventures. There were five of us who played together – Donny, somehow the leader even though he wasn't the oldest; Pam, sneaky and wild for any kind of adventure; Jack and Joey, whom Dad called the crazy Cilento twins; and me, the youngest, the trail-along-behinder, full of dreams and fancies and longings.

Donny and Pam were summer kids like me, but Jack and Joey lived at the back of the tumble-down general store and snack bar, just down the road where it curved sharply and joined the highway. They were a year and a half older than me – almost seventeen this summer.

Wistfully I thought it would be nice to see somebody I knew. But I wasn't sure. Things had been different last year. Uneasily, I remembered the last time I had seen the twins – Donny had been holding court at the snack bar. He was fifteen then and good looking, hot and fleshy, enjoying the way Pam, her sister Alison, and a pair of the second row cottage girls clustered around him. Jack was working behind the counter and Joey was laboriously stocking shelves. He has cerebral palsy. Sometimes his hands would fumble or jerk, and the cans he was stacking would crash to the floor.

There was a particularly loud crash. Donny stood up with a great show and strutted over to where Joey was carefully picking up four or five cans.

"*Heuh*," Donny shouted with a rotten imitation of a southern accent. "Heuh, now boy. *Yo stop thet racket.*"

The girls giggled. Donny grinned.

Joey blushed furiously; his pale long-chinned face still and hard as he stared a moment at Donny. Then carefully, he went back to picking up the cans. But he was nervous and his arms began jerking even more. Three more cans rolled across the shelf and one after another banged onto the worn linoleum floor.

Donny and the girls laughed uproariously. Immediately, Donny went into an exaggerated pantomime of jerks and stutters such as plagued Joey. Stupidly I giggled too, wishing I knew how to stop Donny, and that if I did, somehow I would.

Joey's head hung down a little as he stared at the floor. I could feel my own shoulders tightening and twitching as Joey strained to make his lanky body obey him. Another shudder shook him, this time causing his head to jerk strangely on his neck, just as you'd imagine a mad dog would twitch. I cringed inwardly, a silly grin still pasted on my face, wishing I could hide myself from that obscene twitching.

His chin lifted suddenly. A look of misery and desperate appeal shot to his brother. Jack tossed aside the cloth he was using to wipe the counter and strode over to Joey, roughly elbowing Donny out of his way. For a moment his arm dropped around his brother's shoulders, his dark head near Joey's blonde one, then together they stooped and picked up the cans.

"*Hey boy!*" Donny gave Jack's behind a push with his foot. "*Who you shovin'? Why yore nothin' but pore white trash!*"

As Jack spun around, hands clenched, Donny sprinted out the screen door, letting it bang loudly. The rest of us rushed out after Donny, mostly giggling.

"*Pore white trash! Pore white trash!*" Pam shouted through the screen. Her sister Alison took up the cry, then the second row cottage girls, and soon all five of them were chanting their mindless litany. I stood a little aside, staring down at the shimmering gravel and drooping weeds, telling myself fiercely that there was no reason to cry, that it was really just a joke.

I didn't cry. As I shuffled through the oiled dust of the side road, I imagined about it until it was no more real to me than the stories I told myself every day. Once again, I was my Daddy's Dream Girl.

*   *   *

The mid-morning sun was stronger now and the clouds that scudded across the sky were swirling white and fluffy rather than banked-up grey. I began wandering around the boarded-up cottages of our neighbors, idly circling them so that I could return and walk in my own footsteps. A child's game I had often played – pretending that I was being chased or spied upon and that this artful maneuver would confound my enemies. But soon the sun began drying the crusted sand, and my footsteps melted into the patterns of tiny dunes on the midday beach.

Resentfully, I reviewed my boredom. I was fifteen and too old to play at the games I'd loved a few years ago, or even last year. There was no one around – wouldn't be for five or six weeks. At best a few people would poke about on the long weekend for the annual ritual of "opening up the cottage." My mother was out of her mind in bringing me here to live – poor white trash now, like the twins. She had told me on the first night in the summer house that she had withdrawn me from East Lakes.

"I can't afford it," she told me calmly. "I've lived off and for your father for years and it nearly killed me. I'm not taking any alimony or child support from him. We're going to make this life on our own, Sandy. I'm going to write again." She tried to smile at me, but I wouldn't have it now.

"You can't just take my life!" I rasped out. She was choking me with her anger and her dreams. "I don't care about your life. I'm going back to Daddy and I'm going back to East Lakes!"

"No, I'm afraid not." My mother stubbed out her cigarette. "East Lakes is no longer good for you, and unfortunately, neither is your father. The regional high school is fairly good. This is going to be our new life together."

"No!" I shouted. "I'm not going to that... that crap high school. This may be your life, but it isn't mine! I'm not staying here with you." All the anger and scorn I'd ever felt for her laced through my words. She stepped back from me, her eyes nearly black and closed off again. I slammed into my room.

The next morning a package was delivered to me from my father. I crouched on the sagging sofa, cradling it unopened in my arms until my mother came in.

"Who was at the door, Sandy?" she asked. "Oh, I see. From your father." She stiffened a little. We both knew the package was a painting. One of his. A gift of himself to me. Under her gaze I began to pull away the wrappings. A note fell out.

To my Dream Girl – so she won't forget her old man.

"Oh Daddy...oh Daddy..." I chanted under my breath. It was the painting that mattered: *Dream Girl Catching Toads.*

He had painted it during the winter I was ten. It had hung in a New York gallery for a long time, but despite his growing reputation, no one would ever pay the amount he was asking for it. Daddy had said it was one of his best works.

It was the only other painting he had done of his Dream Girl. He had used me occasionally as a model, but in these sessions he was creating a mood or a tone of his own devising. He was not painting me – only a girl my age. This painting made me real again.

The painting, *Dream Girl Catching Toads*, had been loosely created from a snapshot my sister Joanie had taken one summer. I had been carefully peering under a wild grape vine for a big toad that had just escaped me. While I tried to stalk him, he scooted around my legs, later to hop to safety under the porch. My mother had watched all of this, squatting on the sand a few feet away, laughing at the toad's daring escape.

My father looked at the snapshot and created art with it. The sun glinted hazily over the sand, and the impressionistic form of me, the Dream Girl, caught all the intensity and expectation I felt. Even the toad was beautifully done, although he was much uglier than I thought Daddy should have made him. He had always been repelled by my toads. But still, it was my favorite of his paintings. Even the critics said it was a masterpiece. My father had changed the original picture slightly – it was the only self-portrait he ever did. He painted himself in my mother's place.

I pulled back the wrappings and triumphantly displayed the painting to my mother.

"Damn him!" she hissed. "It would be that one – that lying picture."

I smiled a slit-eyed smile as she walked out the door and down onto the beach. In lingering triumph, I found a hammer and nails and carefully hung the painting on the blank wall facing my bed. Every morning when I woke up, and every night when I went to sleep, the first and last sight I would have would be of Daddy and his Dream Girl.

*   *   *

I had the painting, but three weeks had passed, marked only by cold anger between my mother and me. I continued obstinate and refused to go to the regional high school. And so here I was, prowling around on the lonely beach while my mother single-mindedly attacked her typewriter.

A toad suddenly hopped out from under a vine, desperately scrambling for refuge. I pounced, catching it on its first hop. Sitting on a cottage stoop out of the damp sand, I slowly opened my hands.

"Hey, little toad," I whispered, turning its body so that I could look straight into its face. It was a big toad, but old man thin from its winter hibernation. It gave a frantic shove with its legs, almost dislodging itself from my hands. When I held it still, it fell back on its best defense. It peed all over my hands.

"Oh *God*," I muttered in disgust. How could I have forgotten that a scared toad always wets all over you? After all, I was a toad catcher from way back. We all were. In the velvet dusk the toads came out from their hiding places by the thousands. Big ones as large as your hands, tiny ones no bigger than your thumbnail. They leapt like scraggy shadows between the vines, across the beach, around the cottages. And we caught them. Hollering in triumph, dancing in desperate maneuvers to avoid stepping on them. Our cache was always an old rowboat that had bottomed out and lay adrift in the sand. The sides were high enough to keep the creatures contained. One by one we'd drop them in, tallying our prowess.

One night, the hunt went on and on – past the supper cleanups, into the near dark. The assorted parents drifted out onto the patio, drinks in hand. Talking, laughing, mostly ignoring us. That night we caught a hundred and six before the adults noticed us and ordered us to bed.

They did not appreciate our joy in the hunt.

"*Come on, kids,*" a deep voice would call out. "*Time for bed.*"

"We're almost done!"

A lull of a few minutes before another adult voice, indistinguishable through drink and dark, repeated the order. "*It's late. Bedtime, now.*"

No response from us.

"*Did you hear me?*"

When we identified Donny's dad, we sullenly muttered and slowly started the final count. My Dad heaved himself out of his chair and strolled down to the boat, drink in one hand, cigar tip glowing in the other. Then the count would speed up as Pam and Donny reported enthusiastically about the hunt. Jack and Joey faded back a little.

My father emitted an amused grunt and watched while we released and counted. It looked Biblical (we had to go to Sunday School at East Lakes) as the toads raced away across the sand – a plague of frogs.

"They weren't playing with those slimy things again, were they," Pam and Alison's mother said peevishly, and, "Don't come near me until you've had a shower!" As Alison leaned over to hug her good night.

"Look, Mom!" Pam held out a big one. Shrieks. Spilled drinks. Scolding and sulks. We were all sent away to our beds, tired, resentful, but giggling a little anyway at the adult upset.

I never have been able to understand why most people think toads are ugly. Do they ever really look, I wonder. Do they see how my toad is so solid and earthy? Have they gazed at the liquid black and gold eyes, clay patterned knobs and stripes, cushioned with a creamy soft underbelly that can sometimes shimmer like a rainbow?

I remembered Jack talking about it once, his gravely voice almost without emotion. But as he spoke, his eyes looked sharp and liquidy like the toad he gently held.

"You know, Sandy, the poor little thing isn't ugly. People just don't bother with looking or feeling. Someone says, *'That's great!'* or *'That's horrible!'* and everyone else just agrees and never wonders how come, or even who thought so in the first place."

His square face became jaw-hard as he watched Joey trying to flush out more toads.

"I'll tell you what's ugly – the only ugly things are in people."

Joey jerked obscenely and I understood what Jack meant. It must be awful to have a half-crazy father and a practically deformed twin brother. That's what Pam and Donny said. It's what everybody said.

Except me. I just drifted into my imagination. That's what I liked about my dreaming – everything was shining and perfect the way it should be.

Not the way it was now. Not when my family had disappeared like a dune in the winter storms.

I put the toad I had caught down and watched him scramble desperately to a space where the porch met the sand. He scrabbled with his front paws and was almost underneath before I caught him again.

"I'm doing you a favor," I told him as he peed on me again. Not much this time but it made me feel queer inside. Funny how you change – I had never used to care.

"There!" I placed him under the leaves at the edge of the undergrowth. "There's nothing to eat under a porch. You need some meat on your bones," I joked. He didn't even smile.

Joey had taught me about the toads, even though his cerebral palsy had been worse when we were little, and it was harder for him to talk. Jack could always interpret Joey's words if I needed it, but somehow then, I rarely did.

Even on days when Jack was trying to run the store after their father had gone off, Joey would help me act out my fantasies. We were Arabs hiding in the dunes, pirates burying treasure and then holding us for ransom, or even a band of children shipwrecked on an island. If the others didn't want to play, we took all the parts ourselves. We lived the adventures. Sometimes Joey's shaking was because he'd been given poison by the enemies (he could die for hours) or had been tortured or badly wounded. We were both fierce, brave, and strong.

In the evening, it was another adventure. Most nights if you were seen by an adult, you had to let the toad go. I don't know why, but that was the rule we played by. Joey knew all about toads – all the book things about what they ate and where they laid their eggs, and all the important things about where a toad would hide and how to hold him so he wasn't hurt, and how deep a hole had to be dug to keep him from jumping out.

Jack and Joey hunted for toads as a team, and I tagged along. Joey wouldn't catch one himself because he was afraid he might jerk and squeeze it too hard. Once Donny did it as a joke. The poor toad croaked and then some of its insides squished out its wide mouth. It died on the sand after a couple of jerks like the kind Joey made.

Donny grinned and yelled, "Yuck!"

I just stood there, feeling sick and hurt and ashamed, and wishing someone would hurt Donny. I guess Joey felt the same way because he tried to punch him. He missed, of course, and so Jack had to do it for him.

Chapter 2

The cold, silky dust slid between my toes as I began walking down the road toward the highway, my footsteps in a carefully even line. People would stop and wonder how I did it.

I liked that road. Even in the height of summer season, there were never many people on it – a couple of cars might pass you, or maybe one or two people. I pretended the kids weren't there, but adults had to be smiled at and offered a "Good morning" or "Afternoon," toned in a way that resembled a good business handshake. Pleasant. Noncommittal. And you were alone again between the tall pines and poplars. If you were a nosy like me, you could look between the trees and watch other cottage people as you passed, consider flapping laundry, or listen to snapping voices that were quarreling.

I always hurried past the quarreling voices, my stomach churning, hating them all for their anger. So much like our summer home. Quarrel after quarrel, no purpose, no beginning, not even an end.

"God I wonder how I could ever have saddled myself with a female – note I don't say woman – as stupid and insensitive as you!" my father would rage. "I am trying to paint Andrea! To create!"

"I'm sorry, Bryce," my mother would whisper in the kind of "poor me" voice that made me want to scream.

"Sorry," Daddy would repeat, "Yes, you're always sorry. 'Sorry, Bryce...sorry dear...I'm so sorry!' But still you disturb me, interrupt me, badger my Dream Girl when she should be playing in the sun!"

"But Bryce..." my mother would begin more strongly.

"Enough!" He held up his hand. "I suppose you can't help yourself. So we'll just forget about it – again – and I'll try to get back to work."

No wonder they got a divorce. Yet what puzzled me then was why it was my mother who started proceedings, for how my father could have shared his house and nights with her, year after year, was more than I could understand.

And then there were my fears that I could barely think – fears that the vicious quarreling was because of me, that I was at fault somehow. So many of their fights ended up or started with me that I learned to play them against each other. Who loved me really? Dad said this; Mom said that. And at last there was The Girl. So obtuse, I thought Daddy had spent too much time with one of his freshman students. I was enraged beyond reason. Relief – it was a woman. I relished my mother's cold agony while I felt sick at her betrayal. I hated him. She deserved it. I knew my Daddy could never betray me.

Each season I returned to the boarding school, glad to escape the rounds of quarreling, yet bitterly lonesome for something I could never explain. Sometimes I could almost grasp it here on the beach while I chased the night toads with the twins. But even after all the summers of it being so close, I could never quite name it, never quite hold onto it.

*   *   *

I hesitated now when I reached the curve in the road, half hoping for and half dreading a meeting with the twins. I knew I'd run into them sooner or later, but now that I could see the tumble-down store ahead of me, the echoes of *"Pore white trash!"* had returned as clearly as if it had just happened.

The store was even more dilapidated than I remembered, paint half-gone and the roof tiles uneven from the winter storms beating on them. How could the twins stand living in that dump? Even the red pick-up carelessly parked beside the building looked worn and beaten.

I wandered along the road, wincing as my winter-softened feet picked their way across the gravel. Where the road joined the paved highway, it was always well-graveled for perhaps twenty yards before it reverted to soft, red-brown dust. Ahead, across the highway stood the general store. Beside it, on my right, but separated by an empty field of scrub, squatted the local church. I don't recall what denomination it was, only how prim, clean and empty it always looked. On my right sat the scrupulously neat, white, cottage-style gift shop and post office, open only during the summer. Rough boards still covered the windows and door, so even the Creytons, the old couple who ran it, had not yet returned. They were always among the first to arrive every summer. All in one weekend, a crew of straggly young men hired in Simcoe would take the boards off the gift shop and the wide inverted V of their cottage, five down from ours. Everything would be cleaned and aired in a scolding, twittering bustle of activity, and then Monday morning at nine sharp, the post office and gift shop would open for the summer.

I didn't like the Creytons. They were sarcastic and impartially distrustful of most people – children in particular. But they had lovely things in their tiny shop, things I would gaze at daily, not trusting myself to touch them. Every year, a day of so before we left our summer home, I would buy one of the small china figures or some souvenir that I had learned to love particularly. Even Mrs. Creyton's cold distrust could not mar the magic moment of the final Choosing. Each of these treasures I kept with me, and when I gazed at and handled them, I could clearly remember the events of the summers they represented.

My father called them trash, and in bad taste, but my mother would carefully wrap them all so that none would break or chip, no matter how heedless I was when I returned again to school.

*   *   *

"Sa-andy!" The word caught and twisted slightly in the middle.

I turned quickly, pulled away from my dreams and wonderings.

"Joey!" A smile slid upwards and across me. He grinned cheerfully, his pale, long face the same but a year different. He grabbed my arm, pulling me across the highway toward the general store.

"Had lunch? Hot...hot dog on us!" he demanded, all warm and joyful, in the way I had almost forgotten was so special to him.

"Jack!" he shouted, and I noticed his voice was man-deep, without the trembling waver of the summer before.

"Yeah?" Jack answered from the dim places behind the screen door.

"Look, Jack! I...I...It's Sandy!" Joey's words caught and twisted as they always had. But he was excited so maybe it really was better.

"Hi, Sandy," Jack said pushing open the screen door. The gesture was welcoming, but somehow the voice was not. I hesitated, suddenly feeling as though I was seeing Joey and Jack for the first time. Whereas everything about Joey, from his long face, lanky body, and loose, light-striped shirt radiated his easy joy in things, everything about Jack was tight and hard. He stood staring at me, his wide, angular face inflexible. His hands hung down causally, but they seemed relaxed the way an athlete relaxes, ready to spring into controlled action. His tight, red T-shirt clung to his stocky chest and muscled shoulders. I knew our minds were one – tolling a vicious chant of *"Pore white trash!"*

For an instant, I saw myself as he must – a coward who could turn on old friends without cause. Shallow. Without substance.

Maybe I could have mended it then and there with an apology, even an appeal, but for me, the right words never come on time. The uncertainties I hid from surged up and I froze. Joey watched us watch each other, then surprisingly, he suddenly draped his arm loosely around my shoulder. Jack's eyes flickered surprise as the brothers exchanged glances.

"Sandy's g..going to have lunch. On us." His voice held the same deliberation he always needed to accomplish the simplest tasks.

"Sure," Jack snapped. "Old friends always get a free lunch to welcome them back." Joey's glance didn't waver. Then suddenly Jack shrugged and smiled.

"C'mon in, Sandy," he said easily. "What'll you have? Same as the good ol' days? Malted milkshake and a hot dog with our own home-made fries?"

I tried to mutter something appreciative that he had remembered that, but the words stuck in my throat. I wished I could draw myself up with dignity, issue a cold apology, and walk away.

Instead, I shuffled into the store and slouched down onto a counter stool as close to the door as I could get.

"No, sit at a table," Joey insisted.

Bewildered, I looked around. The store had been changed since last year. A wooden partition, waist-high with artificial plants trailing along the top, separated a small dining area from the rest of the store. Each table had a red-checked cloth hiding the worn arborite, and a candle in a colored glass vase, ready to light. A new air conditioner was set into the outside wall so that for the first time, the little restaurant would be cool in the summer heat. The general store itself had been changed around. The shelves had been painted and the stock was neatly piled on them, with three narrow aisles between. New shelves lined the walls.

"It looks great," I said, glad of the real enthusiasm in my voice. The place had always been such a mess that if you didn't know Roy Cilento and Jack and Joey, you wouldn't have bought any groceries there, let alone a hot dog or sandwich.

Jack and Joey grinned.

"Joey figured out the arrangements," Jack explained. "Whole thing only cost a hundred and fifty-eight bucks. Got the shelves and air conditioner and stuff from a place in Simcoe that went bust during the winter. A lot of scrubbing, some paint, and the material for the table cloths and we were all set. I sure hope it was worth it."

"Yeah," Joey added somberly. "Dad h..had to borrow the hundred and...and fi..fifty from the bank."

I had had no experience with being poor. Of course, I had heard my parents wonder aloud how the Cilentos kept in business, but it meant nothing to me while we three had adventures and chased the evening toads.

"I thought your dad was a lawyer and made a whole bunch of money and retired here!" I blurted out.

Jack looked at me coldly. Joey blushed.

"What, poor white trash like us?" Jack mocked.

"But...but...Joey told me," I stammered out.

"Y..you remembered th..that?" Joey ran a jerky finger over the edge of the partition.

"Dad was a lawyer all right," Jack said. "But he didn't make much because he was just starting. Then Mom died when we were two, so he packed it in and moved us here. His folks used to have a summer place on the Point when he was a kid."

"I...I told her when we were little that Dad had been a famous lawyer," Joey explained uncomfortably, "that he'd made a ...a million dollars and re..retired. It was that s..summer the Children's Aid w..wanted to take us away, because Dad kept wandering off and for.. forgetting about us. And we pretended he really was a m..millionaire, and we were going to hire ser..vants and have new bikes and...and everything."

Jack stared at the wall for a moment and I stared at him, feeling as though I watched something that was not meant for me. But still I watched him. His hard face held a look I couldn't understand – of bitterness and hurt and many other emotions that I was too ungrown to know. I know now, so many years later, that that briefly mentioned time while we caught toads in the evenings and had dream adventures during the day was Jack's focusing hell.

Suddenly Jack looked at me fiercely and then his face gentled. "Jeez, you've always been a dumb kid, Sandy...Goddammit!" he swore suddenly, turning his back on us. "Do you like your hot dogs char-broiled?"

We laughed then, all of us, and once again we were the three who had caught toads together. But there was a difference of passing time and understandings that made me feel a little lost, a little forlorn – lonely for the old days when everything was sand fairies and adventures.

*   *   *

I had known the twins' father, Roy Cilento for as long as I could remember, but I find it hard to see him in my mind as a body and a face. He was a warmth – sure as the sun and just as remote.

I remember wondering occasionally why he would go off leaving Jack and Joey who could barely top the counter in charge of the store. But I never wondered long enough to find out. As I grew older I began to understand from overheard snips of conversation and my own vague sense of how things should be, that Roy wasn't "quite right." I would become afraid to see him again, but once the meeting was over, once I had faced him over the counter of the snack bar and felt the warmth of those pale, blue eyes that occasionally looked at you sharply from above the soft, brown beard, then the fear was gone. He was once again, just Roy.

Roy was woven into my memories of sand and sun and the daily pilgrimage to the general store, a dime, or if Daddy was pleased with me, even a quarter clasped in my hand. Choices of riches could be turned over and over in my mind. Comic books were most coveted, but new ones only came out once a month. Maybe an ice cream "drumstick", or perhaps a large bagful of two-for-a-penny candy to last a good part of the day. For two summers in particular, the two-for-a-penny won out because the gumball machine that stood sentinel outside the store was not working properly. For a penny, sometimes two or three of the hard, chewy gumballs would drop into your hand. Once on a glorious start to finish day, the gumballs overflowed my hand and dropped into the gravel – eleven!

I remember old Mr. Creyton watching as he picked up the morning paper. Then we heard him telling Roy about the gumball machine.

"Y'know, Roy," he said with an amiable voice that didn't mean it, "that gum machine out there is broken. Gives out too many gumballs for a penny. That's how you lose money all the time. And this penny candy here takes up a lot of shelf room and hardly pays anything in profit. If you don't wise up, man, you'll end up in the poorhouse."

The old man laughed then, but it was the kind of laugh that twists the desire for your pain to sound like a joke.

We five stood outside the screen door, holding our breath, raging with the hurt anger of children who have no recourse against the disguised cruelty of an adult. We could just barely see the blurry outlines of Mr. Creyton gesturing sharply with his rolled-up paper while Roy wiped the counter top.

"The children like the candy," Roy said. "And you're getting slow in your old age, Les. Don't notice things so fast. That machine's been giving out too many gumballs for almost two years now. The children like it."

Mr. Creyton snorted and strode out of the store, snapping the paper against his palm. He looked at us as if we were thieves, but said nothing.

He must have put a jinx on the old gumball machine, for the next day when we put in our pennies, nothing at all came out. Jack and Joey were working on the counter and stocking shelves, but somehow it didn't seem right to tell them. They'd been so proud over how their dad had told Mr. Creyton off. Pam wanted to do it anyway, but for once I refused. Maybe I was being loyal, but I think perhaps I was just too shy to ask for my money back after all the extras. Afterwards I was glad I did keep quiet, because that was the summer the Children's Aid tried to take Jack and Joey away from their father.

He would wander off fishing in the marshes far back behind the store, or follow the tiny herd of deer that I only once caught a distant glimpse of. Roy said they would eat from his hand during the hungry winter months.

Pam, Donny, and I had always been carelessly proud of our fathers. I like to think that even then, I had a glimmering of the rare and wonderful pride that Jack and Joey felt when their father became a hero in our childish eyes.

The gumball machine didn't work properly for the rest of the summer, seemingly paying us back for its previous bounty. Every once in awhile it would become generous again and would dole out perhaps two or three gumballs for a penny. But most often it just took the penny and gave out nothing.

We never did tell Roy, or even Jack or Joey, but after a while we never tried it any more. The next summer it was gone, replaced by an inside counter-top machine that dispensed gumballs that were big but hollow inside. It was an impersonal machine, fairly doling out one gumball for one penny spent. I didn't bother to buy gum any more.

*   *   *

I bit into the charred hot dog my friends had given me, wondering with acute embarrassment if they could afford a non-paying friend. I resolved not to go to the Causeway, a big fancy store two miles up the highway, for milkshakes or french fries this summer, even if that was where all the teenagers hung out.

We ate silently but not uncomfortably now. I wondered if they knew why I was here so early this year. As if reading my thoughts, Joey suddenly spoke up.

"We heard your M..mom and Dad got their divorce," he said with a sympathetic lack of emotion. "I..It'll be great having you here all the time."

"Yeah, well..." I blushed furiously. "I'm only part-time with Mom," I lied. "I'm going back to my private school and probably spend a lot of holidays with Daddy."

I stared down at my plate, then sucked noisily on the straw of my milkshake. Jack and Joey stared at me, twins now in thought. I had forgotten how much I resented their closeness.

"We thought your Mom had full custody," Jack said with barely any inflection in his rough voice, "and that you've been enrolled at the high school. That's what she told Dad a couple of days ago."

"Yeah, well, smarty," I shouted, "if you know so much, how come you're stuck in a dump like this!"

Maybe it was the terrible words I said, or maybe it was because for the first time, I was with friends, but all the grief washed over me and I began to cry. I laid my head on the table and buried it under my arms, feeling my shoulders shake as I wept hard, loudly then softly, then in long tearless shudders that came in waves. Throughout I had been aware of nothing, but now as the trembling shook me, I felt Joey's jerking hand stroking my hair, and the warm heaviness of Jack's arm across my back.

Even when the shuddering stopped, I didn't move, afraid of their eyes, of their sympathy. I felt Jack pull back his arm and heard the chair scrape as he moved away from the table. Joey's hand slowed and then it too was taken away, but he still sat beside me.

A moment later I hear the tinkle of ice in glasses, then the scrape of Jack's chair as he sat down again.

"Take a drink, Sandy," he said in a matter-of fact voice. "Your throat'll be dry."

I reluctantly lifted my head, feeling the coolness of my wet face. Joey handed me a paper napkin and I blotted away at myself.

"I feel really dumb," I mumbled, my voice not quite my own again.

"You're not the only person who cries," Jack replied, pushing one of three glasses of coke towards me. I lifted it shakily. Jack and Joey lifted theirs too.

"S..so, here's to pore white t..trash," Joey said and grinned. Jack jerked and his jaw clenched. Then he smiled, a quick quirk of his lips.

With a half-hysterical laugh, I drank the toast, choking a little as a final shudder caught me after all. I could only drink a little and then I needed to escape. I felt half-blind as I stumbled to the door. But I remembered to shout, just before the screen door banged. "Thanks for lunch...and I'll see you!"

Susan Brown

Chapter 3

It was a few days later that I displayed the painting – my treasure – to the twins for the first time. My breath caught in my throat as I gazed at my Daddy in his red, open-necked shirt, laughing happily with his Dream Girl. It was a portrait of all my dreams and fancies. The twins stared at the canvas for a long moment.

"Can you paint like that?" Jack finally asked.

"No, of course not," I replied. "I didn't inherit my father's genius. I'm more like Mom – she used to be a writer before she had kids."

"That's too bad," Jack replied.

"Being able to write isn't that bad," I snapped, angry that he would criticize my mother – that was my prerogative. He blinked at me, then suddenly grinned.

"No, not that you can write – that you can't paint."

"Yeah," Joey added. "D..during the summer, there's a craft exhibit in Simcoe. Could m..make a lot of money selling p..pictures. You..ou're sure you can't paint? Doesn't have to be much good. M..most people can't tell the difference anyhow."

"Of course I'm sure! I'd know, wouldn't I? Besides, if Daddy thought I had any promise he would have taught me himself. He always said my artistic sense was as hopeless..." I trailed off. I didn't want even the twins to know he had compared me to my mother.

My friends didn't notice the unfinished sentence.

"Too bad about the painting," Jack repeated with a resigned air.

"But don't you think this is fantastic?" I demanded. "Daddy's a great artist, you know."

"It's a great pain..painting," Joey said hastily. "W..we wouldn't know anyway." He grinned at me. "Trouble is, w..we're so worried about making money that we're n..not much able to think of anything else."

"You worried about your dad's store?" I asked as we wandered out to the verandah. How could they not have felt the power of the painting? The two boys flopped onto the comfortable furniture. I perched on the rail, facing them.

"No," Jack answered in bitter laziness. "Dad doesn't want much out of life. Being poor white trash is just fine, so the store makes enough to look after him."

"Th..thing is," Joey went on with an air of intense anticipation, "Jack and me have both been accepted in uni..university in Toronto. We even got a small scholarship."

"How could you go to university?" I demanded. I knew as well as anyone that everyone was eighteen or nineteen when they finished high school in Ontario. At that time, the course was five years – grade nine through thirteen. "You're not even seventeen yet."

"We finished all the high school courses at Christmas," Jack replied.

"How could you do that?" I scowled, sure they were pulling my leg. "You guys probably just quit school and are trying to act big, that's all."

Jack made a noise of impatient disgust and stared out at the grey lake, obviously deciding I wasn't worth discussing his life with. I was just starting to get hotly furious when Joey explained.

"Th..there's not much to d..do out here in the winter. Snowshoe if there's snow, but there's n..not much around here. And we haven't got a TV, so ever since we were little we'd read and study together, a..at nights. They kept promoting us because we knew everything b..before the teacher even started it."

"Besides," Jack spoke up, apparently deciding to grace us with his conversation, "we've got brains – especially Joey. Even our teachers were knocked out by his IQ scores once they made allowances for his shaking – way up in the genius category. And so we're not going to rot here much longer."

Joey blushed as I stared curiously at him, rather like at an odd exhibit in a museum.

"I didn't know you were that smart."

"Well, I'm not," Joey protested, then temporized. "A..at least it's not much g..good if you can't use it."

"Why can't you?"

Jack let out a crack of laughter. "That's why I've always liked you, Sandy," he said. "You're so dumb, you've got to be an original."

I shut my mouth with a snap. Just let Jack wait until I bothered to talk to him again. I looked remorsefully at Joey though, feeling the matching prickle of a blush in my hairline. His face was scarlet still as he stared out at the waves rolling over the shore.

"Use your head, Sandy," Jack went on, this time without the sarcastic snap in his voice. "Joey's cerebral palsy holds him up. He's real slow on exam papers because he has a hard time writing. He can't even use a lot of big words or talk a lot, like a genius is supposed to, because it affects his speech. Most people can't be bothered waiting for him to put together what he wants to say."

"Ja..ack bails me out m..most of th..the time," Joey explained, embarrassment twisting his words. "I..it's a g..good par..partnership. I can thi..ink out a lot of theory, then Ja..ack can make it operate. He c..can do anything mechanical or..or elec..ctrical."

"Can't you make the things you think up?" I asked. Even when we were little, Joey was practical about constructing toad houses or arranging our adventures.

"Well," Joey smiled shyly, "I c..could I guess, but with my sp..spasms it takes me a lot l..longer than it would anyone else."

I sniffed, disbelieving.

"You do okay any time I've seen you. And you talk pretty good too – a lot better than when we were little. Except maybe when you're excited or embarrassed or something."

"Yeah," Jack interrupted, "and the world is full of people like Donny Muller. They give him a hard time so he has more spasms."

"He doesn't have them around me much, do you Joey?" I argued.

"But I've known you since w..we were little," Joey explained.

"So we have to stick together," Jack continued

as if neither of us had spoken. "Joey needs me to look out for him."

I was getting madder and madder at Jack. I'd forgotten how he always thought he knew better than everybody else.

"Yeah," I snapped. "Well, I bet all that happens is that Joey never does anything for himself or has to stick up for himself. It makes you feel good that he has to run to his big brother Jack all the time, I'll bet anything. So there!" I slammed into the house.

Why hadn't he understood how important my painting was?

*   *   *

I didn't see the twins for several days after that. At first I had thought they were avoiding me as carefully as I was avoiding them. But after several days of my own morose company, I swallowed my pride and wandered slowly over to the store. They were nowhere in sight. The store was open though, so I went in and sat down at the counter, planning to order a chocolate milkshake. When several minutes passed and no one appeared to wait on me, I began to get annoyed and uncomfortable. I knew the twins wouldn't ignore me as a customer no matter how angry they were with me as a friend.

I had just made up my mind to leave, when the door from the tiny apartment at the back was pushed open. It was Roy.

I was startled to see him, though why I thought I would not barely occurred to me. He was the same as always – brown and disheveled, slight like Joey and short like Jack, and his eyes a vague, pale blue like neither.

His soft mouth under his beard crinkled slightly in the gentle smile I had almost forgotten.

"Ah, Sandy," he said softly. "The boys told me you were back. You've come early this summer, haven't you?" The question was vaguely puzzled as if he also asked reassurance that it was early.

"Yeah," I replied, feeling my face redden with unreasonable embarrassment. "Mom and Dad are divorced now. Dad's living in the city, but Mom decided she wants to live year round in the summer house. She's trying to pick up her old writing career and she thinks this is a good place to write – says there's no distractions."

Roy's smile widened. "No, there are no distractions around here. No busses, no offices, no crowds. It's a lovely place."

"Yeah, but it's boring," I said sourly.

"Maybe," Roy admitted, "but there are things here that are worth more than excitement.

Of course, you're young yet to look for them. They're an old person's dream."

I laughed with him.

"But you're not old," I protested as I realized for the first time that he wasn't.

Probably he was less than forty. My father then was close to fifty-five. Even my mother was forty-three. But my father literally snapped with vitality, and even with her natural reticence and unhappiness, my mother never seemed as vague and frail as Roy.

"Are the twins around?" I asked after a minute.

"No," Roy said more briskly, his easy smile widening proudly. "They've taken the bus up to Toronto for a couple of days, to see about the courses they're going to take at the university this fall. It's funny – I never pushed them the way my family drove me, because their ideas – my family's, I mean – didn't do me any good. But Jack and Joey are just seething with ambition. They're so strong and young and sure. They despise it here. They figure that together they'll put together space rockets and cars that don't break down and a thousand other things."

"Will they?" I demanded skeptically. I couldn't imagine my shabby old friends conquering the world like that.

"Might," Roy answered. "Then again, they might not. Life's full of things that can cripple you, so you're no use to anyone after all." His voice had gone soft again and he stared at the wall, apparently forgetting me. I didn't want to be forgotten.

"You mean like Joey being spastic?" I demanded.

Roy blinked and looked back at me. "No," he said slowly, "that's something on the outside that doesn't really matter."

"It matters to Joey," I pointed out.

He smiled. "Yes, it does now. And to Jack too, probably more than Joey. Jack's one to take things hard, but Joey rolls with the punches. He'll manage just fine once he finds himself."

I kept silent then, sensing that I didn't understand, and a little impatient with Roy. I never did like riddles. I always wanted everything spoken out plain so that I could make it mine. I didn't understand then, that the things I thought were plain were often deeper riddles – riddles that could take years to unravel for what they truly were.

"Well," I said finally sliding off the stool, "if Jack and Joey aren't around I guess I'll go home for lunch. Will you tell them I came around?"

"Sure, Sandy," Roy murmured.

When I glanced behind me just before the screen door swung shut, I saw him staring at the blank wall opposite him, an expression of what – sadness perhaps – etched deeply over his face.

I ran from him, across the highway and down the dirt road to our summer house, angry and panting and straining to obliterate what I had seen of him.

The mailman had come early, so eagerly I rifled through the medley of returned stories addressed to my mother, looking for the letters my friends at school still faithfully wrote. As I opened the one from my best friend, I remembered I had forgotten to order my milkshake.

"That's the trouble with Roy," I muttered irritably. "He always makes you forget what you wanted."

*   *   *

For several weeks I saw little of the twins. Early spring passed into late spring and then crept, dragging day by dragging day, toward summer. I spent my time reading, wandering up and down the cold beach, watching the very few programs that came on the one TV channel we could receive, and being as surly as possible to my mother.

It was hard to understand why she didn't hate me. I knew myself as a disappointment as a mother's daughter. Like my father I was lanky and without much of a figure. My hair was chopped off at shoulder length, supposedly in a page boy cut that was very stylish then, but did not become me or suit my naturally wayward hair. Even the color was unremarkable – a sort of paper-bag brown that streaked white-blond during the summer. Both my mother and father refused to let me "cheapen" myself by letting me bleach my hair to the white-blond that ensured I would have more fun.

I was agonizingly, if inarticulately aware of my own shortcomings. My mother was so pretty – dark-haired with clear blue eyes that quietly absorbed you. All the while she and my father were married she had been painstakingly careful about her appearance, and so as a child I accepted that how a person looked meant a great deal to her. That was one of the reasons I gravitated toward Daddy. I was sure he didn't care so much about my disappointing looks.

I barely wondered, strangely enough, why my mother had become so careless of her appearance after we moved to the summer house. She moved quietly about in slacks with baggy sweaters wrapped around her small frame. She washed and set her own hair, allowing it to fall in natural waves. And sometimes she hummed and whistled off-tune when she didn't know I was around.

I let my looks, such as they were, go too – more to aggravate her than anything else. I barely brushed my hair in the morning and if my shorts were ragged at the edges, well, too bad. I wasn't going to mend them.

In the evening we often made popcorn. I think my mother was trying to make our time together warm and cozy and happy. I didn't respond but I ate the popcorn. Then we would sit reading together (Mother wouldn't let me hole up in my room all the time) or occasionally we would round out the evening with a nice, old-fashioned argument.

I remember one fight in particular, though why, I don't know. It was neither the worst nor the last fight we had. Perhaps I remember it because it was so repetitive of all the others we had had that summer. Once again, I'd started on returning to the private school.

"Melany wrote me today," I muttered at her. "She said they're starting a new European culture course and an equestrian class at school next year."

I could care less about European culture, but I knew that was one of Mother's shibboleths – that North American people don't know anything about the rest of the world. Personally all I could think of was learning to ride.

"Don't start again," my mother said wearily. "You're not going back to East Lakes, Sandy. How many times do I have to repeat myself?"

"But why?" I demanded. "You don't care about me! You never did! You sent me there in the first place and didn't care whether I liked it or not. Well I do like it and I'm not letting you drag me off here forever, just to spite Daddy!"

"I'm not trying to spite your father," Mom said in the tight voice of fury she sometimes used now. "And I didn't want to send you there, ever! The girls who go there are wealthy and we're not."

"I know," I snapped, "you just don't want me to mix with people I'm not fit for."

"Sandy, stop," my mother pleaded. "I've told you before. If all your friends are wealthy, you'll be left behind. We are not rich – especially now," she added.

"You're just too cheap to pay the tuition," I raged. "And you're too damned mean to let Daddy do anything for me. You don't want me to have anything to do with him – you're trying to take me away from him! Well you can't! Because I love him and I hate you!"

I slammed into my room and threw myself on the bed, too angry for tears.

Seeking comfort I stared up at the painting, but by some trick of the moonlight shining in the window, Daddy's face looked as though he was laughing cruelly, not cheerfully as he should. In hot panic I flipped on the lights and the saturnine face was gone. Daddy laughed with his Dream Girl once again. But several times during the night the face reappeared in my dreams and I woke up crying, twice with my mother bending anxiously over me.

Perhaps it was that series of nightmares that crystallized my sullen insistence that I would return to East Lakes. I saw the choice as mine now, not the gift to be offered or withheld by my parents. If I could earn the tuition for the year, surely my mother couldn't stop me. Jack and Joey were trying to earn the tuition for university – also expensive.

Perhaps they would include me in their plans.

I threw on my clothes, banged out of our summer house, and raced barefoot, as always, through the shifting sand. Then for an instant I stopped. It was warm – the first balmy day of the season. As I trotted down the road, I held out my arms to catch the welcoming sunshine. For weeks I had stubbornly been wearing summer clothes and shivering a lot. But today the sand felt hot under my feet and I was perspiring by the time I reached the post office. A sullen looking young man was slapping the annual coat of paint over the white sides of the building.

I sucked in my breath happily and held my lower lip between my teeth as I expelled the air. Summer was so close after all. Only a few more weeks before the cottagers would all be here. Some had already come briefly to open up their cottages.

I'd seen Pam and her younger sister down the beach a week ago, but they had gone inside before I'd reached their cottage. Feeling foolish, I hung around for almost half an hour before I gave up and left. Their father was a bad-tempered man who shouted indiscriminately at any of the kids who came to his door. He owned a discount store in Simcoe and liked to tell everyone about the "sharp deals" he pulled and how he "put one over" on someone else. Even as a child I understood that these were the words an adult used to brag about cheating someone else. I couldn't understand why it was alright for parents to do that, but any child caught cheating was punished.

Eventually I decided that the difference was that no one caught the adult. My father laughed uproariously when I explained it to him and, despite my mother's objections, told everyone my childish observations. It made me feel very clever.

I paused for only a moment to watch the painter, not so much that I wanted to see what he was doing, but to savor the approach of summer. When Mr. Creyton stalked around the side of the building, obviously checking up on the paint job, I took off again, barely bothering to look for cars as I raced across the highway.

One honked its horn loudly as the driver swerved to miss me. I licked my lips in satisfaction. The summer traffic had begun.

Chapter 4

I ran around the general store, past the battered red pick-up, through the knee-high weeds that sprouted each spring, only to be burned off by the summer sun, and to the back door leading into the Cilento's tiny apartment. I was just about to knock when Jack and Joey pushed open the screen door to come outside.

"Hey, Sandy," Joey said cheerfully, "thought you...you'd gone back to the city."

"No," I mumbled, suddenly embarrassed. "You'd gone to Toronto when I came to see you, and...and Mom's kept me pretty busy. I do the housework while she writes."

"Has she had any luck with her writing?" Jack asked amiably. Apparently he had forgotten the rotten things I had said to him.

"No...yes...a little, I guess. None of the big magazines have taken her stories yet, but a few of the little ones that hardly pay anything have. She says it's a start. But listen," I said in a rush, "I've got to make some money too. I'm going to pay my own school fees this year. Mom can't afford them," I added scornfully.

"If you're short of money, why waste cash on a private school?" Jack demanded.

"Well, you're going to spend money on school," I argued. "And we're not that short. It's just that...that...well, it's expensive, that's all. And I'm used to going to a good school."

Jack snorted.

"Th..there's nothing wrong with the high school here," Joey told me. "If y..you want to do extra studies the pr..principal will help you. She's the best!"

"Yeah, well," I snapped, "all my friends are at East Lakes. And it's none of your business why I want to go there. I came to ask if you needed an extra partner for all your business ventures." I injected as much sarcasm as possible into my voice.

"W..well, I don't know," Joey said, eyeing Jack.

"Might," Jack answered with a shrug.

"The bike," Joey argued with a tip of his head and a slight involuntary jerk.

Jack nodded. "Might for the pies," he admitted.

"Change too," Joey added.

"Yeah," Jack agreed decisively.

"Will you guys stop that and talk English," I snapped. I felt like a child who hears an adult conversation floating incomprehensibly over her head.

"W..we were," Joey said with a grin. Jack smiled slightly in amused contempt at my annoyance.

"Okay, you're in," Jack said. "We've got a couple of good ideas that might work out if we could handle it, but during the summer we're not dependable as a team. You'd be able to fill in the gaps."

"What are you talking about?" I demanded.

"C..come on," Joey said, putting his arm around my shoulder and guiding me toward a broken-down shed at the back of their property. "You are abou..out to see a mechanical marvel. We're going to make our fortunes with it."

It didn't look like much – a welded together bunch of bicycle parts, but once I came to understand it, I was amazed at how carefully the twins had designed and built it.

It was a motorized tricycle of sorts, started by peddling, and then kicked over to a small engine. On either side of the bike hung two large boxes about the size of the freezers used on ice cream bicycles. A wooden bin straddled and joined these compartments over the back of the bike, behind the seat.

"What is it?" I asked.

"Our delivery van," Jack explained running his hands proudly over the frame.

"We're going to use it to deliver papers all down the beach, take orders for groceries and the baked goods that Mrs. Patterson makes and deliver them to the cottages. That way, it'll save the cottagers trips into town, and we'll have a charge for what we deliver."

I peered again at the bike, envisioning what Jack had described – particularly Mrs. Patterson's pies and bread. She was an elderly woman living in an old farm house on the road into Port Rowan, who partially supported herself by baking and selling an array of mouth-watering goods. During the summers, I'd often gone with my mother, vying for the chance to order one of her pies, a loaf or two of bread, or some sweet buns.

We would stand in her summer kitchen, redolent with baking smells beyond description. Mrs. Patterson would sit at the small table under the window and open an exercise book. If you were lucky and had come early enough in the week, she would look up and say, "Yes I think I can take your order." She would smile and we would smile. If you were not quite so lucky, she would allow you to order a pie, or a loaf of bread, or the buns, depending on what had been promised to those ahead of you.

She only baked so many of each, and they were so incredibly, home-baked-on-the-farm good, that it was never sure you would be one of the lucky families who were allowed to purchase some. While I gazed at the three old-fashioned stoves that she used, Mom would give her our name and it would be entered in the book for the next lot of baking.

Occasionally some foolish family would neglect to pick up their order. If you happened to be going by at about four o'clock, you could stop in and inquire if there was anything left. Mrs. Patterson would answer in a voice of grave displeasure that someone had not picked up their order and you may as well have it.

She would explain peevishly that she was an old woman and couldn't afford the time or money baking for people who didn't honor their obligations. Those unlucky people, if she were angry enough, might never be allowed to order again. As a child, I could never understand the stupidity of anyone not picking up those baked pleasures.

But now Jack and Joey were planning on carrying them in their delivery service.

"Will Mrs. Patterson let you order that much?" I asked in wonder.

"Yeah," Jack said with a grin. "We shoveled her out two or three times this winter when the snow stayed around, so she's agreed to let us have six sweet buns, a dozen loaves of bread, and eight pies a week. We guaranteed we'd pick them up and pay for them whether we had orders for them or not."

"And if there are extras, we can eat them!" I exclaimed.

Jack and Joey both grinned, and Joey licked his lips.

"We thought of that," Jack admitted, a rare twinkle in his eyes. "But anyway, the plan is to deliver the morning paper for a quarter extra a week. At the same time, we'll pick up orders for groceries. We'll deliver those after lunch at a rate of ten cents on the dollar, minimum charge twenty-five cents. This box," he pointed to the one on the far side, "is fixed up to take ice to keep everything cool, so we can deliver perishables like milk and butter and such."

I was more impressed with how well the twins had planned than I had wished to be, for I had not wanted to follow their lead entirely.

"You sure you need my help?" I demanded as carelessly as I could. "It'll cut down on your profits."

Jack's eyes narrowed but he grinned.

"I have a job setting up pins at the bowling alley for the summer. And a lot of times I have to help at the store. Joey can't drive this thing because of his spasms." Jack touched the blue frame with his foot. "We've got to be reliable to make this work, and for a while we didn't know if we could. We'll teach you how to run the bike and then you can drive it for the deliveries and pick-ups."

I opened my mouth to protest, then shut it again at Jack's challenging stare. He was so ready to think badly of me. Well, not this time.

"When can I learn?" I tried to sound eager. In those unliberated days, girls of the class I thought I belonged to didn't ride motorcycles or motorbikes. Even bicycles were socially taboo once you'd passed eighth grade.

Even more important, in any days, I hated loud noises – particularly the roars of engines.

"How about right now," Joey said. Without waiting for a reply, he wheeled the bike out of the shed onto the hard ground around it.

"You can practice out here." He pointed to the lush expanse behind the store that gradually melted into a marsh.

Just as the wide beach lined one side of the eighteen-mile point, marshes bounded the other side. An industrious swamp-draining program had been undertaken years before, and so there were areas like the few acres behind the general store that were technically swamp, but actually just damp meadows. At regular intervals of perhaps three-quarters of a mile (my memory is hazy about this) cuts had been made through the swamp, almost to where the highway bounded the beach area.

These cuts were long, narrow channels that ran straight through the marsh area. I never knew precisely how they worked (although I remember my father once explaining it), but I think the water that drowned the swamp land could drain into these regularly dredged channels.

The marsh was full of wild growing things, gigantic bullfrogs that kicked and jumped like jackrabbits, nesting cranes, and all kinds of mysterious creatures. The scraps of land that had been drained were coated with coarse sun-burned weeds, a few butterflies and endless droning insects.

One of these cuts ran to within thirty feet of the Cilento's shed before coming to an abruptly squared-off end. Each spring before the channel was dredged, and each fall, long after it had been done, the banks were crowded with bulrushes and the water floated with lily pads.

We wheeled the bike to a track along the cut. As tiny leopard frogs dived for the shelter of rushes and water, and the coarse weeds slapped wetly against our legs, I felt as though the rest of the world had never existed and never would.

We stood silently awhile, listening to the calling birds and the *plop*, *plop* as frogs dropped into the water, watching the beauty of tiny wildflowers opening to the early summer sun, feeling the kind of peace you often hear or read about but rarely experience.

*   *   *

I was free.

The steady drone of the motor became lost in the rush and slap of the wind. I opened my mouth to shout in exultation and the gusts, cool and sweet, filled my mouth and throat. All around me tall weeds and marsh grasses lay aside for my passing. Above, the sky shone clear, summer blue, jeweled with white puffs of clouds. The wheeling seagulls spiraled far above my head, their cries faint and broken as I made my own sounds in the summer air.

I had learned to ride the bike.

At first the grips had felt heavy and awkward as I learned to balance and steer. But the three wheels gave the vehicle a solidity that would be hard to overturn. I bumped over the trail slowly, trying out the steering, then the brakes, and finally some abrupt turns and stops as though I had been confronted with an emergency on the road. The bike responded as though designed for me alone.

My confidence soared. I kicked her off and pedaled until I could catch the motor. Then joyfully I left the half-overgrown trail and followed a deer path.

The weeds gave way to rushes and thick marsh grass. Redwing blackbirds and other swamp-nesting birds chirped and cackled at me, furious that I had invaded their isolation. In response I shut off the motor, feeling again the silence and peace.

After a while, I reluctantly started the bike again and slowly returned to where the twins were waiting. I resented coming back. Today the marsh was mine and I didn't want to share it.

When they asked me in for a milkshake, I refused, escaping instead across the road to the undergrowth by the beach that had housed so many of my childhood adventures. As I sat there, hidden by the dappling leaves, letting sand run through my fingers, I tried to push the jigsaw pieces of my life together in my mind. Nothing fit. My old life of carefree summer adventures, my new life marooned at Long Point, my old life structured by school routines, my new life with my mother, adrift like poor white trash, my old and new lives with my father who had somehow lost me.

Nothing fit.

I didn't fit.

Desperately, I wondered if I could ever fit anywhere again.

A week later, I had another erratic letter from my best friend, Melany. School was over for the year and in two weeks she was leaving for France with her mother.

It's such a DRAG going with Mom, she wrote, *because I won't know ANYONE! But, there's all those gorgeous Frenchmen to fall in love with. Paris! L'Amour! Here I come!*

But wait 'til you hear THIS! ... I asked Mom if you could come too and she said YES! Why should you suffer because your Mom wants to 'go it alone'?

I had complained in my letters to Melany about my mother, but somehow I didn't like her echoing my own scornful words.

We're staying in a villa, so there's no hotels or meals, and if you can't come up

*with the airfare (it's only a few hundred,
I think) I'll tell Mom that as an invited
guest you shouldn't have to pay. So I
know my parents will buy your ticket
too. I can always count on them!...*

The letter went on in an equally haphazard style, but I barely read it. I should have been ecstatic about the invitation, but I wasn't. After all, the twins wouldn't begrudge me a trip to Europe.

But I had to get some money. Maybe Melany could get her folks to give me the ticket, but my mother's words kept running through my mind.

Another reality of becoming poor white trash.

Well, I wouldn't be "left behind" or the one "everyone would feel sorry for and patronize." My father was a famous artist and he made a lot of money on his paintings. I wouldn't give my mother the satisfaction of saying no. Daddy would help me.

We had a rarely-used telephone, a black, desk model in a small curtained alcove we called the den. Most of the cottagers never bothered with telephones and most of the calls had to go through an old-fashioned operator. I rushed from my bedroom to the den and told the operator the number of Daddy's studio. I had to repeat myself twice before she could get the number right.

"Hello Daddy," I almost shrieked. "It's Sandy!"

"*Sandy, Dream Girl,*" he laughed, his voice warm and rich. "*Why are you calling? Did your mother sink into the lake or something?*"

I giggled.

"No," I said quickly. "Oh Daddy, you'll never guess what. I'm so excited I could just about die!"

"*Well, don't do that,*" he replied cheerfully.

"You remember Melany? Well, her mother's taking her to France for the summer and they've invited me to go too! All I need is money for the airfare. They've rented a villa – probably on the Riviera or something – so it won't cost anything else!"

"*Hold on,*" Daddy said. I tried not to notice that his enthusiasm had lessened somewhat. "*There are always extras – what about spending money and clothes and all that? Did you think about that?*"

"I won't need much," I pleaded. "I'll never get a chance like this again. It won't cost that much, really Daddy."

His voice was cool now. "*What does your mother think of all this?*"

I hesitated a moment.

"She thinks it's a great idea," I lied. "That's why she said I should call you, because she knew you'd think so too."

"*Did she now!*" he raged suddenly into the phone. "*Well, you tell the bitch for me that if she wants to go trotting off with her nose up in the air – too damn proud to take the money she was glad to get for years, then she can pay for this little jaunt of yours! That's your mother all over sweety.*" His voice had gone hateful and hard. "*And now she's teaching you her tricks. Forget it Sandy! You've got your mother now!*"

"But Daddy..." I wailed. The phone clicked.

I stood holding the phone, looking stupidly at it. How could he have spoken to me like that?

It was all my mother's fault for taking me away from him! I slammed the receiver back onto its hook and turned around, suddenly seeing my mother leaning against the doorpost. Her face was white with anger and hurt.

I opened my mouth to shout at her, take out my own hurt, but she spoke first, her voice breathless and hard.

"You shouldn't have lied, Sandra – not if you wanted to get your own way with your father. If you'd just told him that you knew I wouldn't have given you the trip – it's not the money is it? You're so sure that I wouldn't give you anything – then he would have given you a trip around the world. He would have called you his Dream Girl again, Sandra. You'd like that of course. And he'd have given you the money to spite me. He'd enjoy that, spiting me, making himself look the hero and me the villain. He's always..."

Her voice broke then, and she turned from me and ran to her room, slamming and locking the door behind her. I stood where I was, shocked and frightened.

"That's not true!" I screamed, but she didn't answer.

It was one of the longest days I have ever spent. All day I wandered about the summer house, swung on the tall rope swing that had always stood in front of the house, and sat on the beach, watching the waves roll in. My mother did not come out of her room until the supper hour.

I was resentfully ready to defend myself, to tell her exactly why I called Daddy. I had kept my anger whipped up all day. It was the only defense I had against my guilt, and my hurt and fear at what Daddy had said to me.

I was curled up on the sofa, trying to watch a stupid comedy on TV, when I heard my mother's door open. She had changed her clothes and washed her face, although the crying marks were still clear.

"Do you mind if I switch this off," she said calmly. I shook my head and the blare of canned laughter stopped. She sat in a worn upholstered chair beside the TV, opposite me.

"I've known I'd have to talk to you sooner or later, Sandy," Mom said so quietly I could barely hear her. I bit my lower lip, wondering whether I was going to get yelled at or just a lecture.

"Your father was furious that I wanted a divorce," she went on evenly.

"He didn't want you to take me away from him." I was so afraid she'd criticize Daddy, that she would make it sound my fault. "You don't like it that I love him more than you!"

A spasm of pain crossed her face. I didn't care because I had wanted to hurt her for so long.

"No," she said softly, and her face looked old. "You're right. I don't like it that you love him more than me. I should have left your father years and years ago, Sandy. But I couldn't. You know as well as I do that he's the kind of man who is loved – not just by us, but by many people."

"Especially by us, because we're his family," I objected.

Mother waved this aside with her delicate hand, no longer manicured.

"He's a genius. You can forgive someone so much when he can create such passion and beauty for the world. It makes you feel that everything you give and give and give has been made worthwhile, has been made noble. We were married for twenty-six years, Sandy. For a long time he needed me because he wasn't a success. It took a while for his talent to mature.

"I should have left when he reached his success. When that first article was written about him in *Time*. When he stopped needing me and before he started destroying me."

"Daddy never did anything to you," I protested. "You just wanted credit for what he did, that's all. You wanted everything for yourself and didn't want to share anything."

I thought she would get angry, but she almost chuckled – a sad sound that had no relation to laughter.

"Me, Sandy?" she said. "I shared everything. I even gave away most of myself for him. I loved him so much."

"Then why did you divorce him?" I demanded, trying to keep away the tears, the lump in my throat. "Why did you take me away from him?"

"Why?" Her voice sounded hard suddenly. She jumped to her feet and began pacing the room. "Because I learned to hate him. I woke up one day and saw what he had done to me, what he was trying to do to you. You're too young Sandy, to hold out against his personality. He's just too much of everything – too clever, too genial, too handsome…"

"He's everything a father could be!" I told her.

She looked at me sadly. I sensed she wanted to say something, but I didn't want to hear anything else. Too much had been said and not said at the same time.

"I'm going to make dinner," I announced and jumped from the sofa.

"Sandy," my mother's voice stopped me. "Remember something for me," she said. "I love you very much, and when…if things don't work out…or things happen differently than you think they should…just remember please, that you're very much loved by me."

"And by Daddy," I said loudly and ran into the kitchen. I banged the cupboards and pots so loudly that I couldn't hear whether or not she answered me.

*   *   *

I stayed up late that evening, hugging my knees and staring at the picture of Daddy laughing while I tried to catch the toad. The moonlight shone through my window across the ugly little toad, exaggerating the grotesque features Daddy had given him. I wondered suddenly if Daddy had ever really looked at the toads I used to show him – if he had chased them as a child too. Suddenly I had a horrible vision of my father, black-haired and handsome and young as Donny, squishing a toad and yelling *yuck* as it jerked helplessly on the ground.

I pushed the stupid thought out of my mind, or at least tried to. But it was night and I was tired. My mind rolled and turned into channels I couldn't control. So many images twisted through my thoughts, beyond my wishes, responding to my fears.

"Oh, Daddy," I whispered to the laughing face. Sadness seeped up from within me, from thoughts I would not think and feelings I had to hide from. I cried for a long, long time staring at the picture through my tears, seeking desperately for the happy time where I played in the sun-lit sands as my Daddy's Dream Girl.

Chapter 5

I dropped the letters – one for Daddy and one for Melany – into the mail slot inside the gift shop and post office. I had spent all morning on them, finding the right tone and the right words to refuse Melany's offer with dignity, and to assure Daddy that even though I lived with my mother I still loved him dearly (and WHY didn't he come down for a weekend to visit me!).

I had shown them to Mom because I was rather proud of them and she was a writer of sorts. She smiled wryly, suggested that I change a couple of words, then agreed they were excellent letters. I stared at the mail slot for a moment, wondering about Mom. Since our argument or discussion or whatever it was, the sullen air of emotional guerrilla warfare had lifted. I suspected that Mom thought she had explained herself to me. Maybe it had been bothering her.

"Can I help you with something?" Mrs. Creyton asked suddenly at my elbow. Her tone implied that she'd like to help me out the door seeing as I was obviously a hooligan bent on destroying every treasure within the four walls.

"No, thank you," I replied with sophisticated coolness. "I might buy some postcards," I muttered resentfully when she continued to stare at me with pursed lips and hard grey eyes.

She was a plump little woman who bustled about with an air of suppressed anger. Her grey hair was crimped at the front, and swept into a tightly pinned, French roll at the back. As always, there was an aroma of faintly metallic floral cologne clouding about her. Her rhinestone-edged glasses hung on her full bosom, strangled by the firmly knotted, black silken cord that encircled her neck.

I disliked her even more than her husband.

I stepped around her in order to look at the souvenirs and gift items they had stocked this year.

Some of the things, such as little birch bark canoes (one purchased the year I was seven), peace pipes, and tom-toms (the summer I was nine), were perennial items intended for the lean purses and undiscriminating eyes of children. Others, gift cups and saucers with "Long Point Beach" printed on the rims in gold script, for instance, were intended for the fatter purses but equally uneducated tastes of adults.

But there were other things that were real treasures to me – inexpensive china figures of birds and animals, delicately colored, and items of fine china imported from England. The really expensive items were locked in a glass cabinet but everything else was arranged on the open shelves, to be admired and perhaps carefully handled.

Every year there were many items the same and a few different. I saw nothing on the open shelves that particularly appealed to me for my summer's treasure. The items that had charmed me even a year before, I felt too old for now. Yet the souvenirs intended for adults – cups and saucers and cake plates – interested me not at all.

With a growing feeling of resentment and half-panic I picked out a half-a-dozen post cards to send to my friends from school. Surely there had to be something for me to treasure this summer? I was afraid, so afraid, that with my family life in shambles, even this small ritual of my own would be broken and then lost.

And so I held the post cards rather too tightly, and despite Mrs. Creyton's following eyes, began a slow search of the store again.

And then I saw it.

It had been locked in the cabinet with the fine china – a small toad under a spotted porcelain toadstool. I was entranced by the delicate creaminess of the toadstool and the whimsical expression on the sleepy face of the toad. The little creature was as it should be, compact, earthy, cream-throated with golden eyes as it crouched amid tiny porcelain flowers.

"Are you sure there's nothing I can help you with?" demanded Mrs. Creyton.

"I'd like to see that, please," I pointed to my treasure.

"Oh, the little frog," Mrs. Creyton replied, her lips pursed again. "I believe it's quite expensive."

"Could I see it, please," I repeated.

Reluctantly, Mrs. Creyton unlocked the cabinet and handed me the little toad. It felt smooth and cool in my hands, almost opaque in its fineness. The little toad nestled in my hands.

"Are you finished with it," Mrs. Creyton asked impatiently, "or do you wish to buy it?"

"How much is it?"

"Let me see," she took the toad from me and turned it upside down to read the sticker. "As I said, it's quite expensive – thirty-two dollars."

I tried to maintain my dignity in face of such a staggering amount – even the Royal Doulton figurines were considerably less than that. But perhaps it was so expensive because of the flowers, ripples of grass, and obvious artistry.

"I won't get it today, thank you," I said. "Just the post cards."

Mrs. Creyton sniffed, her mouth and nose wrinkled as if I had farted.

The toad was locked up again. I paid for my six post cards with a quarter, and then with a vague sense of a narrow escape, left the store.

I knew I had to have the toad – I had to save a treasure from this summer just as I always had. But where was the money going to come from? I had seventeen dollars stashed in my drawer, and I could count on more when our business got underway. But if I used so much for the toad, how could I ever pay for my year's tuition at East Lakes next year?

I thrust the thoughts away, tried to bury them amid the detritus of all my anxieties. As always, I walked slowly to the beach.

There is a ridge of sand like a dune lying between the cottages where the back road makes a ninety-degree curve to settle into its parallel course with the highway. This was the public access to the beach, but it always seemed a secret trail to us as children. The tree-covered dune rose almost as high as the low-peaked cottages on either side, and because of the trees, we were completely hidden.

On impulse, I trotted from the road up along the top of the dune, toward the beach. Where it sloped down, I paused and looked over the sand and water – a queen surveying her lands. And they were my lands now. My loose-limbed form and sloppy blouse were part of the hot, dry winds that shaped the sand and rolled the waves.

They were all mine. I sniffed the water smells and gazed about me, savoring the silence. The cottages on either side were boarded up. Only three sunbathers lounged on the beach.

The gulls cried loudly to me, wheeling and screaming at the waves that rolled in the small fish and debris they fed on. At my feet, a narrow, rope-ribboned pattern wove across the sand. A snake had passed by. The delicate trail led across the dune, at one end disappearing into a small hole between the boards of the cottages on my left. The snake would be safe from its worst predator – the cottagers.

I stepped over the trail, careful not to mar its dainty pattern, and slid down the steep drift to the beach. The sand was hot, making me run, hop-footed and gasping, to the shore. Broken waves swirled over my feet and sucked at my toes. The wind was high today, whipping the lake into angry, caramel-colored rolls. When the lake was calm again, there might be a new sandbar started by a submerged branch or a rock. It would disappear again in a few weeks.

But today the high waves were dangerous, signaling a fierce undertow.

On hot summer days when the wind blew fierce and the waves rolled high, Daddy and I had sat in water no deeper than our ankles, our hands and feet burrowing into the sand like crabs to fight the undertow. Some days we were carried thirty or forty feet down the beach before the wave would lose its grip.

In shallow water, the waves merely rearranged our position, as though we were driftwood being cast ashore. But had we ventured out to thigh-depth, no one could have saved us. The tow would have heaved us to the surface, yards and yards out. And then in a second or two we would have been pulled under again. Many people were drowned in that lake – people who did not realize the power of the water.

As I walked swiftly along the wild shore, the magic of my childhood experiences eluded me. Finally, I gave it up and strode up to the summer house, banging through the screen door. My mother was sitting, curled up like a kitten on the comfortable sofa, a magazine spread unheeded on her knees.

"Sandy, I'd like you to look at this."

She didn't move when I took the magazine from her lap. She pointed to one side of the page – a black-boxed, exuberant bubbling about a writing contest for teenagers. Prizes ranged from a thousand dollars for first prize, down to a hundred for fifth place.

"So?" I muttered.

"Don't be dense, Sandy," she said wearily. "You're a good writer and there's always a chance you could win one of those prizes – if you want it enough."

"What good would the money do me here?" I felt hateful and was enjoying it.

My mother's mouth quirked into a very slight smile of amusement.

"You've fought me every inch, Sandy, and I can't fight you any more. Your conversation with your father made me realize that. I'm picking up the pieces of my life that I gave – no shoveled – away for all the years I was married to you father. And it's not easy for me. But I want my life. You have no idea how much I want this life Sandy.

"I'd hoped that I could bring you along with me, but I waited too long. It took me seven years to decide to leave your father. I hated him the whole time, but I'd made him my life. I'd depended on him for meaning, for love, for my very existence."

"Then what made you change?" I demanded, wanting to stop her, but wanting to know what she was really like. I had never seen my mother as a person before. I couldn't avoid it now, for in an orgy of honesty she was dumping her whole self on the floor between us.

"I don't know," she said slowly, suddenly as puzzled as a small child faced with a dilemma beyond understanding. "It wasn't his girlfriends, for I'd always known he would take a mistress sooner or later."

I opened my mouth to protest, but couldn't speak. I felt she'd slandered my Daddy, yet the almost-woman in me grasped what she had said. There were no words. My mother went on, not noticing that I was floundering between fears and certainties.

"I think it was his true love – his painting. Your father, despite his glib ways, would sacrifice anything to it, Sandy. You. Me. Himself. If I hadn't understood that, I would never have loved him. And in the end, I would never have hated him.

"But that's not the point," she said suddenly, rousing herself to look at me. "I want myself. I've given until I can't and won't give any more – not even to you, Sandy. You can do what you want now. If you want to go back to East Lakes, I won't stop you, even though," she said, her face looking weary and sad, "I know it's not right for you to go there. It's the Dream Girl who goes to East Lakes, Sandy. Not the person you are."

"You don't know the person I am," I said, my voice and suddenly my thoughts hard and clear.

"No, I suppose not," she said with that slight smile again. "But I doubt if you do either. There's always a time of choices, Sandy. I've made mine, and maybe soon you will make some too. I can't give you any money for school because I don't have it to give you. If you can earn it, or coax it from your father, then I won't try to stop you from going."

I had a sudden vision of her casting me off in the Biblical sense – driving me from the summer house with curses and a writhing dish towel.

"Will...will you be angry with me," I asked. I meant, would she still love me – feel herself my mother. I could not bear to be abandoned by my mother.

"No," she said simply. "I'm letting you go, not tossing you out. If you ever want to come back to me, I'll always want you."

She walked out of the summer house and away from me. After a few minutes I went out on the verandah to watch the waves and the sand. I could see the dark green of her slacks and the blowing billow of her cloud-white blouse far down the beach, her back still to me as she walked and walked. After a while I could no longer see her.

I wanted to run and cling to my mother. I wanted my father to stride into the house, his laugh booming and his arms strong as he swung me into the air.

And suddenly I wanted to be free of it all. I wanted to be sure and happy, flying with the wind, rolling with the waves, untouched by the pulling and tugging of personalities, of needs, of wants. I wanted to be empty like the shells on the beach.

I wanted to be the Dream Girl.

I ran into the house and clutched the telephone. The operator was inclined to be chatty, explaining that the call might take a minute or two. I didn't answer.

At last the phone began to ring. When he answered I tried not to cry.

"Daddy," I said, "it's me, Sandy."

"Well, Sandy," he said. There was little welcome in his tones. "I hope you're not phoning to take another crack at that France trip."

"Oh no," I whispered. "I just missed you, that's all. I wish I could see you."

"I'd like to see you too, Dream Girl," he said easily, but his voice didn't long for me as I did for him. "You know you've caught me at a bad time, Sandy. I've got a dealer coming to see my new work. He's going to bring a fellow from one of the New York art museums. You know what that means."

"Yes." I felt small, unimportant.

"I knew you'd understand, Sandy," Daddy went on, his voice warm and easy again. "I can always count on my Dream Girl, just like you can count on your old man, right!"

"Yes."

"Cheer up," he said, his voice warm with sudden concern. "I know it's hard living with you mother. God, don't I know! But one of these days I'll take a run up there and we'll take a swim and go for a milkshake together – just like the good old days."

"Please come soon, Daddy," I whispered, my voice unruly from the welling tears. "I really miss you a lot."

"I will, Sandy. Don't worry. I'll come soon."

Chapter 6

Jack knocked on a cottage door, the eighteenth that morning. When the lady answered, he handed her a flyer.

"Good morning," he said. "I'm Jack Cilento. This is my brother, Joey, and our friend, Sandy Welsham. Did you receive the flyer we left in your mailbox last week?"

"Why, yes," the woman smiled. "I think this is just a wonderful idea – I hate the walk to get milk or the paper or whatever three times a day. My husband has the car, you know, to go into the city..."

We all nodded, mesmerized by the gush of words. Then we smiled and chuckled at a couple of little jokes. But she ordered the paper and a loaf of bread and a bottle of milk daily, with special orders to be given as needed.

I marked her down on our growing list.

We had been knocking on doors all week, systematically calling on every cottage whenever Jack and Joey could get away from the store. In an unusual fit of energy, their father was doing most of the cleaning and stocking of shelves in preparation for the summer business.

"Your father's being a big help," I remarked, thinking bitterly of my own father. "You guys are lucky."

Jack muttered, "Yeah," and Joey turned his head away.

"What's wrong?" I demanded.

"Nothing," Jack said shortly. "Come on, let's get to work."

And so we rapped on doors, introduced ourselves, and tried to hustle a little business from the cottagers. All in all, I found it was fairly easy – Jack did most of the talking while Joey and I smiled with moronic cheerfulness.

Jack and Joey kept running figures, their voices intense and hard as they calculated and coaxed the numbers into a promise. I was impatient with all this. After all, things always worked out – I wonder now how they were able to bear me. I suppose I was part of the uncertain promise of the money and escape.

"Oh hell," Joey said suddenly when the figuring was done and no more promises could be coaxed from the lists. He stood up quickly and jerkily brushed the sand off his cut-offs. "Let's go g..get a milkshake."

We ran and yelled down the beach, our feet slipping in the sand, plowing and straining for footholds until we reached the hard wet water edge. We ran on, hollering ourselves back to our childhood – before I became long and lanky and before the boys' voices changed.

I had noticed the change in them a year or two before – the hairiness of their legs in their shorts and bathing suits, the depth of their voices that sometimes made me feel odd.

Both Jack and Donny had tried exploratory kisses with me the year before. I played at it for a little bit, then resentfully pushed them away. Maybe my hormones weren't up to par. I don't know, because even the memory is hazy. I remember clearly though that while we swam together, even Joey's hands seemed to be boosting me by my bottom more than my arms and legs. Donny was the worst (of course). Jack and Joey didn't bother me, for somehow their touches were as innocent as my own uncertainties about the changes I could see in all of us – especially myself.

But Donny was different. He touched as a man does, though I didn't know it then. His hands would be laid tightly against the parts of my body that were private to me, always at times when I could not protest or move away.

And then he would look at me, his blue eyes fierce and blank at the same time. His mouth would be moist but without expression. I saw him do it with Pam, but she did not seem to feel as angry and curiously hurt as I did.

I was very innocent. I knew all the facts and quite a few of the possibilities. But I didn't know the emotions or the fears, the hurts or the pleasures. I had information, not understanding.

And the feelings I had as we ran down the beach – perplexing new feelings. I let Jack and Joey run ahead of me, though I could easily have beaten them. But I liked to watch Jack's muscles knot and flex as he twisted and leapt with exuberance. And I liked the glint of sun on the pale hair that coated Joey's legs. When he pulled off his shirt and threw it into the air, the sight of the hair under his arms made me feel dizzy in my stomach, but not my head. I wanted to be close to them both. And I wished I could hold them, stroke them, and know the feel of them as I would with a kitten or a dog, or even a little toad. When we were little I would demand they flex their biceps and we'd have contests. For years I won as easily as they did. But with my new feelings, I knew I could never ask to see them again. It was very frustrating and very exciting.

We ran and shouted and finally ended up at the summer house. The boys ran ahead and spread out, lying full length on the redwood lounges, gasping and panting. I hesitated by the rail, still uncomfortably aware of them. But Jack laughed and spread his legs so that his feet hung to the boards on either side.

"Siddown," he invited breezily.

I grinned and sat on the end, my back to him, facing Joey. Everything felt easy again. But Jack hadn't finished with his spurt of good humor. Suddenly he closed his legs around my middle like a vise.

I shrieked and Joey laughed while Jack shouted that I'd never get away. His leg muscles were as strong as the rest of him, so I threw myself backwards against him, planning to knock the wind out of him and so triumph. But he knew my fighting techniques from years of tussles and was ready for me.

"Jack, I hate you!" I shrieked as he cocooned my arms and legs with his own. There was a hazy swirl of impressions in my senses – of smell and sound and feel of Jack, and much laughter, when a new voice washed over us.

"Who gives her the first roll in the hay?" Donny demanded loudly. The grin I hated widened his cheeks.

Jack's arms and legs relaxed instantly and I pulled away quickly, feeling as though I'd been caught once again by my father in a kindergarten game of show and tell.

"Nah, she's too mean," Jack said offhand, his face devoid of the smile that would have included Donny in the joke. He didn't look at me. Donny did. His look was speculating but friendly. Any other time I would have grinned and welcomed him back, one of the gang, absent for almost a year. Instead I leaned on the verandah railing and stared at the blue mirror of the lake, rippled at the edges, waiting for the fire to retreat from my cheeks.

"Wh..en did you get here?" asked Joey. How grown-up he sounded to me, even with the catching twist in his words. I turned around and faced them all again.

"Last night," Donny responded with a smile, his voice equally friendly and mature sounding. I understood that they were testing, feeling out relationships that were changing, looking for strengths and weaknesses in each other. For some reason I was not included in the testing.

"We were going to come a couple of days ago, but Dad ran into a problem at one of the high schools. They made him superintendent of five high schools, so he had to work longer into the summer this year. You're here early this year, Sandy," he rounded on me suddenly.

Startled, I opened my mouth to speak, but the words seemed impossible.

"Sandy's living here full-time now," Jack intercepted for me.

"Her folks have go..otten a divorce," Joey added. I felt as though they had erected a shield for me with their words. I could stay silent behind it, or when I chose I could leave it with my words.

"Jesus, you mean you're going to have to go to that crap regional high school, and bus it, as well?"

"I haven't decided yet," I said, feeling cool and angry and in control again. "I might go back to East Lakes in the fall. Mom thinks I should earn part of the money, so it all depends on whether or not I think it's worth it."

"God, I wouldn't think there's any choice," Donny exclaimed with an expansive gesture. Even in my anger I noticed the fleshy muscles of his chest and shoulders, revealed by the unbuttoned shirt that hung loosely around him. I bet he plays football, I thought suddenly.

"Pam'll be up this afternoon," Donny told us. "Hail, hail the gang's all here."

And suddenly I remembered the easy fun we had all had at one time. Donny wasn't the enemy. The make-believe bad guys and phantoms were. We were comrades-in-arms then.

"It's getting hot," I said suddenly. "How about we go swimming then I make us some hot dogs or something?"

"Sounds great," Donny said.

"Yeah," Joey agreed with a grin and a slight shudder in his shoulders. I barely noticed his quivers now but Donny quickly averted his eyes. It angered me again.

"Go put your suit on, Sandy," Jack said, heaving himself out of the chair. His eyes were still cold, but he seemed happy enough I decided. I slammed into the cottage.

"Sandy," Mom said to me as I passed.

"We're going swimming," I told her exuberantly. She had used her "will you" voice, but this time she just smiled and turned back to her typewriter.

"Okay," she murmured. "I'll catch you later."

I had a new bathing suit and last year's discreet one-piece. Uncomfortably I laid the bikini out on the bed, remembering Donny's fierce-blank eyes. Slowly I stripped off my clothes, trying to decide what to wear.

"You'll have to wear it sometime," I muttered to myself in the mirror.

But the Sandy-in-the-mirror told me I was

scared of something I didn't have words for. I gazed at myself, noting all the disheartening details.

Like my father, everything about me was long – my arms, fingers, neck, torso, and legs. Like my mother they were thin. Where I should have had a lovely curve between my ribs and hips, there was just a slight indentation. My breasts were fairly respectable but kind of small.

"I look like a sack of potatoes with a couple of potatoes bulging out," I muttered resentfully. I angrily pulled on the bikini. Once it was on, I still felt thoroughly undressed. But, stifling my unruly emotions I ran out of my room. Grabbing a blouse I'd left draped over a chair earlier, I pulled it on as I slammed outside. The boys were already in the water, lazily floating about and talking in loud voices.

I picked my way down the beach to the water, feeling totally self-conscious. It seemed to me that the world was full of bodies that everyone was looking at. I was desperately afraid that someone would look at mine. And I was equally afraid that no one would.

"What's it like?" I yelled out to the boys.

"C...c'mon Sandy!" Joey called, standing up waist deep. "It's not that bad!"

I waded around up to my thighs with my blouse still on. My arms seemed paralyzed when I thought of ripping that slim covering from my unprotected self.

"C'mon!" Jack shouted.

"It's too cold," I lied.

"You just have to plunge in," Donny said with a wicked grin.

"May..maybe she needs encouragement," Joey agreed.

"Well, let's help her then," Jack grinned.

They came after me, all three. I shrieked and yelled. They caught my arms and legs, shouted "Heave ho!" and tossed me, blouse and all, into the lake.

It was cold, but once I was in, I liked it. There's something about the feel of cool water whirling and pressing around you. I dove down, seeing if I could still swim under water as well as last year.

My blouse hampered me, and so I pulled it off and flung it dripping onto the beach, almost forgetting my fears. I don't know whether or not the boys noticed the amount of me they could see, for now I no longer cared. I ran back into the deeper water, diving and swimming in a well of joy. Under the water I frog-stroked lazily, watching the movement of sand rippling across the bottom. Here and there tiny fish nibbled at my toes and fingers, but disappeared in darts of speed if I tried to capture them. Once in a while, emerald green strands of seaweed clung to me, wrapping like wet cotton around my fingers and toes.

A little to one side I saw the bottom half of Joey standing, legs spread widely. His upper half was just a wavy swirl of light above the water. Impulsively I tried to shoot between his legs, just as we always had when we were young. I got stuck. Then I felt his hands, big, hard and strong on my behind as he gave me the necessary shove to go "under the bridge." When I came up for a lungful of air, I gasped and immediately dived down again, not willing to face him. I could still feel the pressure of his hands.

We swam lazily for most of the time, occasionally falling back into the screaming hilarity of years before. Then we would dive between disembodied legs, or try to pull each other under the water. It was just the same as when we were small, but it was so different. After each touch, I could feel the sensations on my skin. With each casual brushing of skin or hands, I was opened to a flood of sensation. I smelled new smells, felt new touches, heard sounds I had never listened to before. It all pulled me and frightened me until I felt a stranger to myself, but somehow even more known to myself all at once.

We left the water at last, struggling cold and exhausted up to the summer house. Inside the boys draped themselves around the furniture, leaving wet circles whenever they moved. None of them bothered to pull on their shirts. Mom came in and sat down to chat with them. I wondered how she didn't notice their muscles and arms and stomachs. Probably, I decided, it was because she was old.

"How many hog dogs?" I yelled from the kitchen.

"Four!"

"Three!"

"Four!"

"Do you want one, Mom?" I asked, trying to add up these incredible amounts.

"No thanks, Sandy. I had something while you were swimming. I'm going for a stroll down the beach."

I heard her go out and the door slam behind her, while I added thirteen hot dogs to a pot of boiling water. Then, while I heard the boys begin a desultory conversation, I opened bottles of Coke for us all.

"Hurry up woman," Donny shouted out to me. "Don't you know we're about to die of hunger!"

"Go ahead!" I replied cheerfully.

We went outside to eat the hot dogs, lazing

in the hot sun, the smells of the water the best relish for our food.

I don't remember what we talked about, but I do remember the good feeling that all was as it should be, as it used to be. I forgot about the feel of their bodies and drowsed in the warm pleasure of the sun on my skin. I think I dozed off. When I awoke suddenly, the group had changed. Pam had joined us. I had thought myself daring in my bikini, but now I felt like a child dressing up in her mother's clothes.

Pam had let her hair grow longer, so that it hung straight and thick and auburn down her back. She had curves where I had indentations. And she had breasts where I had potato bulges. Her bikini was a white string that thickened slightly at the interesting parts. She had the most gorgeous tan I'd ever seen.

"Hi Rip Van Winkle," she laughed with a lilt she'd added since the year before.

"Hi!" I muttered feebly. I shut my eyes, wanting to remove this body from the beach. When I opened them again, she was still there, still looking like an advertisement for something. And the boys were all turned toward her the way compass needles turn north.

"Hail, hail, the gang's all here," I muttered under my breath. When the boys laughed in unison to something dumb Pam said, I wished the gang had remained the way it was that morning.

Chapter 7

The sun was setting, flaming behind the trees and cottages down the beach. I sat motionless on the lounge on the verandah, magazine spread across my knees, trying to ignore the mosquitoes and make sense of the afternoon.

After Pam came, everything had turned around. She and Donny went to the same high school, were in the same grade, and chatted easily about parties and people I'd never experienced. Jack and Joey were apart from me, mesmerized by the glowing curves of Pam's body. I did not feel jealousy. But I felt bitterly alone again, unsure, and without a time or place of my own. I had latched onto Jack and Joey, and now I wondered if they felt any affection for me at all, or if I had given their actions emotions that had never been there.

I remembered little coldnesses, especially from Jack. And Joey, so easy and kind – was his gentleness the same as Roy's, offered to anyone who hurt inside? I didn't know. I only knew that my friends had become strangers.

And where was the Dream Girl?

Daddy had not come. Three weeks had passed since I called him, and he had not come. I wrote to him two or three times a week, but he rarely answered. If my mother knew of the hurt I felt every day when the mailbox was empty, she said nothing. When the phone bill came with the long distance charges on it, she still said nothing. I had tried to explain them guiltily, because money was not easy for her.

"Don't Sandy," she said gently. "I'm not trying to cut you off from your father. He's the only father you'll ever have. I know I can rely on your good sense to only call when you must."

She was so reasonable about it that it enraged me. Good sense! What had losing everything that mattered to me have to do with good sense? How could she make what I was feeling a matter of good sense and financial management?

"How's it going?" she asked me suddenly. I hadn't heard the screen door. "Ugh! How can you stand the mosquitoes out here?"

"I can stand anything if I have to," I snapped.

"I don't like the tone of your voice," my mother said. "I don't know what's bothering you this evening, but I'm tired of being the brunt of every bad mood you fall into."

"Good, then I'll leave," I shouted and ran up the steps, dropping the magazine as I went. I slammed into the house, then into my bedroom. Furiously I threw myself onto the bed and looked up at my picture. Daddy laughed down at me, as if we were sharing a secret joke that Mom could never figure out. I began to relax.

I was still his Dream Girl. He still loves me, I thought drowsily. But why doesn't he come?

*   *   *

I watched my mother bending over her typewriter, typing, typing. Always typing yet another story. I wondered how she could go on, day after day, with nothing to show for what she had done, no appreciation for the part of herself that poured into the words and sentences and the stories she patiently put on those pages. Sometimes she paced, smoking furiously in frustration. Sometimes, when she didn't know that I was around, she swore long staccato strings of curses. But she always went back to the typewriter.

"Mom," I said hesitantly. She was typing so furiously that I was unsure whether or not

I should disturb her. But she looked up and smiled, light seeming to dance in her eyes. The writing must be going very well.

I held out the magazine with the invitation for young writers to send in their short stories. "I don't know what to say, what to write about," I told her.

"Looking for advice or permission to quit?" she asked. I blushed then stuck out my chin.

"Advice," I said, suddenly changing my mind. I plopped down on a chair. "Everything I write sounds like a lurid romance between the kind of people you know couldn't be for real. I'm not really very intellectual," I confessed.

"You and me both," she replied wryly.

"I can't write about what I know, because that's so ordinary – or too personal."

I thought about the divorce. Sure, there were strong emotions there, but I couldn't blithely put myself on paper – stretched out naked for every disinterested editor to prod with a superior toe. And the things I did write – I could hear them now – *'Hey Joe! We've got a live one!'*

"I wish I could tell you what to do, Sandy," my mother said. "Write about something or somebody you care about – even if you make that person up. If it's any good, you'll feel like you're mentally touching steel. It's so sure, you don't have to wonder what someone else thinks. It'll be so strong, you'll know it doesn't matter one way or another."

My mother's eyes lit suddenly and she looked into the distance seeing a landscape I'd never known, radiating a sureness that I'd never seen in her before. Suddenly she reminded me of Daddy when he was creating a picture. I remembered how he would caress the painting, his long hands gentle and tender over the canvas. It was always his best ones that drew his gentled fingers.

I sighed.

"I guess that's not much help," she said with a smile. "It's Tuesday. Why don't we run into town and go to the library. Maybe you can find a good how-to book. Or at least some books of short stories that will show you how to structure a plot."

"But I don't have a plot to structure," I wailed.

"Well, that's got to come from there," she tapped my forehead.

I sighed again, but went into my room to change.

I enjoyed trips into Port Rowan, even when I was trying to avoid Mom. After the highway had run the length of the beach, it turned sharply northeast, and the scenery changed abruptly. Instead of pines and beach and sun-browned grass, it was as though we had suddenly plunged into the everglades.

For a couple of miles we drove through swamp where oaks, elms, and willows hung thick with trailing wild grape vines and other creepers I never knew the names of. The trees lined the highway, surging up from beds of bulrushes and marsh grasses. Everywhere it was green, green, green.

Here too, you could often see flocks of birds, small animals, turtles and bullfrogs. These creatures represented a glorious, free wildlife to me after the half-tame squirrels, sparrows, and starlings of the city house and school. And I loved them all, with a yearning kind of love that perhaps everyone shares, or perhaps no one. Some people go to great lengths to experience nature. This was where nature was mine.

Beyond the marsh area, the land becomes gently rolling, marked with old farm houses, all neatly kept. A bit farther, past the town, is tobacco country where fields of leafy, dark green plants, turning to sandy yellow at the bottom, are hand-picked by gangs of migrant workers. The drying sheds, kilns, always looked to me like play houses or decorative barns, for the ones we saw from the road were always freshly painted green or brick-color. It was a pastoral painting – neat, green, orderly with a quiet appearance of human industry and contentment. I'm sure it was not so, but I watched from a car window only. From the car window, it was lovely.

Port Rowan was, I think, an agricultural town serving the farms of the area, and in summer, the cottagers. I don't remember what the inhabitants thought of the summer people (if anything) but the cottagers rather liked it. I remember only a few of the stores – the selective memory of a child. I remember the five and ten clearly, with its slightly sloped wooden floors and the musty smell of treasures to be discovered. I remember the bakery with its warm smells and baked goods, not so good as Mrs. Patterson's but much better than we ever got in the city. I remember the post office, the doctor's office (where I was once treated for an ear infection when I was six), and I remember very clearly the library.

It was situated in a small, ivy-covered building – an old house, I think. There were just two rooms with the books so tightly wedged onto the shelves that I never pulled one out to glance at it unless I was almost certain it was the one I wanted to borrow. Everyone moved about in a solemn, hushed fashion, presided over by the librarian. She was a nice woman, neither fat nor thin, old nor young. I think perhaps she may not have been a trained librarian such as I was accustomed to in the city, but she had a detailed and intimate knowledge of almost every book in the little library.

I let Mom walk in ahead of me, feeling a bit uncomfortable and out of place. I didn't know how to ask for what I wanted. In fact, other than a hazy notion of what Mom had told me to get, I was lost.

Unless I won one of the prizes for the contest, there wasn't much chance of me going to East Lakes. My most optimistic tally of my share of the delivery service profits probably wouldn't cover more than a semester's tuition, and Mom had said nothing about spending money. I couldn't, wouldn't go back as the poor relation. Maybe Daddy...

I brushed the thought aside and looked around. Three kids, all younger than me, stared at a bird's nest perched on a shelf, and boasting in stage whispers of ones they had seen. I wandered dispiritedly around the two small rooms, suddenly overwhelmed by the tight-packed books that marched in unfamiliar order. I lightly fingered two or three, then withdrew my hands. The titles didn't intrigue me.

It's an odd thing about libraries. Most that I've been in either feel like an old-fashioned front parlor – only slightly less hallowed than a church; or else they feel like a country kitchen – bustling, busy and friendly. In the latter, their chief delight is to share the treasures of their hearts with anyone who walks through the doors.

In a front parlor library, the books are just as treasured, but before being permitted to see these treasures, the patron is judged. If found worthy, all unbends. If not, the borrower slinks outside again, one or two books plucked from the shelves in the undiscriminating haste of a thief. The books will be returned to the bookdrop later, unread.

This was a front parlor library, and I was not at home in it. But I loved libraries and refused to leave a thief. I sucked in a large breath of air, straightened my shoulders, and approached its mistress.

"Excuse me," I spoke up as firmly as I could. "I'm trying to find some books about how to write short stories. Or maybe a book of good short stories to study."

The librarian looked at me for an instant without expression, then smiled. I had been found worthy.

"I think we have two or three books that might help you," she said with another sudden smile, and led me to a nook I had overlooked.

Twenty minutes later I left bearing treasures. Two books of short stories, two how-to's, and a manual of the English language. I didn't want the last, but it's impossible to refuse a treasure being thrust determinedly on you.

*   *   *

I sat on my bed, paper, pencils, and my how-to books spread around, watching the setting sun's rays grow fainter and fainter on Daddy's face. For three evenings I had sat this way, searching for my story within myself. I wondered how my mother could create story after story, finding that steel-hard ring of truth in each. Maybe it was only in a few. Maybe it was something that eluded her, like the rainbows we chased as children. But when I had run and run until all the breath was out of me, I always hoped that maybe the rainbow would suddenly lie in my hands. I wondered how many do catch the rainbow. And how many only looked for the pot of gold, never seeing the beauty of the rainbow? How many never catch toads, never see beauty?

Toads. Everywhere there were toads in my life. Mixtures of ugliness and beauty that I could not separate, could not find the beginning and end of. Where did one change into the other?

In my mind and unfocused eyes, I gathered all my people in to me, catching them where they hid their lives, all so separate from me, never close when I needed them.

The outside screen door banged suddenly. Mom had come in from the beach, cool and invigorated from a brisk walk or a plunge in the water. Then I could hear the eternal *tap, tap* of her typewriter. I sighed and stared again at my blank paper, wondering where I would find the story that would win me enough money to go back to East Lakes.

But the mood was not quite gone and my eyes strayed to the picture of my Daddy and me, as my thoughts strayed to those easy days of toad catching and adventures in the sand. Days with Jack and Joey and Donny and Pam that flickered warm and happy through my thoughts, the way the sun filtered through the green leaves onto the diamond sparkling sand.

And then my story came to me. I felt the steel hidden in the gentle curves and folds of ideas and laughter and tears. I would write about the twins and me. About all of us as children catching toads in the summers that waved by us. I remembered how I had turned from the fears and hurts that hung in their eyes between flights of imagination – that summer that almost stole their father from them. Vaguely I remembered overhearing the horrified gossip of how they had been alone at night when the social worker came. The twins had been gone for several days, returning only to collect their things. Jack told me their dad was real sick. There was something wrong with his head and he had to go to the hospital. He and Joey spent most of the winter in a foster home in Simcoe. I remembered how hard and cold Jack had seemed that last day, and how Joey had had spasm after spasm until he couldn't even talk. I remember how the social worker looked away from him, the way some people look away from toads – as if they're too ugly to bear.

For the first time I understood their fears. I had lost my father too. I knew I could write about a summer of catching toads – of being children who are afraid and can't understand what is happening.

I wrote all that evening and into the night, sometimes flexing my hands or pacing around the room to relieve my exhaustion. Mom opened the door once but said nothing as I glanced at her, barely comprehending. At two, I wrote the final sentence, then sat back in wondering exhaustion. The world spun by me, and I simply sat and watched, apart from everything. Slowly I left the world I had created on paper and returned to the world I existed in now. I began to shiver, and I became aware of my roiling, starving stomach.

My mother was sitting curled up on the sofa, reading over one of her own typed manuscripts, when I rambled out of my room.

"You still up?" I muttered hazily. I had never felt so tired before.

"Uh huh," she said. "There's fried chicken and rice in the oven for you if you want it."

I got my dinner, a fork, and a glass of milk, then returned to the living room. For a few minutes I ate hungrily, barely aware of my mother watching me.

"I finished my story," I said after a few minutes.

"Is it good?"

"Yes." I replied simply.

I remember the sudden warmth of the smile that flooded across my mother's face. For a brief instant she allowed her love for me to show, just in the way she looked at me. I don't think I had ever thought she loved me before.

"Will you read it?" I asked. "It might need some little changes – spelling and things like that."

"I'd be glad to," Mom answered. "After you've revised it tomorrow, or whenever you feel it's the time, before you're ready to start the final draft."

"I don't think it'll need much revision," I protested. Newly emerged from the chrysalis of the writing, I couldn't bear the idea of hacking at the words I had agonized over.

My mother smiled wryly.

"The first writing is the fun part," she said. "Now you've got the hard work ahead of you – rewriting. Leave your story alone for a few days, then go back to it. You'll probably find there are parts where you didn't say enough, and parts where you said too much, and parts that you expressed very badly and will have to redo. You've got a month before the deadline, Sandy dear. The competition will be very stiff."

I nodded, not really believing her, but too tired to argue. She might need to rewrite, I told myself smugly, but just wait until she reads my story. Then she'll see that she doesn't know what she's talking about....

Chapter 8

Summer had come.

It had threatened to sweep in on hot winds and blue skies before, but always the gods had hesitated, chuckled, then sent another draft of cool spring weather just when I was sure it was at last, true summer.

I leaned against the delivery bike and stared at the cloud-decorated blue, the reflected heat draining my energy into a passive wish for solitude. The sky achieves a certain shade of blue for each season, indescribable, but discernible to the eye that cares to watch for it. And today, the sky arched clear, shimmering, summer blue.

I stared back through the trees toward the cottages, looking for Joey. This was the first day of our delivery service, but instead of elation, I was feeling irritable and resentful of the hard work. The sun was too hot. Joey was too slow. The route was too long. The bicycle was too heavy.

I had reread my story that morning for the first time since I had written it four days before.

I had woken up early, and on smug impulse reached over and taken my story into my hands. It felt thick and full. I felt like a proud mother as I glanced from it to the painting of Daddy. He shared my pride this morning and so, softly, I began reading it aloud to him.

But something had changed. It was as if gremlins had altered my words. They no longer flowed with ease and beauty. At times they limped and stumbled, and even though I knew what the words should have been saying, sometimes the thoughts became knotted or meandered endlessly. I stopped reading and looked up at Daddy's face. He was laughing at me. I stared in confusion at the papers before me, feeling a slow deep humiliation enclosing me, pulling me downward like the undertow of the lake.

How could I have been so stupid? So smug? So sure I had written something of beauty?

"Goddammit!" I muttered and furiously threw the papers on the floor, seeing them scatter with satisfaction. I pulled on my clothes, not bothering to wash, then dashed outside to the beach, letting the door slam in my fury.

The beach was deserted. Under my feet the sand was cool, crusted lightly from the morning dew. As I made my way to the water's edge, I jumped over a pile of dark green seaweed washed up a few days before and stared out at the lake. Cold wavelets washed over my bare toes, sucking the sand from around them. The morning breezes had not yet ruffled the lake up to whitecaps or even the playful little waves of a very calm day. Far off in the hazy distance, I could see the dull brown speck of a fishing boat on the empty water. Fishing was almost finished in the lake even then, because of the growing pollution.

In the cool morning air I relaxed a little, but the humiliation did not leave me. I felt I had been caught in something shameful. And I resented knowing that my mother had been right, that my story needed massive rewriting if it was to be salvaged for the contest. I couldn't understand how this had happened. When I thought of my story, I still felt the hard steel of truth under what I had tried to tell. I knew that my story mattered somehow. But anyone who was forced to read it would only see the ineptitudes, the stumblings, the juvenile meanderings. How could anyone wade through those masses of words to find the truth?

"Sandy!" Mom called from the verandah. My name hung in crystals in the calm air. I couldn't pretend not to hear.

"Breakfast! Hurry or you'll be late!" She disappeared back into the house and, reluctantly, I left the water and slogged up the sloped beach to the house. I had forgotten that today the twins and I began our business venture in earnest.

Mom and I ate breakfast in comparative silence. When I went to get changed and cleaned up for the day, my story had been gathered up and neatly placed on my dresser. I glowered at it, but was too depressed to bother trying to read it again.

"Did you read my story?" I asked cautiously when I emerged from my bedroom. I was torn between dread and hope – maybe she'd found a virtue I had missed.

"No," she said, smiling slightly as · she cleared the table. "I don't think that would be fair until you've had a chance to revise a bit. I know my first drafts always sound like an illiterate wrote them."

"Yeah," I muttered and bit my lip, still resentful that she was right. I had planned on stunning her with a display of genius – a child prodigy, undiscovered until that moment.

"Well, I better go," I mumbled and slipped out the door.

"Good luck," she called after me.

*   *   *

"Get m..many orders?" Joey asked exuberantly from behind me. I hadn't heard him come up.

"Six."

"I got fifteen," he exclaimed. "That's t..twenty-one and we've still got half the route to go!"

He peered at the lists, radiating excitement and pride.

"I can count," I snapped. How could he with his spasms and stutters have done so much better than I had? Well maybe they felt sorry for him.

"What's bugging you, Sandy?" he asked after a minute. "You d..don't want to back out, do you? I r..really need your help."

His face had turned gentle and concerned as he stared at me. I felt like crying and maybe screaming and crawling away to hide.

"Let's take a b..break," he offered suddenly. "I meant to tell you, but I forgot. Last fall I found a s..super hideout – the kind we hu.. unted for every summer when we were kids. Snake tracks and probably t..toads and everything. It's just up here."

I let him take the bike as he led me past three cottages. He chatted comfortably, but he stuttered more as he felt my emotions.

On our right, the sand had been gradually piling up until finally, between the wide-spaced driveways of two cottages, it became a dune about twelve feet high. Like most other places, it was wild here – poison ivy, wild grape vines, and milkweeds all grew unchecked in the sand, shaded by the pines and poplars. The beach curved outward into the lake near here, so the dune was about a hundred and fifty yards from the cottages themselves, well-screened by the towering trees and latticing vines.

Joey hid the bike in a clump of bushes.

"Come on," he urged and scrambled up the steep slope of the dune. Reluctantly I followed, panting as I strained to climb up the sand before my feet and hands slid out from under me. At the top I flopped onto my stomach and tried to slide down the other side. Joey laughed, grabbed one arm, and pulled me giggling and yelping the rest of the way.

"N..now isn't this a..a super hideout," he exclaimed, his hands proudly stuck on his hips.

I sat up, spit out what sand I could, and looked around. It was better than any hideout we had found as children. The dune rose again about ten feet from where I sat. The closely circling trees and webbing of vines must have protected the hollow from the winds that constantly changed the landscape.

"I come here when I w..want to be alone," Joey said, suddenly serious again. He squatted down beside me. "It's si..silly, but I like to have a place like this. A hideout. Just like wh..en we were kids. I used to look forward to the su..summers when you'd come and we'd play together. Y..you never make me feel l..like I'm different. Like I'm going to be b..buried here in the sand."

He stared off at the trees, his face flushing. I felt my own face growing hot in response, and felt cross about it. I didn't know what to say so I stared at the ground and tried again to spit out the sand that had gotten in my mouth.

"S..so what's bugging you?" Joey asked finally.

When I looked up again I didn't know what to say – how to explain all the stupid things in my story and the big things that I avoided thinking about, and how Daddy still had not come to see me. Instead I began to cry, quiet tears building into sobs.

I leaned toward Joey instinctively, and he held me and murmured as I talked. I don't know what I said. I don't know if I told him everything or nothing, sense or nonsense. Sometimes, as if punctuating my hurts, I would feel him shudder a little as a spasm took him, but it didn't matter.

As my crying eased off I became aware of other things – that my head was on his shoulder with my face burrowed into his neck, that he had his own smell, that he held me differently that either Mom or Daddy. I looked up, suddenly embarrassed, feeling as though I was with a stranger. Joey shook slightly, then softly kissed my cheek. Then we both blushed and pulled anxiously away from each other.

I wiped my arm over my face, trying to erase the tear marks, but got sand in my eyes and mouth.

"God!" I muttered, trying to wipe the irritating particles from my eyes.

Joey looked up. "I have dreams tha..at I'm going to be buried in the stuff. But I w..won't. We'll all get out, Sandy..."

We were silent again for awhile, then Joey smiled and stood up.

"You okay? I mean if you are, we b..better get going if we're going to finish the route then pick up and deliver the groceries."

"Oh yeah!" I said as enthusiastically as I could. Then I watched him as he scrambled to the top of the dune. I still felt funny inside in a way that had nothing to do with my troubles.

"Joey," I called when he reached the top. He paused and half-turned, unconsciously taking a pose like the ancient Greek statues.

What would they look like in cut-offs and a tee-shirt?

"Thanks," I said. "And sorry. I feel better."

He shrugged and grinned.

"So now..now you owe me a crying on the shou..oulder bout," he said. "But if you don't hurry up, our business will be screwed before it ever got st..started."

We slid down the sandbank anxious to forget the past few minutes, determined to recapture our sureness in work. Almost wordlessly we each took one side of the road as before. I took the bike and the beach side, as it was harder for Joey to manage in the shifting sand and control the bike too.

I recall the rest of the morning very clearly – our determination to succeed, and the nervous exhaustion I felt as again and again I cajoled cottagers into trusting us with their orders. Many didn't want to be bothered. Some for obscure reasons didn't trust us – apparently expecting us to leave them inconvenienced with an unfilled order. A few gave us orders cheerfully.

At the end of our route, we climbed onto the bike with me steering and Joey clinging onto me from the back; we pushed it awkwardly along until the moving pedals allowed the motor to catch. It took less than ten minutes to ride the distance that had taken us all morning to walk.

At the store, Jack took the lists of orders, bagged each, and stashed them in the bike while we hurriedly ate a hot dog and chips. I was so tired, but elated too. All was going well. Roy came in part way through and sat down with us.

"Well, Sandy," he said, his voice rich and quiet as it had always been. For the first time I noticed the deep masculine timbre in it that was the same as Joey's. I looked at him suddenly with new eyes.

I had been a sheltered child, raised in a world of inscrutable adults who ordered my life with an incomprehensible logic. Even when my child's perception recognized Roy's behavior as different from other adults, I saw him only as one of them – an adult. His behavior was secondary to his caste. I felt today as though I truly saw him at last, or maybe it was just the edges of him, for it's hard to abandon a habit of thinking and seeing. But I suddenly felt him as a person, as lost as myself.

"How many orders boys?" he asked cheerfully as Jack shambled back into the store.

"Quite a few," Jack said crisply. He was so hard and energetic beside the quiet vagueness of Roy and even Joey.

"W..we did better th..than we thought we would," Joey added. "Didn't know we were such good salesm..men, eh?"

Roy smiled. I saw the movement of his whiskers when the skin pulled into the smile. The coarseness of skin and whiskers fascinated me as though I'd never seen such before.

"That's great kids." He seemed to pause and waver slightly. "Did I ask you how many orders you took?"

"Forty-three, Dad," Jack said. His voice hardened in the words and he turned his back to us and began filling another order. Joey glanced at him, his own face white and hard as marble.

"Guess I'm getting senile," Roy murmured with a half-smile and stood up again. "I'm going for a walk, Jack. Look after the store for me?"

"Sure, Dad," Jack said. "Try to remember I've got to be at the bowling alley when they open at four. Have you got your watch?"

"Sure," Roy answered without checking as he walked out the back way.

There was a silence after he left that I couldn't interpret. I decided that maybe Jack and his father had been quarreling about something. But I had enough problems of my own, I thought in irritation. Who needed this too?

"Are the orders filled Jack?" I asked, standing up, not bothering to see if Joey had finished his milkshake. He was staring at it moodily, stirring it round and round with the striped plastic straw.

"What? Oh yeah. This is the last."

Joey suddenly pushed himself away from the table.

"Let's go, Sandy," he said flatly. "I'll try to get back," I heard him say in an undervoice to Jack as I carried the last bag out the door.

"Okay. I can't be late, and I don't think I should close the store."

"No. T..too much talk."

The rest of the afternoon we delivered orders of groceries. Made change. Tracked cottagers down to the beach or wherever to get paid. It was well past four when we finished the last one.

"Whew, thank goodness we're finished," I muttered wearily to Joey.

"It'll go faster when we're used to the route and people r..remember to leave the money for us," Joey replied without much interest.

"Want to stop by for a Coke?"

"No..o." he said. "Dad might need a hand with the store."

"Why should he?" I demanded. "He managed it for years without your help." I resented his indifference to my invitation and so I stood unmoving beside the bike, waiting for him to answer.

"For Christ sake!" Joey exploded suddenly. "Are you going to drive me back or not! Y..you may n..not have any r..responsibilities, Sandy, b..but I do!" He grabbed my arm and pushed me roughly toward the bike.

"All right!" I snapped. "If you want to go back home that badly, I'll take you!"

I was shocked and upset and wanting to say something clever and nasty, but I didn't know how to talk that way to Joey. We had never quarreled much as children and rarely had he ever snapped at me. All the way back to the store, I seethed with anger and hurt – a feeling that grew rather than lessened when it occurred to me that I'd asked for it.

When we reached the store, Joey climbed off the bike before I had a chance to stop it. I almost lost my balance, but he didn't even notice in his haste to see whether the store was open or not.

It was. Roy was busily making sandwiches for a couple of customers and chatting knowledgeably about what fishing was to be had in the area.

I followed Joey into the store.

"N..need any help, D..Dad?" he asked. He shook briefly with a spasm and his head jerked.

"Nope," Roy replied. "Go along and take it easy with Sandy. You've worked hard today. Get some soft drinks out of the cooler. Treat's on me." He grinned for we had always been free to help ourselves from the time we started playing together years before.

"Say, what's it like over by this Turkey Point?" the customer asked suddenly, jabbing his finger at the map he'd spread over the counter.

"Not bad..." Roy began.

I walked outside furiously, letting the door slam. Not knowing what was making me so angry didn't help what I was feeling at all. If anything it made it worse. A moment later Joey followed me outside carrying a Coke and a grape. I'd always loved grape pop, and Roy's store was one of the few that carried my favorite brand. Something about Joey's thinking to choose it for me, warmed me.

He stood drinking his Coke, staring at the scrub bushes across the highway, seeing nothing I think. The look of white marble had returned to his face. I stood beside him, watching unheeded, not bothering to drink my pop.

"You okay, Joey?" I asked suddenly. He turned to me, blinking, startled at my presence.

"Yeah, sure," he said and shrugged. But it was a nervous, *I'm sorry* shrug. "Want to go for a w..walk along the cut?"

We wandered silently out back and along the still, blue-brown water of the cut. There was silence here. It was warm. Dragonflies swept in low formations under our feet as we rambled across the sun-beaten grass and weeds. I heard the familiar *plop-plop* as tiny frogs leapt for the shelter of the water.

"You remember that story I told you I was writing for the contest," I said suddenly. There was a serenity and closeness here that made me want to share a part of myself.

"Yeah," Joey mumbled.

"I wrote it about you and me and Jack – that summer, that you know, your father got sick."

His eyes turned to mine.

"Is it a good story?" he asked.

"My mother asked that. Yes, it's a good story." And suddenly I knew it was. I would rewrite it and it would be a good story.

"That was a weird summer," Joey said, his eyes looking back into the years when we were nine and eight. "Dad got stranger and stranger – wandering off. Getting dizzy. For.. forgetting things. I..we were so scared. We..we were afraid he'd g..gone crazy."

"Had he?" I asked unsurely. Everyone had always hinted at that.

"No," Joey said, and there was a bleak sound in his voice. "He had a brain tumor.

For awhile they thought may..maybe he'd die. B..but the operation worked, and af..after awhile h..e was okay."

Joey's voice was heavy and sad, as if the fears and unhappiness of that summer had surfaced again. I knew nothing of sorrowful memories – how long they lasted or how they twisted a person into a different shape.

We stood quietly together for awhile. I put my hand in his. It was the best I could do.

Chapter 9

It was finished. I had spent days on it, and at last my story was finished. I squatted on my bed, shivering a little, hugging my pillow as I stared at the picture of Daddy and me. There was a bitter, wondering edge to my feelings of accomplishment. He had been here for none of it. How could he not be here when I loved him so much?

Mom was so excited about my story. She said little, rarely asked more than how it was going, but I was beginning to know her. If she asked at all, it was because her excitement and concern were so strong they were leaking out into a few words, no matter how hard she tried to restrain herself.

I am not a reserved person. My thoughts and feelings spill out in every direction, even when I've had years of regretting my impulsiveness. But Mom holds herself to herself. Even her anger is rigidly controlled. And her love...well, her love is rarely spoken.

My mother's silence left part of me empty,

but she filled another part. Stories, and stories, and more stories. She read them. She made them up. She acted them out. How ironic that it was my mother who gave me the dreams and the imagination that my father delighted in. My mother gave me the substance. My father gave me my place. I was his Dream Girl.

And now, as the finished pages lay around my feet, the Saturday morning sun reflecting their whiteness, I suddenly ached to show them to my Daddy. The perversity of it – the knowledge that it would somehow unbearably hurt my mother to do so, only strengthened my wish to go to Daddy. But he was not here. I couldn't bear to call him again, until he had called me at least once.

The phone rang, a jarringly unfamiliar sound in our house. Maybe the twins wanted to do more work on our business, though I didn't know what there was to do. I sighed, then uncurled myself from the pillow and went into the living room. Well, maybe Mom's search for a good literary agent was bearing fruit.

She had answered the phone and was now smiling mischievously, while her voice carried its most sincere note. "Why that's very kind of you to invite us, Alice," she was saying. "I'm sure Sandy will be delighted to come. Yes, thank you."

She hung up the phone and chuckled.

"Pam's family are having, not a wiener roast, Sandy, but a beach party!" She grinned and I grinned back. Nobody, but nobody had ever before aspired to a social occasion on the beach.

"I know it will be the hit of the season!" I responded. "Should I wear the chiffon or the blue silk jeans?"

"The silk, dear. I think I'll wear my chiffon and we simply mustn't clash!"

We laughed a little more, and suddenly I felt cheerful again.

"I've finished my story, Mom," I said a little shyly. "If you want to read it before I type it..."

"I'd love to, dear. Only you must go for a swim while I do it. It will make us both nervous if you're pacing around the house. Besides, you've hardly not worn that new bikini."

I grimaced and went to change. Then as an afterthought returned to the phone and called the twins to see if they wanted to come, too.

"Dad's given us the day off," Jack told me, "so we're on our way."

"See you on the beach," I replied.

The sun was hot, summer hot. I ran down to the packed water edge, each step burning. The lake was calm today. I stuck my scorched toes into the cool water and sighed relief.

For awhile I waded around, trying to get the courage to plunge under. It was odd how just a year or so ago I dove in without a thought for the cold.

"Hey, Sandy!"

I looked around and smiled as Donny waded toward me. He grinned widely and let his eyes stray teasingly over me.

"Did I tell you I like your new bathing suit?" he said.

"You don't have to, Donny," I retorted. "I mean when you've got it, flaunt it!"

Seeing as I obviously didn't have it, or at least not much of it, my brazen remark broke the ice he was building between us. We were just friends again. For awhile we floated around in the water, diving or striking out along the shore as the mood took us. It felt good. After awhile Pam joined us. That didn't feel quite as good.

"Say, how come you hang around with those crazy twins so much," she asked with a slightly malicious grin. "Which one do you have the hots for Sandy?"

"Both!" Donny shouted uproariously. "Sandy's into orgies!"

They both laughed as though Jack and Joey were absurdities. I felt angry and embarrassed and woodenly resentful. But I could think of nothing to say. Instead I slogged angrily out of the water and lay down on the hot sand, closing my eyes against the sun and my two companions. I listened to their staccato laughter and muttered exchanges. Without looking, I knew Donny was getting amorous. All the delicacy of a tomcat, I thought.

"Hi Sandy!" sounded around me. I looked up and grinned. I had forgotten that the twins were coming.

"Go..going in?" Joey asked.

"I just came out," I answered. "What took you so long?"

"We got a delivery just after I talked to you," Jack replied, gazing keenly out over the water. "We stocked the shelves first."

We sat in silence for awhile. I liked the feeling of having Jack and Joey beside me. They could be trusted, at least most of the time. My thoughts strayed again over my story, and I wondered if Mom had finished reading it and what she thought of it. Pam waded out of the water toward us, once again riveting the twins' eyes. She smiled a toothpaste commercial smile and sat down opposite me, holding her knees.

"I haven't seen you guys around for awhile," she said cheerfully. "Are you hiding from me?"

I exercised great self-restraint and did not point out that that coming remark made most clichés seem bright and witty. Neither twin smiled, but I think it was embarrassment rather than coldness. Joey stared at the sand and absently made a cairn of tiny, wave-smoothed stones.

"We been busy," Jack said awkwardly. I winced inwardly over his grammar. Poor white trash!

"I've got to go in for a few minutes," I interrupted. I wasn't going to hang around for these pleasantries. Let the twins make up to Pam – I had my story to worry about.

As soon as I left the water's edge, the sand again became unbearably hot, and so I abandoned my brief attempt at dignity and ran through the small fairy bushes to the shade of the lone poplar in front of our house. I turned and looked back briefly. Donny had joined them but the twins were as they had been. They looked like a scene from a beach party movie – all browned and good looking against the white hot sand.

I leaned against the poplar and tried to remember them as they used to be. Their faces wavered an instant back to the children we were, dashing over the sand summer after summer. But just as the patterns of sunlight on the sand never remained, even in my thoughts I couldn't hold their faces. I had a collective memory, not of one time or place, but of many times and subtly shifting places, and all had become woven in me as thought and emotion, as impossible to hold as a trill of music. There, but untouchable.

I heard the screen door close behind me. I was reluctant to turn, to hear the carefully considered criticisms of my story that Mom would offer me. The story was good, but I had no more illusions about rewrites.

"Hey, Dream Girl!"

I whirled around.

"Daddy!" I shrieked and ran to him. He twirled me around in his arms, laughed aloud, then threw his arm over my shoulder and holding me close, smiled up at my mother standing alone at the top of the steps.

"I told you she'd be glad to see me," he said. His voice was still cheerful, but I caught a note of triumph and challenge. "My Dream Girl knows I was just aching to see her again."

Mom shrugged and went back into the house. My pensive mood must not have quite gone, for I felt a hint of wistfulness when the screen door shut. I loved them both. They insisted they detested each other.

"When did you get here?" I demanded. "Just now? How long can you stay? Oh Daddy, I've missed you so much!"

I chattered on to him. Barely waiting for replies, vaguely realizing that my words sounded more like those of the ten-year-old Dream Girl catching toads in my bedroom than the almost-woman I was becoming. But Daddy never stopped me as my mother would have done, never criticized or tried to change me. Now that he was with me again, I wondered how I could have stood all these weeks and months of never seeing him.

"I've missed you so much," I repeated finally, my voice soft again.

He smiled at me, that warm smile that I knew he saved just for me. He hugged me again.

"Well, Dream Girl, you've got me for the rest of the day. How about a nice leisurely swim and then I'll drive you into town for lunch. We can wander around the shops in Simcoe before I bring you home. I've got to be in the city for an eight o'clock date, so I'll have to be on the road by five at the latest.

He smiled at me again, and I tried not to think that five was less than six hours away.

*   *   *

"Try the sole almandine," Daddy suggested. I looked down at the menu again, trying to make up my mind. I've never much liked seafood, but Daddy had forgotten and brought me to a seafood restaurant. He loved it, and boasted that he knew every good seafood restaurant in southern Ontario and New York.

"I think I'd rather have the salmon," I murmured shyly. The waiter stood beside us with thinly disguised impatience. Daddy raised his eyebrows slightly.

"The lady will have the salmon and a ginger ale with a cherry and a twist. I'll have the sole and your best white wine."

He leaned back in his chair as the waiter left. I could feel his annoyance.

"You should have had the sole, Sandy. You're getting as stubborn as your mother."

"But I like salmon," I protested.

"Maybe, but I've eaten here several times. The salmon is probably frozen. It's tough. But the sole is excellent. You should have listened to your father m'dear."

"I'm sorry," I said wretchedly and stared at the cutlery in front of me. Absently I rearranged it so that it was correctly set.

"Well, don't get upset, Dream Girl," he said with an assumption of good humor. "Probably it won't kill you, but you'll know to listen to me next time."

"Okay," I murmured and smiled shyly at him.

It had been a strange afternoon. We had gone swimming together as he had promised, but Pam and the others hadn't gone away as I'd hoped, and Daddy horsed around with them almost as much as he did with me. He seemed amused by Pam, and apparently enjoyed the sight of her in that excuse of a bikini. I had always thought Mom was stupid when she objected to the young art students Daddy kept around him, but suddenly I had a glimmering of how she had felt. I told myself that Daddy simply appreciated the natural beauty of young people, but I didn't want him to notice Pam while I was there, so starved for his attention.

Jack and Joey swam with us, but at a little distance. Daddy had always disliked them both, and though they never said so, I think that Joey was a bit afraid of him. Jack kept his thoughts to himself.

It should have been a perfect time, but somehow it was not. Daddy was himself as he always was and is, but I had changed I guess. I expected more, wanted and needed more, but I didn't know how to tell him so. He knew himself to be giving me a tremendous treat and would have summoned all the hurt fury of a child had I tried to explain myself. Perhaps the words 'I love you and need you' would have helped, but I didn't know how to say that to Daddy. Maybe I knew it would have become a cord around my neck.

He bought me a lovely silver bracelet in a jewelry store in Simcoe. When he chose it for me and fastened it around my wrist, the afternoon suddenly came right.

"Nothing's too good for my Dream Girl," he said gently and kissed my forehead. I hugged him fiercely.

We drove back along the highway in silence, comfortable and happy.

"Say, Sandy," Daddy said after awhile, "I'm going to be back in a week or so with a friend of mine – one of the top art experts in New York. He wants to see that canvas you have in your bedroom. He saw it when it was on exhibit last year and wants to take another look at it."

"It's a beautiful picture," I said warmly. "I love it so much, Daddy. You know," I added shyly, "I talk to it when I want to talk to you but I can't."

"Oh yeah?" Daddy answered and glanced at me quickly before looking back at the road.

"Could you stop for a minute at the gift shop?" I demanded as we neared the turn-off. "I want to show you something special." I knew that I had to show Daddy the porcelain toad I had my heart set on for my summer's treasure. It was part of the painting and him and the way I felt about everything.

"Sure, Dream Girl, but just for a minute. I've got to be going."

He pulled the car up right in front of the gift shop, making the tiny pieces of gravel crunch under the wheels. Before I could open the door, Daddy hopped out of his side of the car and casually opened my door for me. No one else ever bothered to.

"Do you remember how every summer I would buy something special to take home?" I asked shyly.

"Yes," he laughed. "It was all junk."

"Well, I want to show you what I'm going to buy this year."

He raised his eyebrows slightly but said nothing. I knew he had a very low opinion of my taste, but I was certain that he would be delighted with my choice this year. When we entered the store, the Creytons looked sharply, then smiled. I had forgotten how Daddy made people smile in spite of themselves.

"It's over here," I insisted. We looked in the glass case together. "See, at the side? It's a toad under a toadstool."

"Could I show you something?" Mrs. Creyton bustled up to us and, without waiting for a reply, opened the cabinet. I bit my lip in resentment that she had broken into the twosome that Daddy and I made, but I quickly reached for the figure.

"Isn't it beautiful?" I murmured as the tiny toad nestled again in my hands. It looked at me solemnly from his bed amid the tiny porcelain flowers, all sheltered by the toadstool. I knew I could never find another thing that was so perfect for me.

"Let's see," Daddy remarked. I was reluctant somehow to let it go, even into Daddy's hands. It was so important and suddenly I wasn't sure...

He turned it around in his big palms, studying it from every angle, his artist's eyes searching for beauty and for flaws. I held my breath.

"It's not a bad piece of work," he said indifferently as he placed it carelessly back on the shelf. "The subject leaves me cold though. Price is a little steep, too."

Perhaps he suddenly sensed the shamed hurt that daggered me in his words, for he looked at me keenly for an instant. I lowered my head, told myself fiercely that it was a stupid thing to cry over, that I was stupid to expect Daddy to respond to the tiny toad as I had.

"I can't keep buying every little thing for you Sandy," he said. "Even if you want it a lot.

I must admit," he added humorously when I continued to stare at the floor, "that your taste has improved over the past year. I didn't know that my little girl had begun to appreciate such things. You sure as hell never did before. But it's too expensive and I don't think you should ask me to buy it for you, especially after I bought you the bracelet."

He tweaked the silver bracelet that he had earlier clasped around my wrist. Perhaps it made me angry. Perhaps it was the hurt of the past lonely weeks. But for the first time in my life I stared into his eyes in anger.

"I'm not a little girl any more Daddy, and I did not ask you to buy me the toad. I'm going to buy him for myself."

He was taken aback and so for a moment did not answer me. But when he did, it was merely to brush my anger aside, as if it were of no account.

"You're getting as miffy as your mother," he said cordially, his arm draped around my stiff shoulders as he guided me outside. "And you're right that you're not a little girl any more. But isn't your old man allowed to remember his little Dream Girl?"

He gave me a warm hug, and dropped his arm before climbing into the car.

"I've got to run Sandy if I'm going to be on time. You don't mind walking from here do you?" He reached through the open window and grasped my hand. "Take it easy, Dream Girl. Don't let your mother get you down. And don't forget that I love you."

He drove away, leaving a small spurt of dust roiling over the gravel. I pulled off my good sandals to walk home through the cool dust of the back road, wondering all the while why I wanted to burst into tears.

Chapter 10

Mom was sitting on the verandah, staring out at the lake. I watched her for a moment from the screen door, wishing I could run to her as other girls ran to their mothers. She looked so alone, as if she lived in a separate world, a place of quiet and isolation and loneliness. And I could not go into that world.

At last I opened the door and came and sat down beside her. I too stared at the cold blue waves.

"Did you have a good time with your father?" she asked after a couple of minutes, her voice strained to a cheerful brightness.

"Yeah, it was great. He says he's coming back next week with some art expert who wants to look at my picture."

"Oh," she replied, a slight frown settling more naturally over her features as she appeared to consider what I had said.

"We really had a terrific time," I asserted and thrust out my arm. "Look, he bought me a bracelet. Isn't it pretty?"

"Why yes, it's very pretty."

She got up suddenly and started toward the house. "I have to get moving," she said in her false bright voice again. "We'll never have dinner if I don't start it."

I opened my mouth to say I wasn't hungry yet, but she had disappeared into the house before I had a chance to utter the words. I plopped back against the lounge, angry that she would desert me, resentful that she was obviously jealous of the little time I had spent with Daddy, and desperately trying to convince myself that I didn't really feel an aching hurt.

After a few minutes, I thrust myself out of the chair and slogged through the sand to the edge of the water. I turned to walk toward the end of the Point miles away, then hesitated. A little way down the beach, Pam and her younger sister were swimming and splashing in front of their cottage. I could hear their shrilling voices clearly. They were immersed in one of their endless quarrels.

I grimaced and turned the other way. I detested Pam's younger sister. She had all Pam's sly sharpness, but was sulky and whiny into the bargain. If she could, she always caused trouble. She was only two years younger than me, but seemed even more immature. Pam had always been bitterly jealous of her.

The view in the direction I chose was not as pleasant. The beach narrowed, and cottages thrust out from the trees in a ramshackle fashion just a mile or two down. Toward the end of the Point though, the beach gradually curves into the lake; the cottages are set further back among the trees, and small seedlings and tiny sand bushes grow more profusely giving the beach a progressively deserted look. Right at the end of the Point, past the public campgrounds, was a wildlife park where the deer we rarely saw originated from. As children we had tried at least once a year to walk along the beach to reach it, even though we knew it was fifteen or twenty miles.

Our last excursion had been three years ago. We had traveled further than ever before. Provisioned with hot dogs and bottles of soft drinks, we had begun walking down the beach. Donny had led the way, as usual, and Pam was right behind him. Jack, Joey, me, and Pam's sister Alison trailed happily behind, strung out along the water's edge as we played tag with the waves hurling themselves over the packed sand.

We must have walked miles by the time we stopped for lunch. We had played with some children far down from our cottages, found a sandbar only waist deep, seen some large fish swimming near our toes as we waded, and picked up a few shells. It took very little time to collect the driftwood to roast our wieners. The cottages were yards and yards apart here, the brush sparse but wild. We cut green willow wands, speared the hot dogs, then stuck them over the fire until the wieners were charred and hot. We gulped them down, burning our tongues then swallowing long fizzy draughts of warm grape and orange soft drinks. Someone had thought to bring marshmallows, so we toasted them too, and ate until we felt we would burst. If someone had not gotten careless, Donny I think, and sat on the bag grinding sand into the marshmallows, perhaps we would have eaten until our stomachs gave way. We drowsed for a long time in the sun, tired, happy, and dreading the long, long walk back.

But at last we started. I remember how we meandered along the beach, sometimes stopping to swim, but mostly just walking along, too tired to bother talking. What a raggle-taggle band wandering back to our homes at the end of the adventure.

*   *   *

The breeze had begun to cool as I walked. I had no wish for adventure, just solitude.

I thought of nothing and of everything as I walked, feeling dimly that I must make decisions, but unsure as to what they were or what I should be doing. Everything was turned around in me. I was being pulled in different directions and I didn't even know by what or by who, or in what direction I should go.

I was suddenly sure that my parents were using me against each other, each trying to win my devotion and loyalty to the exclusion of the other. How could they do this? If they loved me, why were they trying to use me this way?

Bitterly I saw that I had been betrayed by them, that neither loved me for myself. All I was to them was a tool, something to be used to make themselves feel better. And what defenses did I have? I stared down the beach seeing the rolling waves, the few late sunbathers, and the dilapidated cottages. I wished I could run away from them all, go out on my own, away from their pulling and pushing and subtleties that were beyond me. Now I knew why kids wanted to leave home. They wanted to get away from devoted parents who didn't care about them.

I hated them both.

And suddenly I wanted my Daddy to come back, to hug me, to tell me I was his Dream

Girl. I wanted my mother to talk to me, to tell me I was the daughter she had always hoped I would be.

How could they do this to me?

A dark little shape hopped before my feet, and I almost fell as I stumblingly changed my rapid footsteps to avoid it.

"Little toad, little toad, something will hurt you way out here in the sun with no bushes or bugs," I whispered, and scooped the small creature into my hands. He shivered in my palms, his liquid gold eyes fixed on my huge, pale blue ones. I stroked his knobbled khaki back, and watched the soft pulsing of his creamy throat. I could feel his fear, not small and gnarled like his body, but as large as I and as fierce as the pain I felt.

"Don't be afraid, little one," I murmured. He wet over my fingers and I winced slightly, wishing he could understand that I meant him no harm. Carefully, cuddling him into my cupped hands, I carried him out between the cottages to the wild growth that lay beyond them. I placed him gently on the sand, hoping he would see this gesture as one of good will.

He darted frantically for the cover of the undergrowth, away from me.

*   *   *

"Sandy, you almost missed your dinner," Mom said cheerfully when I returned at last to the summer house. I was surprised that she didn't seem angry with me. Still unsure, I got my dinner from the stove and came back to sit with her in the living room.

"I had a big lunch, and late, too. You know how Daddy is about meals," I said uncertainly.

"Don't I," Mom said and grimaced. While they were married they fought frequently about Daddy's habit of refusing to come for meals while he was painting, and his later indignation when his dinner was cold or overcooked.

"Your sister called," she went on briskly. "Guess what! She and Alan are coming down next week for the long weekend. She says she has something to tell us."

"That's great," I replied without too much enthusiasm.

I liked Joanie alright, but I didn't know her very well. She was nine years older than me, and I had always suspected that Mom preferred her to me. Daddy and she fought bitterly once or twice a year, especially in the last couple of years. She seemed to think that everything was always Daddy's fault and Mom was some kind of saint or something.

"I wonder what she wants to tell us," Mom went on. "Do you think that at last she and

Alan have decided to start a family? I'd just love to be a grandmother."

I looked at my mother in bewilderment. The last time she'd talked to Joanie she had told her not to start a family yet, that Joanie was too young to become housebound with small children, that she was too young to consider herself a grandmother.

"Did she sound happy?" I asked after a minute.

"Oh yes," Mom said. "I had better go make sure her room is ready." She hurried up the wooden stairs, her hard-soled slippers snapping briskly as she went. I went on eating my dinner, trying to figure out my mother's thought processes.

*   *   *

"Sandra!" Mrs. Creyton called imperiously from the front of her cottage, five down from ours. "Sandra, I want to speak to you!"

Reluctantly I left the water's edge, dropped my load of dry wood on the sand, and walked up to her.

"Did you want something, Mrs. Creyton?" I asked not very politely. Usually all she wanted to do was yell at us for something. When we were kids she'd even yell at us for things we didn't do, never believing us when we told her we were innocent.

"I've heard you and those Cilento twins have started up some sort of grocery delivery service. Is that right?"

"Yes," I muttered, waiting for the lecture.

"Well, tell me about it. I suppose after your father, well...I suppose your mother needs the money. But that's none of my business," she added with arched brows and a tight-lipped smile. I scowled at her, unable to put my anger in words. She made me feel very young and guilty somehow.

"I'm just helping the twins," I lied sulkily, feeling my face flush.

"Well, tell me what it is you're helping them with."

"We take orders for groceries when we deliver the morning paper, then deliver the order in the afternoon. We charge ten per cent of the cost of the groceries, with twenty-five cents as the minimum charge."

"Are you dependable," she demanded sharply. "I can't be bothered with you if you're not."

"Of course we're dependable," I snapped, firing up suddenly. "You don't suppose we'd stay in business very long if we weren't, do you?"

"Well, I can't say I think much of your manners, but I'll try you out," Mrs. Creyton said crisply. She seemed to soften for a minute, to withdraw into herself. "Les, Mr. Creyton, hasn't been feeling too well lately. And he insists on walking to the store as he's always done, then carrying the groceries home." She paused a minute and her normal sharpness of manner returned.

"Well, come into the house and I'll show you where everything has to go. You can stop by the store each morning and I'll give you the list and the key. Mind, I want everything put in its right place or you're no use to me at all. And I want that key returned right away. We have a lot of valuable antiques in our home and I don't want just anybody traipsing through, picking up all our treasures."

I should have said something brisk, cheerful, and businesslike, but I always found the emotional demands of people like Mrs. Creyton more than I could handle. Fifteen was a difficult age for me. I was sure I was an adult, but my emotions would surge willy nilly and I would cry out in the voice of a child. Or perhaps my thoughts would overpower me with a new perception and, in my eagerness, I would blurt out some stupidity in a futile attempt to explain the staggering flashes of my new understanding. Worst of all, I was faintly but uncomfortably aware that my maturity was still a façade, shaky and unreliable, sure to crumble and leave me defenseless before the scornful eyes of the adults. Sometimes I felt their dislike and contempt like a cold chill. At other times though, I was sure I had astounded them with a display of my newfound wisdom and independence.

Mrs. Creyton walked heavily up the steps to the wide verandah that fronted their cottage and I followed meekly but sulkily.

Most of the cottages on the beach were rather plain, square, frame structures, supported by heavy posts sunk deeply in the sand. Long Point was really one vast sand bar, for you couldn't dig down to dirt, only to more and more sand laced with wave-washed pebbles buried years before.

Unlike the cottages around them, the Creytons had a handsome A-frame, with most of the front taken up by huge windows. Probably because of a trick of the wind, the cottage stood high above the sand now, resting on sturdy, partially-submerged pylons. It was raised almost five feet above the beach on the side facing the water and about eighteen inches at the back. As year by year the sand had blown away, a couple of extra steps had been added to the verandah. Another was needed now, I saw, for we stepped first onto a large rock before climbing up the porch steps.

"I'll be giving you the key for the back door," Mrs. Creyton told me. "I don't suppose I have to show you how to work that."

She didn't bother to wait for an answer, so I gave none, only grimaced at her back.

"There won't be any need for any of you to be in the living room," she told me as we stepped into the room. "Wipe your feet on the mat. I don't intend to have to sweep up sand after you."

Obediently I wiped my feet, fuming inwardly all the while. What a horrible person she was. I glanced around the forbidden room and was surprised at its beauty. I knew nothing about antiques, but the occasional tables and wooden and velvet chairs were lovely and just a hint different from any furniture I'd seen before.

Mr. Creyton was seated in an armchair on the far side of the room, reading a newspaper. He looked at us indifferently for an instant, then retreated back into the paper.

"This is a beautiful room," I said, feeling as though my dislike forced me to speak up. It would have been dishonest somehow, or spiteful to say nothing about this beauty. Mrs.

Creyton smiled as she surveyed her home. For a moment she looked quite pleasant.

"Well, then you can understand why I don't want you wandering through my house, getting things dirty and sandy," she said with a little of the sharpness gone from her voice.

"Yes," I said, "but we wouldn't anyway. I mean we have too much to do to spend extra time someplace," I finished lamely. Why, oh why, could I not just speak gentle words of dignity that would convey my disdain for her insults?

"Here's the kitchen," she went on, leading me through a narrow doorway. "Canned goods go on the bottom shelf, here." She indicated a three shelved cupboard lined with black gingham-printed paper. "Boxed goods on this shelf, and the bread, tea and coffee on the top shelf. Can you remember all that?"

I assured her I could.

"Well, don't go forgetting then, please. Now make sure the eggs go in the egg tray, and the milk on the left hand side of the door. Butter fits here in the dairy box. I daresay you're a skitter-scatter girl and won't remember where thing go no matter how many times I tell you."

"I'll remember," I protested.

"Well, we'll see," Mrs. Creyton said with a lifting of her thin brows. "But if you forget and I have to spend hours rearranging my cupboards, I'll not pay you that commission you are charging."

"There won't be any problem," I insisted, feeling sulky again.

She sniffed and opened the back door for me.

"Don't forget to come for that list and key," she reminded me again as I stepped out past her onto the low stoop and down onto the sand. I bit my lip, refusing to say any of the things that were hovering in my thoughts. But the door swung shut so quickly behind me that I knew she had not been waiting for any answer I might give, apparently assuming I had nothing of importance to say. The fact that this was true just increased my fury as I slogged through the hot sand, back to the pile of wood I had left on the beach.

Jack was enthusiastically piling it higher and higher into Joey's overburdened arms.

"Jack!" he shouted.

"You don't understand, brother," he said loudly. "It's good for the muscles. Improves coordination. Stuns the women with your resourcefulness and ability to procure the necessities..."

"Hey, that's mine!" I yelled. Everyone always brought at least one armload to a bonfire and wiener roast. I had no intention of scouring the beach for another hour for my share.

"Sa..ay, it's Sandy," Joey said cheerfully, and promptly dropped his entire armload.

"Finders keepers," Jack informed me with a malicious grin.

I scowled at them, refusing to join in their good humor until I could unburden my indignation.

"I do believe the f..friend of our ch.. childhood is disturbed," Joey remarked conversationally, leaning against his brother as though he were a wall. Jack stepped sideways, allowing his brother to sprawl onto the sand.

"What's up, partner?" Jack demanded.

"Mrs. Creyton," I exploded, "has condescended to permit us to carry her groceries for her, providing of course, that we can keep from prowling through her house or forgetting on what shelf the cans go!"

"Ha! Old b..bitch been givin' you a hard time, eh," Joey remarked with a grin.

"Probably hasn't been getting hers lately," Jack observed winking at Joey who hooted loudly.

"Getting what?" I demanded crossly.

They laughed loudly then, and began loading me up with the dropped wood.

"Never mind, child," Jack said. "You'll know one day!"

"H..hold those arms out," Joey admonished. "We're going to have a great wiener roast tonight."

I grumbled a little, then laughed. Already the sun was sinking down toward the far cottages and the lake.

"Well, come on then," I hollered and began running down the beach, leaving them to pick up the wood as it scattered from my arms. Who cared about Mrs. Creyton anyway, with the wiener roast pyre growing man-high just down the beach!

Chapter 11

The people were shadows in the deeper shadows of night as the flames rose higher and wilder. At my back, the waves surged, hissing and whispering, as each wave lost its hold on the sand and slid back into the lake. In front of me, the fire crackled and spat, roaring in an ecstasy of brief existence. For an instant, I had a vision of fire, the eternal dancing creature, beloved by the lake.

The flames laughed merrily, tantalizing. The waves moaned and sought to creep up the beach to the flames, to embrace the dancing life before both died, smoke and steam mingling in the air.

It was the silent time now, when we stared into the flames, entranced, locked contentedly within our own beings. I was warmly aware of Jack on my left and Roy Cilento on my right. Vaguely I sensed the others, parents and children. We were like a nomad tribe that gathers in season. We knew each other, but except for the fire, we would go our separate ways.

I shifted a little from my cross-legged position.

"Anything wrong?" Jack asked.

"My back's cold," I muttered then laughed a little, "and I think my eyebrows are scorching."

He smiled and groped behind him, finally laying his hands on his windbreaker. Casually he draped it over my shoulders, then laid his arm over it to give me a squeeze. I leaned toward him, grateful for the warmth he gave. He looked at me for an instant, the firelight making his face a strange pattern of exaggerated features. He was like that, firelight and shadows. I was aware of him suddenly, the hardness and the litheness of him beside me on the sand. He smiled a small smile and leaned over and kissed me briefly, gently. Then he dropped his arm and stared at the fire.

About a third of the way around the circle, Pam was leaning against Donny, yet managing somehow to be too close to Joey. Donny had his arm around her, and occasionally I saw his hand stray across her stomach or breast. But they were a mile away, across the circle of firelight and no part of me.

I was aware finally that Joey was watching me, and so I smiled at him, my special friend. I wished then that he was sitting beside me in Roy's place, that both he and Jack were against me, their strong arms around my waist and shoulders, their warmth being shared with me. Joey knew my thoughts for he returned my smile, reaching me through the blazing firelight and dancing shadows. I wriggled a little, feeling the physical heat and the emotional warmth enveloping me in sensations of beauty and pleasure.

Roy looked down at me, his pale eyes darkened and given depth by the uncertain lights. He smiled, and I read his awareness of the new feelings that were stirring between the twins and me. For a long moment our eyes held each other, then he smiled his gentle smile and patted my knee before looking back at the fire.

"When I was a boy," he said softly to Jack and me and the shadows, "these bonfires were the best part of the summer. I met your mother at one. She was as warm and alive as the firelight. It was three years before we ran into each other again, but we both remembered the firelight and stars in the black night, and the sound of the waves washing over the beach. Those things stay with you your whole life."

He lapsed into silence then. I felt I should lean against him as I would Jack or Joey, or say something. But he was an adult and I was fifteen and didn't know what to say, so I kept apart. Beside me, Jack still stared into the fire, but I felt a knot of coldness that had not been there before. He had tensely grasped his hands together, and was working at his fingers in a wringing motion. There was no weakness in his movements, just strength and a furious emotion I could not understand. I put my hand on his knee trying to return some comfort, but he made an explosive noise, pushed me away, then sprang to his feet and disappeared from the circle of firelight into the hovering dark.

"I didn't..." I started to say, but my voice dwindled away. I turned to ask why of Roy, but he too had slipped away into the darkness. I looked toward Joey, but the dark had claimed him too. The magic warmth gone, I hunched forward toward the fierce heat of the fire.

I stared at my bare toes feeling stupid and embarrassed as tears slid out of my eyes. The fire was too hot and there were too many people. Silently I slipped backward into the quiet, impersonal night.

My eyes were accustomed to the blazing red light of the fire, and so for several minutes I walked blind in the velvet shadows. Once I almost walked into the water, but the sound of the waves, suddenly too close, and the damp chill under my feet gave me a little sense of direction. I looked up at the sky. The stars hung piercingly bright, but silent. A sliver moon was there, but its pale light did not seem to reflect other objects into my eyes.

After a long while, I began to perceive shapes and shadows on the beach. The swishing blackness on my left was the lake. The waving blackness off at my right, was the trees and cottages huddled together against the true night. My fancies of the dark flared, and for a long moment I stood paralyzed with primitive fears, almost screaming when a cold wavelet suddenly sucked at my toes. But the physical cold shocked me away from the emotional chill. I moved to run back to the fire, but suddenly made out the shadows of Roy and the twins near the black line of trees. I had no intention of listening in, only of reaching whoever was closest to me, of sheltering from the black night in the companionship of anyone. I ran swiftly and silently toward them.

"You're going to have to accept it, Jack," Roy said in the firmest voice I had ever heard him use.

"Accept it! Damn you! You..you're nothing but a loser! And this is the final bit of losing, isn't it? And you won't even try! You've been trying to die ever since we were babies – ever since Mom died!"

"Jack..." I heard Joey plead, but Jack's voice rose over his.

"Other kids have parents. Their fathers are men." The words curled contemptuously. "All we ever had was you!"

"Jack!" Roy's voice was sharp, "you don't understand! Listen to me..." his voice trailed off as Jack pushed him aside and strode across the sand.

I stood paralyzed, shadowed by the night, not knowing whether to creep away or let them know I was there. As I hesitated, I heard Roy sigh, then Joey's voice, stern and insistent.

"He's right, Dad. You can't just give in. At least give it a try..."

There was no answer. Joey hesitated and I could just see him shudder as spasms took him. At last he too moved away from his father, following Jack. Roy sighed again, and sat down on the sand. As if magnetized, I approached him.

"Roy," I said hesitantly.

"Is that you, Sandy?" he said in his quiet voice.

"I...I'm afraid of the dark," I said in a small voice as I came up to him.

"I wish I was," Roy muttered. I sat down beside him, feeling his gentleness and sad solidity. He put his arm around me the way Daddy used to sometimes, and stared out at the lake, obviously forgetting me. I sat quietly not wanting to disturb him. He sighed again.

"Is Bryce a good father?" he asked suddenly. It took me a minute to realize he meant Daddy.

"Yeah, he's perfect," I said, then hesitated. Somehow with the anonymous dark pressing around, that seemed a silly thing to say. "At least," I said softly, "sometimes he is. I mean when I get to see him he is. He's so busy I don't see him much. I miss him a lot. I wish he were around like you are. But Daddy's never content like you, Roy. He always wants to make something new – find new things, new people. I guess he gets bored with us. I wish he were like you," I said again.

He laughed wryly.

"And my boys wish I was like Bryce," Roy said. "Maybe what you are is never enough... You're a sweet girl, Sandy. Too bad I couldn't have had a daughter like you. Missy wanted a girl..." His words faltered. Then abruptly he stood up, his voice becoming brisk. "We're going to miss the hot dogs and marshmallows!"

I jumped up and began to run because he seemed to expect it, but Roy lagged behind.

"You go on ahead, Sandy," he said. "I'll be along in a few minutes."

I hesitated, then obeyed. Roy was an adult again and I no longer had anything to give him.

When I reentered the circle around the fire, Pam's mother had begun bringing out the hot dogs and marshmallows. Fresh-cut sticks were handed out to everyone who wanted them. Cases of soft drinks were retrieved from a big metal tub at the edge of the lake, each bottle icy cold and wet.

"We have hors d'oeuvres and harder drinks on the patio," Pam's mother announced in her trilling voice.

One of the adults made some sort of comment on the opposite side of the fire, and those around him bust into laughter. I glanced about impatiently, looking for Jack and Joey. Neither were here. Someone thrust a stick into my hand. Automatically I grabbed a hot dog and speared it on the point of the stick. I held it over a red hot spot in the coals and barely noticed as the hot dog began to char around the edges.

Where had Jack and Joey gotten to? I peered through the dark to the lighted patio, or rather the area covered with small beach stones in front of Pam's cottage, looking for Roy. He had disappeared too.

"Crazy Cilentos," I muttered savagely, twisting my hot dog so that the other side would char. Once I judged it to be burnt enough, I thrust it into a cold roll scooped from a passing bowl. When I bit into the hot dog, the juices ran down my chin, hot and good. I burned my tongue. Some of the children were getting overexcited, waving flaming marshmallows around. One almost caught my hair.

This should be a time of rollicking companionship, but I felt alone. I didn't want to be pulled into the Cilento's problems. After all, I had enough of my own, didn't I?

But before coming to the wiener roast, I had read my story once more. They were my friends, maybe my only real friends. What should a friend do? I didn't know and it made me angry. I wanted to be with them, to feel them close around me and to be part of their problems. But I didn't want their problems.

I didn't know what I wanted any more.

"Any of those wieners left?" Jack spoke suddenly at my elbow. "I'm starving."

I opened my mouth then shut it again as Joey dropped onto the sand on my other side. Wordlessly I handed them a bowl of hot dogs. There was only one stick left so I handed it to Joey and my stick to Jack.

"I lo..ove hot dogs done thi..is way," Joey said amiably, only his twisted words giving away that his emotions were roused.

I still said nothing, looking from one brother to the other, wondering. Joey's lips were pressed into a tight, thin line as he roasted his wiener. His face was cold and marble-like, his movements slow and deliberate. Jack was clenching and unclenching his jaws, making a little dent in his cheek go in and out. He twisted about as though he was unable to get comfortable on the soft sand. I could feel the hardness and the anger radiating from each of them and felt caught between it.

"Good, eh!" Jack said in a quick, hard voice as he bit into the hot dog. I nodded wordlessly, angry and confused and bewildered. I wished I could tell them off, throw my uncertain anger at them, but there was nothing to yell at them for. Joey said nothing but I could half see, half feel his mounting spasms. A particularly violent shudder took him, and he dropped his partially eaten hot dog in the sand. For a moment he stared down at it stupidly.

"I'll get you another one," I said.

"No!" he said, his voice harsh. "Let's get out of here." He stood up quickly and turned into the night. "C'mon Sandy," he called back impatiently.

I followed, vaguely aware that Jack had become the dark shadow beside Joey a few feet away.

"Wait for me," I called. "I don't like the beach at night." They made no reply.

We walked fast and wordlessly for about ten minutes. I could barely keep up with their long strides.

"Do you want to go to our place for a Coke?" I asked breathlessly when they seemed to be slowing down.

"No," Jack answered shortly. "Say what's that noise?"

We all listened intently. I thought perhaps I could hear some laughing somewhere, but I wasn't sure.

"Let's inve..estigate," Joey said softly, a mischievous smile finally replacing the ice look. He and Jack began moving stealthily toward the small dunes that banked the cottages around here.

"What...?" I began.

"Shh!" both twins hissed in unison.

I didn't feel like playing night games as though we were kids, but was terrified of being left behind. I wasn't even sure in which direction the summer house lay, so I followed them as they crawled up one of the dunes, careful to keep their heads low.

The breeze carried a distorted ripple of laughter from behind the dune, mingled with other sounds that conveyed nothing to me. I scrambled up beside Jack. We peered over the top, down into the moonlit shadows below.

At first I saw nothing, but then made out some violent movement in the black shadows at one side. Suddenly the movement twisted and rolled into a patch of moonlight. It was Donny. And Pam. And they were...

I held my breath. Revulsion, fascination, and wonder crowded through me, numbing my thoughts and actions. I simply watched, breathing slowly, deeply, feeling strange emotions churning my stomach as I watched my friends' naked bodies heaving about in the sand. I was barely aware of Jack and Joey beside me, or of the time passing. We watched it all until they fell apart, giggling. I didn't notice Jack and Joey sliding away, but I was jerked back to reality when they grabbed my feet and pulled me backwards down the dune.

I would have shouted at them, but Jack knew me too well. He clamped his hand over my mouth, and pressed his face near mine.

"Shut up, Sandy!" he ordered, his face relaxing into the grin I knew from years back – mischief, first class. I glared mutely.

"They..ey'll hear us!" Joey whispered, a similar grin appearing over his features. "Boy...that was something!"

Cautiously, Jack took his hand away from my mouth. I spat angrily but the twins didn't even notice.

"C'mon! We've got to get out of here!" Jack hissed. They grabbed my arms, yanked me to my feet, and started off at a dead run into the blackness of the beach, dragging me along with them.

We ran, propelled by those things we'd seen and felt, joyful, frightened, wildly wicked. It was wonderful and strange and horrible. Our feet pounded over the shifting sand, half-blinded by the night, giggling hysterically as one or another of us would trip and tumble, only to scramble immediately back to our feet, and dash off pel mel again.

We ran until we could run no more. Whether it was by accident or instinct, we dropped at last into a little hollow that had once been our chief hideout summer after summer as we chased the night toads, hid from pirates and savages, and dreamed our many dreams. We lay exhausted in the cold sand, our heads close together but our bodies further apart – the spokes of an unfinished wheel.

"Boy, tha..at was something!" Joey repeated. He and Jack giggled.

"Didn't know old Pam had it in her," Jack replied.

"No..o," Joey snapped back. "It was Donny that h..had it in her!" They laughed hysterically, while I tried to understand what they said and somehow put everything into an order that fitted my perceptions of how things had to be. I did understand, but I was afraid to admit it even to myself. I shut my eyes. After a few minutes I heard Jack and Joey turn over so that they were lying closer to me, looking at me.

"That was really something, eh Sandy," Jack whispered. I suddenly felt his lips pressing against mine, his body close and pressing against my side. My eyes flew open, but I lay where I was, not sure of what to do. I knew I should get up and run, but another emotion, getting stronger and stronger, made me stay where I was. But the war going on inside me left me limp as a doll – unable to respond to either.

Jack lifted his head. His eyes were hard and glittering. Joey pressed against me, and he too kissed me, thrusting his tongue into my mouth. I looked up unsure. They were my friends. I could trust them. But I couldn't admit to myself what was happening to me and within me.

Jack slid one arm under my head. Joey kissed me again and I felt Jack's other hand tight against my breast. For a long time we lay quietly together, our movements slow, their hands exploring me. They took turns kissing me, each time their tongues thrusting into my mouth. Their hands slipped under my clothes, and still I didn't move very much, knowing I should leave, wanting to stay, wanting them to do more and more. To do more to excite these strange feelings that were like the waves slapping higher and higher on the night beach.

With his free hand, Jack pulled up my tee-shirt, then lifted me into a sitting position. Joey reached behind my back, his fingers fumbling stiffly with my bra fasteners. I think he got it open. I felt then as though they were going to fall on me, smother me, as their hands and mouths reached for me. I felt a surging of the wild emotions that had been building and building. The waves here high in me, pulling me under. And then suddenly, the emotions were gone – silently sliding away into the night, into oblivion. I felt limp and angry, but still the twins were pressing themselves on me, stroking and kissing me where I suddenly knew clearly they shouldn't.

Angrily I pushed Jack's face away from my breast and slapped Joey's arm as he tried to explore a little more of me.

"Leave me alone!" I snapped furiously. I pushed them both away, flailing my arms and elbows at them as I pulled on my tee-shirt and then shoved my thin bra into my jeans pocket.

"Hey Sandy..." Jack said in a cloying voice. I smashed him in the face.

"You little bitch!" He yelped.

I stared at them, my anger draining into bewilderment. I sighed.

"I'm going home," I said, my voice somehow like a small child's. I ran into the shadow of the trees, then hesitated. They were sitting where I'd left them, bemused and bewildered. "You'll have to try your...your games on Pam or someone!" I yelled back. "I don't want you!"

Then I turned and ran, somehow finding my way swiftly to the summer house and to my quiet bedroom. I threw off my clothes, pulled on the ugliest pajamas I owned, then crawled into bed. I buried my face in my pillow and pulled the covers up to my ears.

I didn't want to look at the picture of my Daddy watching me catch toads. I never felt less like his Dream Girl.

Chapter 12

When I glared the following morning at the sunlight stealing across by bed, I knew I felt guilty. For a year or so my mother had made me take religion classes, and so I knew guilt when I was finally caught in it. The woman who had taught the class seemed a comfortable practical type – until she got on to religion. Then her eyes got watery with suppressed emotions and her voice warbled unnaturally as she tried to force her extravagant notions of what God did to us and for us. Guilt was one of her big concerns. The worm that ate us until we confessed to God in an orgy of expiation.

I scowled at the sunshine, hands behind my head, trying not to look at the picture of my Daddy with the Dream Girl that felt lost. I had no intention of confessing to God. Or my mother. If God didn't already know what had happened, He wasn't much good. Besides, what could He do? My mother would simply kill me. I decided that confession was much over-rated.

Besides, I reasoned obscurely, I wasn't sure I'd done anything wrong. I mean I hadn't really done anything. It wasn't like Pam and Donny.... My mind hid from that. I didn't want the sight of what they had done lying on top of my emotions, or even what I felt I might as well have done. I didn't want to think about the twins either. In fact I didn't want to think about anything.

It was late in the morning for me. Mom had apparently gone off to the little white church near the general store to hear what the minister had to say. I wandered outside and sat on the swing, eating a bologna sandwich I'd slapped together for my breakfast.

The sand before me was golden-white and the lake was a sky-blue sheet broken only by cheerful ripples that licked like foamy puppies at the shore. When my sandwich was gone, I meandered down closer to the water. My feet picked their way between the delicate fronds of the plants we called fairy trees. They never became brown with the scorching sun or grew more than a few inches. We had always believed the fairies planted them and laid a spell of magic on each so that it could not be pulled out of the sand.

I sank down into a tiny clearing in the garden of fairy trees, a Gulliver in the land of the Lilliputians. Idly, delicately, my fingers began tracing walks through the garden for the fairies, laying out wave-rounded pebbles for little statues and flagways. The sun washed over me, warm, comforting, loving. I felt blessed again by the fairies of my childhood.

Rising smoothly, I stepped away from the fairy garden, back to my world. I ran, suddenly happy and free again, down to the waters edge. The wavelets tickled cold across my bare toes. The water, too, loved me this morning. Every tiny pebble, each smoothed shell could be seen today with crystal clarity. I walked carefully through the water, trying not to disturb the intricate pattern of wavelets. A school of minnows flowed by. Several broke ranks to nibble at my feet, then flashed away when I wiggled my toes at them. I waded out to my waist, not caring that I wasn't wearing a bathing suit. For a long time I floated around in the water feeling the cleansing coolness that flowed over and around me. I dove for shells, then dove again to write my name in the shifting sand under the water. At last I waded back to the beach and flopped down on the sand, waiting for the sun to warm me. My shorts didn't seem to dry very quickly so I went back up to the house, changed into my old one-piece, then returned with a book and a towel to the hot sun.

I had been reading and dozing for about an hour when Pam plopped down on the sand beside me.

"Christ!" she snapped. "I'm going to drown Alison one of these days. You don't know how lucky you are to have an older sister – away from home – instead of a little tattle-tale brat!"

I stared at her wordlessly, sullenly wishing her away, not having the nerve to tell her to go. Pam didn't seem to notice.

"You know," she went on furiously, "I think I hate the little twerp. You know what's bugging her? She's got a crush on Donny! So now she runs and tells my father every time I go off and neck a little. He's straight out of the...of the...I don't know what! So now, after screaming at me all morning, I'm grounded! I can't go out with Donny for a month!" She stared at me, obviously expecting sympathy. I felt none – only a desperate wish for her to go and take my memories with her.

She stared off at the lake for several minutes, her face sullen and resentful.

"I know Donny, too," she went on after a few minute, "girls are after him all the time. He says he's in love with me, but if I'm not around he'll probably start going with someone else. Kristen Sims is just a mile down the beach and she'd do anything to get hold of Donny.

I'll bet," Pam added with a vicious half-laugh, "that if he told her to put out, she would. Just like that."

I stared at my book. I didn't want to hear this. I didn't want to know what she was saying – the lies she was telling or almost telling. I had never known Pam to be frightened, but today she seemed terrified that Donny would abandon her. I couldn't see why, I thought cynically, after all the fun they'd been having last night.

"I'm going to get Alison," Pam snapped. "I'm not letting my father ground me for a month – just like that!"

"Why don't you do like you did when we were little," I said without thinking. "Climb out the window."

She turned and looked at me suddenly, her eyes wide, her mischief grin quickly spreading across her face.

"I think you just saved my life!" she declared. "That'll show them. My father always plays favorites with Alison anyway."

After that Pam was at her nicest with me, but still she didn't go away. I didn't want to be her friend any more. I wanted to condemn her for what she'd done, and somehow purify myself at the same time. I felt small and mean and unsure. I felt years younger than the girl I was the night before.

"You're really down today, Sandy," Pam said after a few minutes of idle chatter and grunted replies. "Got love trouble?"

"Everything isn't always love trouble?" I snarled.

"I'll bet," she said with a skeptical smile. "I don't care. Tell me or don't. Doesn't make any difference to me. You know I won't tell the world."

"Yeah," I replied grudgingly. Pam had never told secrets, even little ones. I felt so lost again, caught between the Dream Girl and the person I was becoming. And all my friends were gone, metamorphosized into other people who would appear as they always had one minute, and then be strangers the next.

Here was Pam now. A stranger Pam, who did things that shocked my aggrieved, naive mind. A childhood friend Pam, who would climb out her window at night to follow her adventures and never blabbed secrets. And safe, sure Jack and Joey. What had happened last night? And what about me? Where had the person I was, gone to? Could I find her again? Did I want to find her again?

"Oh, I'm getting my period," I lied.

Pam nodded and changed the subject.

"Say, which of the twins are you going with?" she demanded suddenly. "Or have you got them both in tow?"

"Neither. Both...Christ!" I exploded. "I don't know and I don't care. What difference does it make."

"Jeez, I was right. You do have love trouble," Pam grinned. "Jack's got a nice body."

I stared at her, then at the lake. I didn't want to think about Jack and Joey's hard bodies. I didn't want Pam thinking about them either.

"Well, I'm going in for lunch," I lurched to my feet.

"See you later," Pam called. She was staring down the beach, the sun shining warmly over her new figure. I could almost read her new thoughts.

*   *   *

My feet dragged the next day as I approached the general store. I licked my lips. I don't think I quite expected the twins to jump out and rape me, but I felt the way I did each summer before my first meeting with Roy – a little frightened, a little confused, a little certain that all would be as it had been before.

"Hey Sandy!" Jack erupted from the store, an armload of papers rising to his chin. "Hurry up! You're late!"

I walked faster, reassured. Joey wheeled the delivery bike around the front. Jack stowed the papers on the back and began putting quarts of milk in the cooler for our customers who had ordered them with their papers.

"All set?" Joey asked. I nodded and felt my face flush scarlet. Jack looked up at me as he fastened the catch on the cabinet, his face as hard as always, but with a little smile quirking his lips.

"Business as usual," he grinned suddenly and punched me companionably on the arm.

"Right!" Joey declared and grinned. But when I climbed on the bike and started it up, he hissed in my ear, "You s..sexy broad, you."

I yelped and almost smashed the bike into the side of the store. Furiously I turned on him, trying to land a good, solid punch.

"Uncle, uncle!" Joey screamed, laughing wildly. I glared at the twins as they roared with laughter. Then suddenly I began to relax and grin too. They were my friends again, sure and trustworthy as they had always been. But finally I faced what I had known for a couple of years – they were boys-almost-men and I was a girl-almost-woman. It made us closer and further, as though we were suddenly different species while we felt new things and thought new thoughts.

As we climbed, still chuckling, onto the bike, that acceptance made my breath come hard. I felt in the churning emotions of my stomach and their difference from me. I was aware of them as I had not really been that night in the sand. It was as though I could feel them. Their man voices vibrated through those churning emotions. Their hands looked so large and strong. I sighed as I kicked the bike into movement, wishing I could disappear back into the days when we caught toads together, yet intensely aware that I didn't want to lose these new feelings either. The confusion pressed on me for awhile, but as we delivered the papers, I forgot the uncertainty in the pleasure of new orders and the money going into our bulging purse. And Joey telling me how well we were doing as the sun shone hot and bright over the shifting sands.

*   *   *

We worked hard all week, delivering papers, taking orders for groceries. Our apparent riches were illusory by the time we paid Roy for the groceries, the newspaper office for the papers, and Mrs. Patterson for the baked goods. Friday afternoon the delivery bike caught a nail in one tire. The gash was too long to be repaired, so more of our small profit disappeared into the price of a new tire that had to be sent at our cost from Simcoe.

I got home around four on Friday afternoon – hot, angry, and frustrated. I banged through the screen door and slouched onto the sofa, glaring at the dull landscape my mother had chosen for the living room wall. It couldn't have been more different from the joyous colors that splashed across Daddy's art.

"Sandy, you're home. Good." Mom said as she appeared, broom in hand, from the beach door. "I've swept the house and the porch and patio. But we need something a little special for dinner in case Joanie and Alan make it here in time. Would you run back to the store dear, and get some pork chops or steak or something?"

I opened my mouth to argue, then shut it again. I told myself it was because I had learned the futility of arguing about petty things, that I did not wish to spoil my mother's pleasure at my sister's visit. I would like to attribute my silence to these possibilities. However, I was just feeling sulky and martyred. A hundred years ago. Yesterday. Today. Tomorrow. It's humiliating how these threads of pettiness bind me into time far more reliably than my rare moments of achievement or virtue. I didn't have many moments of virtue – just lots of anger and those knotty flashes of pettiness.

It felt good, despite my sulks, to be kicking the cool dust of the back road with my bare toes. An old car passed me, the driver shaded by the streaming sun. I could hear some small children squabbling behind the screen of pines in the second row of cottages.

I squinted against the liquid gold the sun was hazing over everything. The Creyton's white gift shop and post office glimmered blindingly. I breathed deeply, smelling the dust, the gasoline-splattered pavement, the indefinable near-water smells. Mr. Creyton was outside, watering geraniums that spiked gaudily upwards from the shiny, black window boxes. I meandered toward the shop, suddenly needing to see my toad again.

The screen door banged loudly behind me. My nose caught the musty, gift shop smells as my ears echoed the muffled, waiting air of the shop. A woman with a beaten, bewildered air was detailing a long tale of her sufferings to Mrs. Creyton. I stepped sideways, around the tables, soft-footed, silent, not quite there. I eased around the nook of the store which hid the glass cabinet of fine figurines. They had been rearranged and I experienced an instant of panic as I realized my summer's treasure may have been sold. It was unlike the other treasures where there were sometimes a dozen of the same thing. My toad was unique.

But he was there still, hiding slyly behind an arrogant lady with a windswept skirt. His liquid gold eyes peeped out at me, confiding, trusting. He was mine alone.

I sighed and smiled, longing to take him safely back with me to rest under the painting of Daddy with his Dream Girl. Then silently promising I would be back again and again until he was mine, I slipped out of the store, the monotonous rise and fall of the suffering woman still droning within.

There were a lot of cars on the highway as the weekenders drove to their families and visitors searched out the cottages of their friends. I gazed down the road, watching for the long clear break I needed to cross. Had I been in the city, I would have dashed between the cars – they were not that closely spaced. But at the cottage, things were done differently. I simply stood and waited, watching the cars and the flickers of butterflies, fishflies, and dragonflies in the scrub along the shoulder. For a moment I understood why Roy and my mother had retreated to this place. It had an illusion of peace, of changelessness, in the drone of cars and insects and the hot, streaming sun. But, I thought with a flash of bitterness, this is a rest and a holiday – not a life.

I ran across the road and banged into the general store. Joey was nowhere to be seen, but Jack was leaning against the counter, too close to Pam. She was sipping on a milkshake, looking blatantly coy. I think Jack's and my mouths twitched identically in irritation – I with Pam for simpering at Jack, and he with me for bursting willy nilly into the store.

"Hi," I muttered. They just looked at me.

"Hello, Sandy," Roy said from the back. I hadn't seen him, but felt an angry flash of gratitude for his presence. Obviously my "friends" didn't want me around.

"Mom sent me over to buy some steak," I muttered, turning my back on the front counter.

"Sure thing, Sandy," Roy answered. "Jack, will you help her dig them out, please? I'm going to take the truck into town for some gas."

"Yeah, sure," Jack said and lounged away from the counter. He led me to the deep-freeze without bothering to meet my eyes. Roy looked at us for a moment, shook his head, and left. I heard the disgruntled rumble of the pick-up as Jack fished around for steaks among the medley of frozen packages of meat. My tongue felt tied in knots of resentment and jealousy.

"This what you want?" Jack asked, pulling a large sirloin steak out with cold-reddened hands.

"I guess," I nodded.

"Two-eighty."

He strode back to the counter and banged the price onto the cash register, pausing only long enough to wink at Pam and murmur something to set her giggling.

"I think I'll have a chocolate milkshake, too," I said loudly, an accent of protest audible even to myself. There was a slow feeling of real anger growing in me now. Jack looked at me in obvious annoyance. Pam seemed indifferent. Had she looked the least bit concerned, I probably would have repented, mumbled a change of mind, and slunk out. But that she could, well, not even worry about my competition, set the slow boil on high flame.

"Seen Donny lately?" I demanded with set belligerence. I was sure my eyes blazed fire.

"Oh, he's gone off to a friend's for a week," Pam answered, shrugging her nicely sloped shoulders. I squared back my bony ones.

"Must be boring for you," I added, taking a delicate sip of the shake Jack smacked down in front of me. I made a point of ignoring him. After all, why pay attention to the soda jerk?

"Oh, I find things to do," Pam said and smiled up at Jack. I spluttered a little, choked as the shake went down my windpipe, and gasped desperately as someone pounded me on the on the back. I regained my breath, but not my composure, after a few minutes. My face flushed scarlet from gaucherie as much as choking and I glared at Joey who had appeared from the back in order to thump me so unmercifully. Pam leaned her head over her shake again, another delicate sip slipping down her tanned throat. We both caught a glimpse of Jack giving Joey the high sign to get rid of me.

"Go for a walk, Sa..andy," he asked easily.

I opened my mouth to protest, but he simply grabbed my elbow, steak, and milkshake cup, and steered me out the door.

"What's the big idea?" I demanded furiously.

"Yeah, what's the big idea?" Joey returned with a grin. "You w..were never a spoilsport be..before. Jack's doing alright."

"Spoilsport! You..." words temporarily failed me. "Pam's trying to get her hooks in him." He raised his eyebrows, and grinned at me.

"*The time has c..come, the walrus said, to speak of many things,*" he quoted at me. "Like an opportunity not to be m..missed." He stared at me a moment, and I at him. A slight spasm shook him. I turned my head and stared at the gravel. I felt sad, as though something important to me had been broken. Without a word I took the steak and ran across the road. Joey followed me. We walked down the dusty road together, our feet kicking puffs of dust, our eyes never meeting.

"Sandy," he mumbled when we reached the mailbox by the summer house.

"What!" I snapped, still not looking at him.

"Do you, I mean, are..are you mad because you like Jack?"

I could have understood, but I didn't want to.

"You know how much I like Jack." I stared disconsolately at the road.

"Yeah, we..ell, I guess he doesn't l..like Pam that much."

I met his eyes then. His face was pale and his eyes were liquidy like the ceramic toad I wanted for my summer treasure.

He shuddered again and his head jerked with the spasm. I searched for something to say, but the words were more than I could utter. Joey turned abruptly and strode back along the road. I could see his shoulders and hands twitch slightly.

"Damn it anyway!" I ran back to the house.

Chapter 13

"Have another piece of pie, dear." My mother's smile was warm and happy as she gazed at Joanie and Alan. The three of them smiled around at each other, all very pleased with themselves. I scowled at the coffee pot.

"I couldn't," Joanie said, and added fatuously. "I still have to watch my figure."

"But you're eating for two now," my mother repeated.

"Excuse me." I thought I was going to throw up.

The air outside had become cool with the creeping dusk. I had missed the sunset – only a rosy haze over the far cottages showing that it must have been a fine one. I put my hands on my hips and breathed the cool, fresh air, glad to be away from the thick cigarette smoke and the thicker satisfaction that had lain heavily over the table.

Why did Joanie's pregnancy annoy me so much? If anything, I had been the one most eager for her marriage to come to this. It wasn't that I was jealous. I didn't want my mother. I told myself so. I told her so. I was dedicated to that idea. I obviously didn't care that she was so pleased with Joanie. Yeah, right.

I stretched a long, slow, cat stretch of freedom and self. Then still a cat, I sprang into a stealthy run along the beach, baring my fangs at the rippling waves and throwing my arms wide to embrace them all. I felt wild for something, but didn't know what.

"Hey Sandy!" Joanie's voice cut across the dream world I had leapt to, hauling me back to humdrum insipidness. She strode, big-boned and loose in her contentedness across the sand. A sudden memory of how she had seemed an almost goddess to emulate to my very young eyes, years ago, clouded over her maturity. She was younger then than I now was.

"So how's it going?" her voice had the firm carelessness that my Daddy rippled to warmth. But like my mother, the words carried questions and summaries that lapped and overlapped anything a person could say.

I shrugged, feeling young and defenseless against her contemptuous knowledge of her baby sister. She stared at me.

"Let's go for a walk," she commanded. I fell in beside her, dragged by the obedience of years before.

"Jeez, it feels good to be out here. Wish we could afford to rent a place for a couple of weeks. But that'd hurt Mom and I don't think I want to spend a couple of weeks with everybody crowded into the summer house."

"You mean you don't want to spend a couple of weeks with Mom at you all the time."

She regarded me coldly. "I'm perfectly able to say what I mean without your help. If you want to throw a tantrum do it at someone else, Dream Girl." She threw all the scorn she could into those words, watching with the amused disdain as I fumed and struggled for words.

"The old man sure made a spoiled brat out of you, didn't he?" she remarked.

"He did not! I...you're just jealous because he loves me so much! I was the Dream Girl, you know!" Even to me, my words sounded like the child in my picture, not a woman or almost-woman.

"Some hope," Joanie muttered. "The old man spared me his tender ministrations, thank God. He wasn't out to get Mom at that point. She was still worshipping the ground he walked on, the way she was supposed to."

"Oh...go to hell!" I whimpered and ran.

* * *

The toad struggled frantically to jump out of the hole, but it was too deep, too steep. The Dream Girl leaned back, her hands on her knees, resting and watching in satisfaction. Her tee-shirt and shorts were bright red, a smear of brilliant color against the deep summer green of trees and vines. In the pale hair on her tanned arms, little sand diamonds left by the fairies shimmered hot and white just for her.

The hole was long and deep. Wet and cold. The Dream Girl had dug it straight down, the length of her arm, handful after handful of wet sand being brought into the air by her scooping fingers. And then the toad had been dropped down, gently, for the Dream Girl never hurt anything. But the hole was deep, close.

The toad jumped and jumped, trying to push and scrabble back to the warm sand, the covering vines, the sunlight. But the hole had been scooped so deep. He could see a big man behind the head of the Dream Girl. Blue, cold eyes, and a smiling mouth. He hated toads, was glad to see the little one struggle against the hole he had casually dug for it. And then the Dream Girl leaned over again to watch the frantic struggle as the toad leaped and clawed again and again toward the little hole of light above. Her knees pushed into the shifting sand, and suddenly, the hole collapsed.

The clumps of damp, smothering sand. Falling over his face, his body. The weight as the hole avalanched full. He kicked and the sand filled the hole and held him. A little air. A little light. All gone.

The Dream Girl scooped desperately at the sand, but it was so loose. Where had the hole been? Where was the toad?

"It's only a toad. Ugly little toad. Leave it. You can't find it. There are too many more."

Her toad was gone.

"Maybe he got out," the Dream Girl whimpered.

"It doesn't matter. All that matters is that you're my Dream Girl."

*   *   *

I was staring at the sand, perched on the steps of the back porch. The summer house was stifling. My mother, Joanie, and Alan were laughing contentedly on the front porch, glasses of iced drinks in their hands. The sky was part blue, part cloud banked. The mosquitoes droned and whined everywhere, biting and tormenting, as the air became thicker with the approaching storm. I hoped it would rain overnight only, leaving the next day clear and cooler for our deliveries.

I heard the blare of the radio before I saw the car. The announcer was talking about the coming storm, but when I caught sight of my Daddy I forgot about it.

"Daddy!" I shrieked and flung myself toward him.

"Easy, Dream Girl," he laughed loudly, joyously, hugging me tight to him. "Phil, this is my daughter Sandy. You know her as the *Dream Girl Catching Toads*. Sandy this is Phil Barnet. He works for the Museum in New York." Daddy hugged me spontaneously as we walked toward the summer house. "Say, Phil, can I offer you a drink before we take a look at the painting?"

"Well, if your wife doesn't mind," Mr. Barnet said, his voice soft, uncertain, and somehow without character in competition with my Daddy's tones.

"Ex-wife, please! Unless you want your head served by her on a platter. She doesn't want anything to do with me any more. Decided to make a career for herself as a writer. I wished her luck of course, but between you and me, she doesn't have any talent at all."

Mr. Barnet murmured something I couldn't hear.

"Mom got a story accepted by *Redbook* last week," I interjected, somehow feeling a traitor to my mother. "That's a good magazine."

"Sure is Dream Girl, but you have to admit no one has offered her the Pulitzer Prize yet."

"They haven't offered one to you either," I snapped, then froze, overwhelmed by what I had said. Only a slight jar in his easy stride, showed that he reacted at all. He laughed.

"See what happens, Phil, when the wife walks out," he explained to Mr. Barnet. "And the sociologists are just starting to document what it does to the poor kids. But my Dream Girl is a good kid," he gave me another crushing hug. "She'll survive just fine. We survive, don't we Sandy? Nobody beats us down."

I nodded, beyond words, drowning beneath the emotions. Mr. Barnet again murmured something that fell below human hearing. We mounted the steps, three abreast, while Daddy pointed out the improvements he had made in the summer house.

"Nicest place on the beach, if I do say so. Mind you I'm always fond of what is mine. Or was mine," he added. "Andrea got the house in the divorce settlement." He smiled again.

"Divorces are always difficult," Mr. Barnet said politely.

They went into the living room and I followed, feeling rather like a stray puppy. Daddy chattered a little more quickly than usual while he poured drinks. I had not understood the words that Mr. Barnet was from the Museum and therefore extremely important. I did understand it from Daddy's nervousness. He said things that seemed strange to me, said things that carried a harshness about my mother. I felt he was making a fool of himself and was crushed by humiliation. I hated that man who made my Daddy, always so sure and wonderful, into an anxious fumbler, too eager to please. I compensated by glaring coldly at this intruder, defying him to think badly of my Daddy.

"Say, where's your mother, Sandy?" Daddy asked, suddenly turning to me. "I thought she'd be in here demanding to know how I dared invade her hallowed ground." He grinned, making it into a joke.

I didn't feel like joking and so only muttered, "I'll go see."

The air was still sultry, hot and breathless, but it was better than the steaming heat of the summer house, and the close, smothering anxiety that that man had caused. My mother, Joanie, and Alan were down the beach, strolling toward the house. I waved at them and they waved back. I went back into the cottage, determined to somehow protect Daddy from that man.

But just as I started up the steps, Daddy banged energetically out onto the porch, rubbing his hands with a sort of physical pleasure I didn't understand.

"Mr. Barnet wanted to examine the painting," he said quickly. "I told him I'd wait here until he was ready to discuss it with me."

I nodded, but pushed beyond him, back into the house.

"Don't disturb Mr. Barnet now, Sandy," my Daddy admonished. I didn't answer. Instead I went into my room and sat on the edge of the bed, glaring with overt hostility at that man. He glanced at me abstractedly, then returned his eyes to the painting. I too stared at it. For a long timeless space we sat together as enemies who loved the painting. My eyes caressed my Daddy, that strong, red-shirted god who laughed with me in my foolish efforts to catch my toad. That ugly little toad that he could not approve of.

...but a toad is so human, I wanted to cry out...

...so far from perfect beauty, he whispered back...

...yes, I agreed, *so far from the perfect beauty. Human. A creature that a person could love...*

"This is a remarkable painting," Mr. Barnet said turning to me with a smile. I noticed the smile lines around his deep eyes, the irregularity of features that made him an attractive person. "You must love it very much."

I nodded. "My Daddy painted me. All of me. He couldn't have painted me without so much love."

"Yes," he agreed after a long pause. "There's a lot of love in these paintings of your father's. He's such a genius." His fingers touched the edges of the painting, gentled with the love of what he saw.

We sat silent for a while longer as Mr. Barnet looked at the details of the painting. I watched only the laughing face of my Daddy. My Daddy and his Dream Girl.

We went back outside eventually. I was still walking in a warm dream. I ignored the strained anger on my mother's and sister's faces – the resentment flushing my father's.

"I'm warning you Bryce, that you had better not go through with this. Just think for once about Sandy..." she broke off when I came out, but I paid no attention – they were always quarreling about me, using me as a reason and clinching argument for every rage they fell into. I wasn't walking into their trap, I thought with distant scorn.

"It's fine, Bryce," Mr. Barnet said, his voice warm and glowing from the love in the painting. "I'm convinced it's your best work."

They walked down the beach together, their heads close as they discussed my painting, marveled at its beauty. I watched them lazily as they shook hands.

"Jesus, let's get the groceries," Joanie snapped to Alan. He nodded, his lean, sallow face set with an anger I was disinterested in.

"I...I'm going for a walk. In the other direction from the genius we all love and adore!" my mother raged suddenly, her face white. She strode away, her anger wild in every pose of her stiff figure. I wondered, with sudden unease what they had been arguing about this time, what was in the air that put my stomach in churning knots. I sat tensed, the good feeling gone in the anxiety that radiated in the sultry air. When my Daddy and Mr. Barnet sauntered back to the porch, I practically threw myself to my feet.

"Daddy," I demanded, "what are you and Mom quarreling about? I mean..." I faltered, suddenly aware of Mr. Barnet staring politely in the other direction. My father gestured in annoyance.

"Never mind, Sandy. You know..." he hesitated slightly, his unease patent, "it's just one of your mother's miffs, that's all. You know. And we don't want to air out our dirty linen in front of Mr. Barnet, do we," he added in the voice he had always chided me with as a child.

"Are you staying for dinner," I asked, dreading and hoping at the same time.

"What, and start World War Three?" Daddy joked heavily. "No, this is strictly business today. Mr. Barnet has to get back. We'll eat on the road somewhere."

I made no answer, but followed them around the house to the car, feeling small and in the way.

"So long, Dream Girl. I'll see you soon," Daddy said, giving me a bear hug. I kissed him, feeling shy in front of Mr. Barnet. He held out his hand to me.

"It's been a pleasure to meet the 'Dream Girl'," he said warmly as I grasped his hand.

It's bad luck to watch someone until they're out of sight, so I turned quickly back to the summer house when the car passed the Creyton's cottage. The sand was hot and sticky under my feet. A toad erupted from under some vines but I didn't feel like chasing him. I felt if I peered into those liquid golden eyes I would start to cry.

I began walking toward the end of the Point, oblivious to the distance, indifferent to the futility. I remember little about that walk now – it's a kaleidoscope of impressions and emotions. I cried. Strangers looked at me with blank faces. The sand was hot under my feet. The air pressed over me like a grey, stifling blanket. The trees were limp and motionless in the air.

In the distance I heard a roll of thunder. A chill of cold air slipped over my skin. I hesitated, then walked a few more steps. Another roll of thunder. A few heavy splashes of water. I hesitated again, then walked quickly, stiffly, toward the water, as though stalked by something nameless. I wanted to look back over my shoulder feeling as though something terrible pushed against me.

At first the lake was flat calm before me. The waves crawled in little ripples along the sand, muttering, complaining. The wind began suddenly. Wild gusts, slapping the water, pushing me one way and then the other.

I stood motionless and stared at the sullen, angry lake. The water turned grey, then as the wind rose higher and higher, it became black. The waves began quickly, each ripple rising higher than the one before it, each wavelet foaming white on the edges, until finally the waves crashed dirty brown toward me. I stepped back from them as they dashed higher and higher, sucking back everything they could reach. Again and again and again and again the waves crashed and rolled over the beaten sand. The thunder echoed and pounded through the air. Everywhere was water – in the air, at my feet, draining silently into the sand as the roars of the elements rolled around me.

And then I became afraid of the water, of the pounding and roaring and lashing. I ran. Back along the packed shore. The waves rose even higher licking over the loose drifts of beach. I ran through the cold sand, each step shifting beneath me. The rainwater streamed through my hair and over my blinking eyelids. The noise still roared around me. Just five more cottages to the summer home. Four. Three. Two. One. I'm home. I burst through the screen door, panting, streaming water – back into my family.

"Sandy!" my mother got quickly up from the couch, clanking her coffee mug on the table. "We thought you were at someone's house, waiting out the storm."

I sighed, exhausted, trying to regain an everyday way of looking at things.

"No," I gasped, "no. I went for a walk up the beach. Got caught in the rain."

"Didn't you hear the thunder," demanded Joanie, still curled distantly on the other end of the sofa. After a glance at me, Alan went back to reading his book on the strategies of the Second World War. I just shook my head, mumbled something about dry clothes and escaped them.

My Daddy still laughed as I changed into dry clothes and absently toweled my dripping hair. I watched thoughtfully, waiting for something to happen, listening for the words that would be said next. I was part of the picture, yet detached and independent from it. Like Alice peering at the looking glass the day after, wondering, sure and unsure.

Chapter 14

We sat on the porch railing, Joanie and I, swinging our legs.

"The lake came a long way up the beach during the storm last night," I remarked, staring at the waves.

"I guess it's the hurricane," Joanie answered, taking a long drag on her cigarette. I wondered briefly what Mom would do if I started smoking. Daddy would hate it.

"What hurricane?"

"Hannah. It's blowing around somewhere south of here. The forecasters are all arguing about whether it'll blow itself out in the ocean or swing back up here and wreak havoc and mayhem."

"I'd like to see a hurricane," I said after a pause. "It'd be more exciting than anything else around here."

"No," Joanie shook her head emphatically, denying the hurricane permission to enter our lives. "Not while I'm pregnant. I mean I have to watch out for the baby."

I grimaced slightly at such a matronly attitude.

"What does Daddy think about his first grandchild?" I asked after another lazy pause.

"Beats me." Joanie took another long drag. I watched with infinite fascination at such daring. Daddy still got angry about her smoking. She shrugged. "I didn't tell him."

"What?" I demanded, aghast.

"No, why should I tell the old bastard anything," she commented, stretching out her long legs.

First shock and then anger froze me, but then, my voice trembling slightly, I snapped at her. "Don't call him a bastard! Nobody ever had such a fantastic father. How could you tell our mother and not tell Daddy! How could you talk about him like that?"

My anger roiled inside me, closing off the words. I remembered with bitter resentment the quarreling that Joanie always started with Daddy. How she acted like our mother was always the one who suffered.

"You keep talking like Mom is a saint or something," I raged. "You just ought to try living with her!"

Joanie stubbed her cigarette deliberately on the railing, then turned and stared at me. I stared back as hard as I could, waiting for her to apologize.

"Someday, baby sister, I wish you'd open your eyes and maybe that mind of yours, too. You've been spoiled rotten by our genius father, whenever the notion occurred to him that he could spite Mom that way. Wake up, Sandy. He uses everyone. He used me and he used Mom. And I hate him more than I hate anyone in this world. You'd better wise up Sandy, because one of these days…"

"You'd better not talk about him like that! You don't understand him!"

"I understand," Joanie said deliberately. "I understand that he's the most selfish son of a bitch I've ever known. I don't care if he is my father. Look what he did to our mother! If you had any brains at all you'd see what he did to you, blaming everything like he does on Mom. You ought to look beyond that cute little Dream Girl conceit, before you go where all dreams go, child. He doesn't care about you, any more than he ever cared about Mom or me."

"You're just jealous because *I* was his Dream Girl."

"That's a laugh. You know why I left home? I would have done anything to get away from his crushing charisma and ego. I married Alan, and thank God I love him, because I think I would have married anyone who braved our dear old man's displeasure. Get this Sandy, I would have done anything to get away from that bastard.

"I only wish to God I could have convinced Mom to leave him then, but she was still garbling about how a child needs a father. Can you believe it? She stuck it out with him the last eight years for your sake. And look at the result. You're a spoiled little bitch who can't understand that you mother practically killed herself to give you what she thought you should have, and care only about being cute and cuddly and lovable to the Great Man. Just like a toy poodle. But don't forget, that if a dog gets in the way, it gets put out of the way."

I fought for words. I hated her! *I hated her!* I surged forward, fist balled, flailing and striking – trying to push her off the railing, push her to a fall that would end the baby she cared about so much. But she caught herself and twisted back from the railing. Her arm flew forward and her hand caught my face. Everything she felt was in that slap – all her hate. For Daddy. For me, who tried to do that to her.

I fell heavily onto the porch, screaming obscenities, and then struggled again to my feet.

"Girls!" my mother's ancient authority pierced my desperate rage, and I suddenly stopped screaming. But my shoulders shook, and like a person on the other side of the looking glass, I viewed with dispassionate contempt my rising hysterics.

What more can I write about that day? Even now, I am coldly frightened that in such a wild anger I could have tried to destroy Joanie by killing the child that was becoming. I have thought about it for years and I still have no understanding that I could do or think such a thing, even for an instant. I was afraid of the things that are hidden in me. I couldn't fight myself. I couldn't hide from myself.

*   *   *

Joey was hurrying up the dust road toward me as I ran down toward the general store.

"Where ya been?" he shouted over the wind that was gusting playfully through the trees.

"I had to wait to say good-bye to Joanie," I yelled in reply. "And Alan," as an afterthought. "They're going back to Toronto today and I was afraid I'd miss them. They didn't get up until late, and Joanie was throwing up. She's pregnant and boy does she have morning sickness."

Joey grunted his disinterest as I fell into step beside him. I maintained an annoyed silence as we hurried to the store, but Joey didn't seem to notice. His face was white and exhausted looking as though he'd not been sleeping, and he seemed to twitch continuously. As we banged into the store, I wished impatiently that his movements weren't so much like a short-circuited robot's.

It was just as well he didn't want to talk. I felt brittle and frightened and a little hysterical after the weekend and this horrible new knowledge of myself. And I didn't want to think about it. I couldn't stop thinking about it. Perhaps if Joey had been sympathetic I would have blurted out this awful secret and maybe it would have evaporated. I don't know. But I think I had to keep it to myself, for it gave me a new vision, a bitter cold vision of a corner of myself that had never emerged before and I was determined would never emerge again.

"Stop dreaming, Sandy," Jack said cheerfully from beyond the haze of my worries. "We've got a lot to do."

I mumbled something and glared at him. He had no right to look so pleased with himself. That was a trifle odd in itself. Jack and Joey usually mirrored the same emotions. What had happened over their weekend?

"Butter on the right. Cheese on the left. Milk in the door," I droned to myself. I still felt like a housebreaker cum peeping tom while I put away the Creyton's groceries. She had bustled out of the gift shop shaking a list at us while we poked wearily along back to the general store after delivering the morning papers and taking orders.

"I have everything written down here," she announced, swatting the air with her list. "Now don't you two forget anything. And I don't want you tramping around our cottage either!"

She glared while I had visions of huge cakes of mud and clay being stomped through every corner of her cottage. Mounds of the stuff while we peeked and pried.

"And make sure everything is put where it belongs."

Cookies in the shoes. Canned goods in the oven. Dairy products under the mattress.

Joey mumbled something to her and she left again, leaving grey anger residue in the clear air. A few gusts slapped it around, spreading bad temper throughout the world.

I felt weary. I wished I could go home and curl up on my bed under the gentle loving laugh of my Daddy. I wished I could sit with him and be cuddled. I wondered if it would feel nice to be cuddled by Joey.

Pam was in the snack bar again, slowly stirring a straw around in a milkshake. Donny lounged beside her. I slumped down onto a chair.

"Hi!" I said when no one seemed to notice me.

"Well, how's the working girl?" Donny said abruptly. He should have smiled, but he didn't. "Joey." He acknowledged Joey's presence.

Joey nodded but said nothing. He plunked an opened grape pop in front of me, then sat on the chair on the other side, elbows resting on the gaily checked cloth. He stared down at his orange drink, motionless as marble but for the twitches and tremors which shook him every little while. I laid my arm along the table and put my head on it, watching Joey's twitches and the cold sweat running down the bottle with equal indifference. Even the air felt heavy in here.

We had never been so silent before, the five of us. There were no jokes, no conversation, only an apparent weariness. Jack began to hum softly as he tidied up behind the lunch counter. Pam slurped the last of her shake and twisted around on the stool, leaning back on the counter on her elbows, thrusting her breasts outward into the air. Donny and I stared at them. I could almost feel the sensation of lushness exposed to the air, inviting admiration, desire, male hands. I grimaced wryly and watched unmoving as Pam tossed her long hair. She looked like something out of a Grade Z beach party movie. I was only surprised that she didn't simper at the hero. I wished I could enjoy my body the way she apparently enjoyed hers. Maybe she had more hormones than I did.

Jack began wiping the counter, but watching Pam with an odd expression in his eyes, and a cold glint of amusement when they strayed toward Donny. Pam looked backward over her shoulder at Jack, ignoring the rest of us, and slowly licked her lips. Jack's cold self-satisfaction radiated outward.

I felt each of my muscles stiffen as a slow, deep anger welled from some far part of me. I understood. Behind my motionless features a snarl of ancient anger formed – anger without logic, without cause or outlet. More potent, more true for all of that. No one would ever see it.

I wanted to kill her, with my hands and teeth. I looked at Joey's cold, marble agony. I wanted to kill her again.

"Did I tell you guys that I'm going to be an aunt?" I announced cheerfully.

*　　　*　　　*

It began to rain that night, lashing water on screaming gusts of wind. The announcer on the local TV station assured us that the storms would abate, that Hurricane Hannah would not come any closer to our lives. But it rained all night and most of the next few days.

Joey and I struggled through the cold beach colony, carrying wet newspapers and bumper loads of groceries. I had never been so cold and miserable. Joey was silent hour after hour. Sometimes he would look at me, and I would see my old friend's appeal, but I turned away. The new visions and emotions that were tearing through me turned me to cold and ice. Rage and fear. One night I dreamed I was struggling through the storm, searching for the Dream Girl. There was a big hole in my picture where the Dream Girl had torn herself away. Someone called to me, tried to convince me that there was no Dream Girl any more. I struck out in anger and desperation. It was a long, frantic, aching search before I found the Dream Girl. But I couldn't speak to her any more. She acted as though I didn't exist. I woke up in a white agony of sorrow.

I hated my mother. I phoned Daddy twice. I hurled myself through the rain, cold, and gusting winds, looking for something, trying to find something.

Hour by hour the lake rose, licking and grasping the loose sand, closer and closer to the cottages. I stood hour after hour in the rain, my bare toes at the edge of the sucking waves, staring out at the hypnotic dance of white caps on black water streaked by the flashes of lightening. If only I could empty myself into the waves, slide icy warm to the bottom where I didn't have to think or feel anything ever again. Beneath the crashing water was silence and peace. There was no storm beneath the water. I could feel the water sucking around my ankles, my legs...

"Hey, Sandy!" Joey grabbed my arm and jerked me roughly backwards. I stared at him bewildered, groping my way feebly back to thought.

"Those waves might have carried you ou..out," he said sharply, his face white and glistening shadows under the rain and clouded day. He had tied his sopping shirt over his shoulders, so that his chest and arms were bare.

"Well, at least I won't go off with pneumonia," I snapped. "I had the sense to put on a raincoat."

He shrugged.

"Want t..to go for a w..walk," he stammered through his tremors.

I didn't want to. I couldn't be bothered. But then another streak of lightening flashed, highlighting the configurations of his chest and arms. Another snake of emotion curled through me and I nodded.

We slogged along in the sand, under the dripping, moaning skies, barely aware that we were idiots to be out in such weather. Eventually we reached the public path between the cottages that led to the road by the general store.

"Want a hamburger?" Joey shouted above the wind.

"I don't want to see anyone."

"You won't. Dad's stranded in Simcoe and Jack's off with Pam – probably screwing the hell out of her!"

I shrugged and wondered a little. Bit by bit I began to come back to myself and to my world. I even wondered hazily why Joey's bitter obscenities would do this. I smiled to myself, suddenly feeling alive and slightly fierce inside. I slid my hand into Joey's and squeezed it. Both our hands were icy cold, and somehow that struck me as funny. I laughed.

"You're my best friend," I told him when he glanced at me.

"Sure. B..best friend," he muttered sourly. "T..terrific."

I couldn't stand looking at him without his shirt any longer, so I grabbed his arm and tugged.

"Race!" I hollered and tore off down the road toward he store, barely glancing to see if he was following. He was trotting slowly without much enthusiasm. I didn't care as I raced past the gift shop. I was taken with a sharp ache to see the little toad who understood me so well. Suddenly wistful, I paused, pushing the streaming hair out of my eyes. Mr. Creyton slammed out of the shop, a trench coat pulled loosely over his clothes. Even through the wind, from the other side of the road I could hear the oaths he was shouting at his wife as they struggled together, with her on the inside, to fasten a window and shutter that had come loose from the wind and rain.

"We should help them," I told Joey solemnly when he reached me. Suddenly he grinned.

"You're right," he agreed firmly.

We laughed aloud joyously then, and ran across the highway to the general store, banging in through the unlocked screen door.

I peeled off my coat and slouched into a chair near the counter. Joey dropped his shirt on one of the bar stools, turned, and slapped some frozen hamburger patties on the grill. He didn't look at me as he cooked and wiped, but I watched him. For some reason, even his occasional twitches appealed to me. He was like my toad, beautiful and ugly in a way that could not be separated one from the other. Each melted and merged and made him himself.

Daddy found him obscene. It occurred to me suddenly, strangely, that Daddy was a fool. Joey had a beauty that was much more than his classical golden body. But Daddy saw only the parody of twitches.

But the thought frightened and hurt me, so I pushed it away, thinking instead of the rain and the cold and the smell of hamburger.

"If the water comes much higher, some of the cottages will get washed out," I said suddenly.

"Maybe," Joey answered.

"Creyton's place is the closest to the water, and their foundations are hardly buried in the sand any more."

He plunked the hamburger down in front of me, and took his place on the other chair, leaning his elbows down and his body over, so that he seemed to be crouching over his plate.

"I was hungry," I mumbled through the bun as I took a large bite.

I wanted Joey to say something, but he remained silent. We ate without speaking while I waited for him to tell me what was wrong. But even when he finished his hamburger, he still said nothing.

"Why were you out in the rain?" I asked finally. I'd never seen him so white and silent before. I didn't want to see him like this. "What's wrong?"

"Let's go in the apartment," he muttered and jerked out of his chair.

I was irritated, but followed him anyway.

The apartment was just four rooms – a bathroom, kitchen and two bedrooms. My memory of it was always the same – a dark, confused clutter of old furniture and possessions. The kitchen was always scrupulously clean, but there were untidy piles on the tables and counters. We passed through into the bedroom. Jack's bed was made, but Joey's was a jumbled heap of sheets and blankets. I slouched down amid the bedclothes, sticking my almost numb toes under the blankets.

"You don't mind, do you?"

Joey grinned. "Are your feet sterile?"

"Of course."

He picked up a pair of jeans from a pile in the corner.

"I'm freezing," he muttered, not looking me in the eye, and pulled off his still dripping pants.

I still don't know what my emotions were. I think I was faintly shocked, mildly considering of what he intended, and generally numb. When we were children we had often skinny-dipped. We were children no longer. In fact, my semi-dazed consciousness recognized that Joey was definitely a man. And, my judicious thoughts pointed out, I had never seen a man before – except in marble or a painting, and believe me it's not the same thing at all. Amid the disorienting shock emotions, I was torn between awe, revulsion, and mesmerizing fascination.

"Pretty good, eh, S..Sandy?" Joey demanded fiercely.

I dragged my eyes up to his face. Everything about him was clenched, every muscle and nerve was pulled tight as he stared at me. But his body couldn't take that, and the spasms began twitching him, pulling and tearing at him. He twisted and jerked the way the little dream toad had as the sand piled over him, suffocation him, shutting him out from the light.

In a panic, I pulled Joey down onto the bed and began rubbing his forehead and trying to talk to him until he relaxed. But he pulled away from me and leaned against the wall, his face averted. I could feel his rage as he willed his wayward body to relax, to stop twisting and jerking. I watched and waited until his body would become his own again.

I wanted to hold him, to protect him from the agony he was feeling, the way I would hold a little toad hoping to protect it from danger as it tried to survive. But there was so much more to Joey. I clenched my hands tightly and just waited, hoping that we would be friends again.

The silence lasted a long time. Joey leaned still against the wall, even when the shudders had all but ended.

"I w..wouldn't hurt you, Sandy," he said finally, unmoving.

"I know."

There was a long, aching silence. His shoulders seemed to tense again. He laughed suddenly, harshly. I knew he was crying.

"I...I could..ouldn't anyway!" he exploded. "I...I don't th..think I c..can..." He jerked around and stared at me. Anger and fear. "D'you know w..what I mean?"

I shook my head. He plopped down beside me on the bed, his elbows on his knees, staring at the floor.

"On the week..end Jack and I decided t..to screw Pam. A..at least try to, y'know..." He didn't notice my clenching fists or rising flush of anger. "We're almost s..seventeen and w..we've never laid anyone, and Pam's been m..making eyes at us."

"Bitch," I said. "Did you?"

Joey hesitated.

"S..sort of. I mean Jack did. I t..tried but.. but I couldn't," he looked at me, his face distorted with misery. "I..I couldn't get it up, y'know. She s..said it was probably my b..brain damage. L..laughed and said she'd never known anyone who w..was impotent before."

"Bitch!" I repeated.

"Oh, it isn't h..her fault." He leaned back on the bed, lying out beside me. I looked at him for awhile, aware only of his body and my growing rage. I didn't understand any of this. I didn't care. I knew so well Pam's laughing, careless daggers. They had shot out when we were children and it seemed they were shooting still. The twins were mine! She would not hurt them like that.

"She doesn't know anything," I insisted. "I mean..." I trailed off, not knowing any of the things I should say to Joey. I didn't know what was true and what I just wanted to be true. There was a hard core of realism that told me there was something wrong with all this, but I didn't know what it was. All I knew was that Joey had been bitterly hurt by her.

"What did Jack say?" I asked abruptly. Jack was Joey's other half. They couldn't think a thought separately – at least they never had before.

"I w..won't talk to him about it," Joey said sullenly. "Why should he be...I mean, I..I shouldn't hold him back any m..more. And besides, all he c..cares about is screwing P..Pam now."

My thoughts changed again as I looked at him. If there was something wrong with him, it didn't show. I lay down beside him.

We lay against each other for awhile, then he rolled on his stomach and looked at me. He took one of my hands in his two hands and kissed it gently.

"Can I ki..iss you?" he asked shyly, as though he thought I would hurt him too.

"I guess," I mumbled.

He kissed me hard, but his movements fumbled. There was none of the hard, lusting glee he and Jack had used toward me before.

I can't even say how I felt. There was such a core of bitter anger. But everything was confused by my new emotions, surges and gales of feelings that thrilled and frightened me. And superimposed above it all was the pulsing reality of the summers in the sun, Daddy and his Dream Girl, and my friend Joey. The friend I shared everything with. The stranger who was kissing me, making me feel so strange.

Above the emotions and the sounds of our own breathing, came another sound, shrill, insistent, demanding. Joey sat up suddenly.

"Somebody's s..screaming out there, in the store!"

Chapter 15

We jerked upright, bewildered – startled into movement. Joey gave me a push.

"Go see what it is," he commanded. "I've g..got to put some clothes on."

I started to giggle. He grinned and we were friends again. Like before. Almost.

"Go on!" he gave me another shove.

I walked slowly toward the kitchen and the door into the store, uneasily aware of the calling and screeching that shouldn't be there, and Joey's naked body which I was certain no one would understand if they guessed.

I pushed into the store.

Mrs. Creyton, dripping, disheveled, wild-eyed, turned on me.

"A dime! I need a dime! Have you got one?"

I stared open-mouthed. She had been trying to pull open the locked cash register. Joey appeared behind me.

"Wh..what's wrong Mrs. Creyton?" He asked calmly. I could have sworn it was Roy speaking in those tones.

"Len...Len! I told him he was getting too angry. He's dead! I think he's dead!" We stared at her blankly. "An ambulance," she shrieked, the tears streaming down her face, smearing her rouge.

"Dr. Parker," Joey said quickly, giving me yet another shove. "Go get him Sandy. I'll call the ambulance."

I grasped suddenly what had happened. I slammed out of the screen door and ran, panting and pounding down the road past the gift shop. With a sense of physical shock, I saw that the shop door was slightly open, held ajar by one of Len Creyton's feet. I looked away and kept running. The Parker's cottage was two over from the public access. I slogged through the water-heavy sand to the door and began pounding with both fists. Mrs. Parker opened the door.

"Mr. Creyton!" I gasped. "He's...I mean... he's had a heart attack I guess..."

She looked at me for an instant, startled, then turned back into the cottage.

"Tony!" she called sharply into the recesses. "Len Creyton's had a heart attack!"

One of their kids looked out in the bemused fashion of children watching something not affecting themselves directly. Dr. Parker came at a run, carrying his bag of instruments.

"An ambulance?" he demanded.

"Joey's calling one."

We ran side by side through the sand and across the road to the gift shop. Joey and Mrs. Creyton were there already. Joey had brought an armful of blankets and had laid them across Mr. Creyton. His dripping face was slack and grey. I bit my knuckle to keep from screaming.

Dr. Parker tossed back the blankets, felt Mr. Creyton's neck for a pulse, then ripped open his shirt. I had seen a film demonstration once of first aid techniques. I never want to see the real thing again. Silent fear thickened the air. The only sound was Dr. Parker's heavy breathing as he pounded and pressed Mr. Creyton's chest, pausing briefly again and again to feel for a pulse, before going back to his "massage."

At last he leaned back gasping, perspiration mingling with the rainwater that dripped from his hair. He pulled some of his instruments from his bag and began listening and gently feeling.

"Heart's fairly steady now," he said wearily. "You called the ambulance?"

"Yeah," Joey affirmed. "It'll be a l..little while because some of the roads p..past the marshes are flooded, but it's coming."

It was almost an hour before the ambulance arrived. Mrs. Creyton sat on a chair, alternately moaning and crying and repeating over and over, "I told him not to. I said he shouldn't get so angry..."

Dr. Parker crouched by Mr. Creyton the whole time, checking constantly. Joey and I leaned against the counters, looking back and forth at everyone. Once Mr. Creyton seemed to drift back to consciousness and moaned from deep in his body. Mrs. Creyton cried out in response and clunked to her knees beside him, clutching his hand. Mascara laden tears dripped onto her husband's knuckles as she gripped his hand in both of hers. She rocked slightly and made noises like the air being squeezed from a rubber balloon.

When I couldn't stand it any more, I stared at a display of birch bark canoes and drums with *Long Point Beach* printed on them in large flowing letters. At last we heard the wailing of the ambulance siren. Joey ran to the door and peered through the rain down the highway.

"It's a..almost here," he called back.

It pulled up in front of the store, and almost too quickly, Mr. Creyton was strapped on a stretcher and carried in. Mrs. Creyton climbed in after him, seeming suddenly uncertain when no one tried to stop her.

"Heart beat has been fairly steady the last half hour," I heard Dr. Parker say. "I think I may have broken a couple of ribs."

The attendant nodded and climbed into the back with the Creytons.

"You broke his ribs?" I demanded. That seemed horrible somehow. Dr. Parker just grinned.

"Ribs they can mend, Sandy," he told me. "Dead they can't.

He waved then and walked down the road toward his own cottage.

"We'd b..better lock up the store," Joey said and touched my arm. I sighed and went back into the gift shop with him. We searched for the keys, finding them at last in a small drawer in an old table.

"Well," Joey said wearily, "let's go."

"No," I replied, suddenly remembering my little toad. "I want to show you something."

I took the keys and carefully unlocked the cabinet. The toad was still there, his eyes liquid and comforting. I held him for a moment, then put out my hands for Joey to see. He took him carefully, gazing into the eyes, examining the exquisite details of the porcelain.

"He's a funny little thing," he said softly. "You go..going to buy him at the end of the summer, Sandy?"

I nodded and Joey put him back in the case. We locked up then, taking the keys with us.

"Want a shake or anything?" Joey asked.

"No. No, I want to go home."

He touched my arm briefly and we turned toward our own homes. The rain had almost stopped by now, if only for awhile. The road was slimy goo under my feet, cold and cloying. I wanted to run, but I was just too tired. At last though, I turned up the driveway and slogged through the clinging wet sand. My mother met me at the door.

"Sandy, what happened? You've been gone for hours."

I looked up at her face, suddenly seeing how lined and softened it had become since I was a little girl. Since before I had became the Dream Girl.

"Oh, Mom..." I said and began to cry. My mother hugged me.

*　　　*　　　*

Business as usual.

The rain dripped and sputtered and poured over Joey and me as we delivered load after load of groceries. The delivery bike was almost useless because of the sticky, oily mud on the road. The muck clung to our legs, stiffening and weighing down our jeans and tennis shoes. No matter how tightly we closed the delivery cases, it seemed to ooze in. I thought we would be smothered in mud, but the rain that dripped and spitted fitfully over us, driven and indifferently dropped by wild gusts of wind that burst then died, would wash us down again. We shivered constantly as the rain seeped through the cracks in our rain coats and soaked our clothing.

But the stream of money into our pockets swelled with the rising winds and dashing waves that crept closer, hour by hour, to the cottages. But just as the money began to seem never-ending, it trickled away. Hurricane Hannah had not slunk away or blown itself out. For several days the eye of the hurricane had hovered sullenly, barely moving one way or another. Then abruptly, the great malevolent storm had turned and begun a slow wavering movement across the natural funnel of the Great Lakes toward the waiting ocean. It was like a huge dying monster staggering across the country, hour by hour growing weaker, yet still rousing into wild strength again and again as it drifted to the Atlantic, to its death.

Families began packing belongings hurriedly into cars, shuttering cottages as if for the storms of winter. We watched the exodus with a strange mixture of fear and exasperation. The wind made talking almost impossible. The mud and empty cottages made our service futile. On Wednesday, we made our last delivery and told our customers we'd start up again if the cottagers returned in force and the weather cleared. Joey and Jack looked white and haggard as we sat in the store, staring at the red-checked cloths, wondering why there no longer seemed anything worth doing. We had earned a hundred and twenty-seven dollars and eighty-three cents each. A lot of money. Not enough money. No East Lakes. No university. Nothing.

"We worked so hard," I protested again. "It's not fair!"

"Oh shut up!" Jack said savagely. "Things aren't ever fair. It doesn't make any difference."

He stood up violently, then hesitated, looking around. There was nothing to do with his rage. Nowhere to put it.

"I hate this place," he said. He stood a moment longer, looking bleakly around the store, then went to the cooler for a Coke with the appearance of someone who has just found himself and his life so bewilderingly useless, that even routine motions are suspect and unsure. He looked at the soft drink a moment before putting it into the opener and popping off the cap. He leaned against the counter staring out the window at the driving rain.

Throughout this, Joey said nothing, merely watching his twin bleakly as if waiting for Jack to find the answer for him. Yet knowing there was no answer.

I was beginning to wonder if I should go home, if getting away from all this might make me feel better. I hadn't fallen into a bleak despair like they had, I thought with sulky smugness. Their misery was boring.

The wind and rain lashed louder as the door suddenly swung open. Roy pushed through the weather into the store, smiling wearily at us.

"Dad!" Joey's voice cracked out. The twins remained as rigid as death, their eyes wide and demanding as they stared at their father.

"Lord, I'm tired," he mumbled, looking down at his coat as he slowly unfastened the buttons. "A two hour drive – took me six and a half hours. The old truck stuck to it though."

"Y..you should have stayed at the hospital," Joey said sharply. The twins' eyes raked angrily, anxiously over him.

"No," Roy replied firmly, yet with still a hint of uncertainty. He sat down beside me, smelling steamy and warm. "They can't do anything for me."

As long as I had known him, Roy had always been the most direct person in my world. But this time he looked at the salt and pepper shakers as though they fascinated him, refusing to even glance at the faces of the boys. Jack made a sharp, angry explosion of noise, then turned his back to us, leaning against the cold steaming window. Joey got slowly up from his chair, his head and shoulders twitching but his face somehow as motionless as marble. He moved slowly and silently, and left the room.

I felt bemused, realizing that I didn't understand what was happening to them – what was being said and not said that mattered so much.

Roy took a deep breath and looked at me. I could see the little hairs growing singly from his cheeks before they melted into the mass of his beard. His cheeks were an odd shade of white and brown under those little rivers of hair. When he looked at me I was almost shocked by the paleness of his blue eyes and the tiny pit black pupil.

"Well, Sandy," he said softly, obviously straining and reaching for something normal to say. "Aren't you and your mother leaving the beach?"

I stared at him for a moment, frightened. But his words were normal. My words too became normal.

"No. We've nowhere else really to go – can't afford a hotel or anything. But mostly we're staying because the summer house is a long way back from the lake, and...and Mom seems to find inspiration in the storm. I mean she's writing a lot and she says it's really good..."

I trailed off uncertainly.

Jack whirled around suddenly and faced us, his face contorted with emotions I didn't understand...didn't want to understand.

"Damn you!" he said with a quietness worse than a scream. "Why didn't you do something about it before – before it was too late? Don't you even want to live?"

Roy just looked at him, his face pleading and somehow certain at the same time.

"There was nothing to do," he said simply. "I've known about this tumor since the day after the first operation. It's inaccessible. They can't do a thing about it."

"There are treatments, aren't there?" Jack pleaded. "Couldn't you have taken treatments ... or something?"

"They might have slowed the growth a little, son," Roy said gently, still staring at the tablecloth. He looked up at Jack suddenly. "But I would have had to spend months recovering and the end would have been the same – just taken a little longer."

"But don't you want that little bit longer?"

"Not particularly. But damn it Jack! While I spent a year or so in a rehabilitation center, where would you and Joey be, eh? Where would you have been? Joey would have ended up in a hospital too, or maybe even an institution. You saw what happened to him in just the two months I was away before.

"Remember those leg braces? And the crutches? And he couldn't talk any more for spasms. Joey needed me Jack. He needed his home and quiet – not a foster home with a half a dozen brangling kids. And even you weren't in too great shape. You cried out in your sleep and had nightmares for three years after that. Don't you understand – you boys needed me! You may not think so, but you did. I'm not much of a father, but that much I am! I would have had to sell the store, found a job somewhere – with a history of cancer. And you and Joey would have had to stay in foster homes for still more months. Think Jack. Just try to think!"

"It may be true, damn you!" Jack shouted at him. "But you're still not trying to live. You don't even care! You're ready to step into a grave right now!"

"Jack..."

"I don't want to talk to you!" Jack yelled and slammed out into the storm.

Roy sighed and stared awhile at the table cloth.

"You don't...I mean you can't really want to...to..." I faltered, sickened, frightened, desperately wanting to understand.

"You mean, do I want to die?" Roy asked me gently, a smile suddenly hovering over his lips. "Well Sandy, yes, in a way I do." He sighed, and then added harshly, "They're well rid of me now. Because...because I want to go... I can't make anyone understand," he muttered, his voice aching with futility. "The boys don't understand and I doubt if you can either, Sandy. I think it will be a great relief to die – to be done with all this." His hand gestured around the shabby store, but I sensed that he meant much more.

"Aren't...aren't you afraid?"

He gazed at me a moment, our eyes meeting, but his were focused still on the vistas I could perceive only vaguely, as though shrouded in a morning mist.

"Of course I'm afraid," he said softly. "I'm so afraid that...that I don't know. But I'm more afraid of not dying, of going on and on and on like this. There's no purpose to this life any more. The boys are grown. I keep telling myself that it's natural to die. After all, we're all dying – you're dying too, Sandy." He paused while I froze in revulsion and fear. A smile –

no and outright grin, identical to Jack's spread over his face as he looked at me with narrowed eyes. I'd never seen him grin before.

"Well," he went on with a brisk note in his voice, "I'm just dying with a little more determination and efficiency than you are."

"But don't Jack and Joey need you?" I pleaded. I felt I had to argue somehow, that his pleasure in death was wrong – obscene.

"No," Roy said, turning the salt shaker around and around in his fingers. "They don't need me now. They've always had each other anyway. And they're grown up – ready to leave me. Though they don't realize it. Missy, my wife, needed me a little. I've always been a drifter, Sandy. Some people drift around the country. I just drift around people, never seeming to get anchored to anyone."

"Maybe if your wife hadn't died," I whispered.

He looked at me kindly.

"It would have been the same, Sandy. In the end. Sure I would have stayed physically with her and the boys, but I couldn't have stayed anchored for many years. It seems to be in my nature to drift away into myself. When you're older, love – the way you're thinking of it now, Sandy – isn't as strong as you'd think. It will modify a person, but your soul belongs to yourself, and it's your soul you follow sooner or later. My soul is tired of my life, that's all. It's as though I've always been waiting to leave."

We sat in silence for awhile longer, Roy turning deeper and deeper into himself. I felt cold and sick.

"You don't understand!" I cried out finally, feeling something hard wrenching away from me.

Roy looked up at me, his old warm smile spreading slowly across his face, rippling his soft whiskers.

"Do you ever read poetry, Sandy?" he asked. I stared at him blankly, wondering if perhaps his mind was no longer right.

"No?" he went on. "Well, I do – constantly. Most poets have at one time or another written about death – some beautifully, some stupidly – but that's the way people are. Have you read Dylan Thomas' poem *Do Not Go Gentle Into That Good Night*? Well, he wrote it when his father was dying. And you know, it could have been Jack who wrote that.

> *"And you, my father, there on that sad height,*
> *Curse, bless, me now with your fierce tears, I pray.*
> *Do not go gentle into that good night.*
> *Rage, rage against the dying of the light."*

"Then how can you just...just..."

"Just die?" Roy finished for me. "That poem could have been written by Jack, Sandy, but John Donne wrote one for me. He just called it *Death*. No raging of youth whose life lies precious before him. But the end is the same. You know there's one other poem by Wordsworth – you know the first line a least – *The World is too much with us*. It's all too much for me, Sandy, and I just want to get away from all this."

He looked at me kindly again, then as if his very soul echoed the words I couldn't accept, he sighed, long and deep.

"Don't worry, Sandy," he said as he stood up. "You'll understand one day maybe. I have to go and try to make it right with the boys. God, I'm a coward. I wish I could just slip away." He looked at me again wryly. "You have no idea how hard things are when you really love someone and they refuse to understand the part of you that makes you alive – even when you're talking about death."

He straightened his shoulders, unconsciously, I guess, then went into the back of the store.

I slowly did up my rain coat, trying not to think about Roy and the twins, but unable to think of anything else. The rain had petered out for the time being, but the mud clung oily and heavy to my boots, weighing me down. The trees dripped constantly. I stepped over branch after branch that had been torn down by the rising and falling gusts of wind.

"Hi Sandy," my mother tossed over her shoulder as she banged furiously on her typewriter.

"Do we have any books of poetry?" I asked.

She turned and looked at me, momentarily jerked back to the real world.

"I didn't know you liked poetry."

"I don't. But Roy told me about some he liked... and I thought..."

My mother looked at me, seemed about to hold out her hand, then let it drop.

"On the bookshelf in my room, there are about a dozen poetry books. You should be able to find the poems you want in them."

It only took me a couple of minutes to find Roy's poems. I carried the books back to my room and lay down on the bed. Daddy laughed down at me still, or rather at that joyful Dream Girl of long ago – if ever – I thought, savagely morose.

The ugly little toad, not understanding that I loved him, still scooted away. I looked away and opened my books.

I can't remember how many times I read those three poems. All I remember is crying for a long time afterward, and realizing as I wept, that I didn't know who my tears were for.

Chapter 16

"Don't you think you're being just a little unreasonable, Andrea?" my father said coldly, his dignity austere and at odd variance with his usual vivacity. "And perhaps just a little selfish?"

I watched my mother and father battling for my favor yet again. Or rather they were using their supposed affection for me as a weapon against each other.

"No, I don't think I'm particularly selfish," my mother said with equal frigidity. "The hurricane will shortly blow itself out or end up in the ocean."

"You are, of course, the expert."

My mother flushed slightly. I tensed, hurt and resentful, as they tried to shaft each other. But usually Daddy won.

"No, I'm not the expert, Bryce. The meteorologists reporting over the radio and TV are," my mother said evenly. "It was entirely unnecessary for you to drive all the way here – as touching as you concern for our welfare is," she said bitingly. "We are not about to be flooded out, blown away, or washed into the lake."

My father stopped pacing about the room and glared at my mother. She stared back, her chin lifted, an unconscious imitation of a child's gesture of defiance. How vulnerable she is, I thought suddenly. So obvious. So hidden. Such an astonishing thought for me.

"We won't discuss it any more," Daddy commanded. "You're obviously not fit to make a responsible decision about my Dream Girl." He turned and smiled at me. Coming so hard on his anger it seemed a deception. "Go pack a bag, Sandy. I'm about to whisk my Dream Girl into the city for the time of her life!"

"Bryce! No you're not!" my mother cried, springing to her feet, her small hands clenched. "You can't, you can *not* just show up now and lift a finger for your daughter to come running. I won't allow it, Bryce. I won't allow you to use her the way you've used everyone else!"

"Like you, Andrea?" He smiled slightly. "I'm afraid your mother has developed a persecution complex, Dream Girl. Hurry and get that bag now!"

"The storm's been blowing for days, Daddy," I replied instead of running to do his bidding. "Except for the lake still rising a bit, the worst is over. The wind's almost gone, and the rain's just a drizzle. Why, if you were so worried about me, did you wait so long to come for me?"

For a moment he looked at me hard, his face grim. I braced myself for his anger, but he seemed at the last moment to damp it down. When he spoke, his voice was quiet and patient.

"I was involved in a new painting, Sandy," he said simply. "You know that when I'm painting the house could fall down and I'd barely notice it."

God, that was true, I thought bitterly. How many times had I come to him, desperately needing comfort, and been brushed aside while he painted. Oh, there was always the treat-drenched whirlwind afterward, but not at the moment I had hurt.

"Yeah," I said harshly. "You're busy painting, and Mom's busy writing. In our family, it's crisis by appointment only, isn't it!"

I stared at them, watching to see what they would say. My mother looked at me, startled, her eyes wide and her mouth half-open. Then she turned away quickly so that her back was to us. Daddy returned my stare.

"Don't act younger than you are, Sandy," he said harshly. "Part of growing up is realizing that your concerns are not more important than everyone else's. Now go get your bag."

"Sandy," my mother said pleadingly, "it's not like that at all. If I could explain to you..."

"Write a book about it!" I snapped. "And thank you, Daddy, for your invitation, but right now, I think I prefer to stay where I am."

"Sandy, Dream Girl," he started.

"Damn it!" I screamed. "I'm not your Dream Girl any more! Don't ever call me that again! I hate it! I hate it!"

I ran past them, out through the trees that had been my friends, heard my crying when no one else bothered to listen, then down to the beach and water.

I sat a long time at the water's edge, cold, shivering, crying, so aware that I had behaved like the child I was tired of being. I drew patterns in the sand. I twisted to stare back at the broken, limp, storm-torn leaves.

I was so frightened.

I hated them for doing this to me.

I despised them.

I wanted my Daddy.

I crept back to the summer house, slunk through the door when I saw the room was empty, edged like a thief in the night to my room. I lay on my bed and stared at the laughing giant and his Dream Girl. I had never liked fairy tales. They had seemed so empty somehow.

"And just maybe I don't like this one any more," I muttered bitterly.

Then I laid my head down in my arms and thought longingly about my Daddy.

*   *   *

The lake rose closer and closer to the cottages, even while the grey clouds broke and the sunset shone blood red and golden through the sky. Pam and Alison came and hammered excitedly on the door of the summer house.

"Did you see?" Alison asked breathlessly. "The Creyton's cottage is being washed away!"

"Don't exaggerate," Pam snapped sourly. "The water is reaching around the supports, but you know the pull of the undertow!"

I pulled on my sweater and went with them to see. The water had not seemed so near the cottages to me, but I saw as we came to the Creyton's place what was happening. A chance shaping of the beach had allowed the water to pound higher and higher in front of their cottage, until a wide curve of water reached inward to pull and strain at the foundations of the summer cottage. We joined the steady stream of silent cottagers who came to stand in reverent awe before the power of the lake. Everyone jumped from a hill of sand to the edge of the steps and up onto the verandah, swaying in a mass as the supports groaned and fought the power of the waves.

I took my place beside Donny and his father. Pam pushed inside beside Donny. I glared ineffectually.

"I've got to talk to you," I heard her whisper desperately to Donny. He looked at her resentfully, but followed her to the far edge of the railing, as though they were going to examine the supports on that side. Alison followed tossing her head defiantly at their backs.

"Place'll go by morning," Donny's father announced in the voice of one making a revelation beyond argument.

"Anyone got hold of Mrs. Creyton?" someone asked.

No one answered.

"God, that's a shame though," someone else volunteered. "Len's heart attack, and now their place going."

"Old bastard deserved it," someone at the back muttered sotto-voice. A few watchers snickered.

"You can't help but feel sorry for him, poor sonuvabitch," Donny's father declared with commanding decision. "He's still in critical condition. Don't know whether he'll make it apparently."

There was a depressed silence.

"Place'll go by morning," he repeated.

I stared at the caramel-colored water, ripping and pounding at the supports at our feet. The waves still rose over three feet high, though the wind was dropping hour by hour. The day before yesterday I had stood at the shore watching them rise higher than my head, crashing and roaring and warring against one another.

I wondered why my Daddy had come for me. What drove him to ignore me then demand my love?

"Won't be long now," Donny's father spoke up again. His voice had taken on a meditative tone, and he shook his head slowly as if pondering the uncertainties of life.

"If the cottage goes, all of their furniture will be ruined," one of the women said. "It'd be a shame. They have beautiful antiques in there."

"Yeah, power should be turned off, just in case," their next door neighbor added.

"The furniture ought to be moved," Jack spoke up suddenly from the shadows. I started slightly. I had not seen the twins.

"You can hardly expect us to break in," Donny's father told him. He eyed Jack with dislike. Jack shrugged his indifference.

"I have the key," I spoke up suddenly. "When Mr. Creyton had the heart attack, I didn't have a chance to give it back."

"I don't think there's a real reason for us to do anything so drastic as to go into their home," Donny's father said severely. I said nothing, but felt my face flush with a mixture of anger and humiliation.

"If the cottage goes," Jack spoke up again, "everything will be wrecked. We can move the best things."

Mr. Muller snorted and turned his back on us. That seemed to be some sort of signal, for almost everyone began to leave. I leaned against the railing, not looking up, feeling embarrassed. I looked sideways along the railing into the dark. Donny was leaning close to Pam, so close they had become one shadow in the darker shadows flowing over us. I could see the stiff shadow of Alison trying futilely to come between them with her presence. And I could hear the wash of water slapping against the wooden pillars of the cottage, smell the cool water smell of the storm-washed air. I was aware of Jack and Joey silent in the shadows behind. And yet I felt alone, removed from their emotions and actions, from their existence. The night and the sound curtained me, held me safe, held me lonely. Everyone had left the porch except us.

"Oh Donny," I heard Pam ripple. "Why should I?"

"I'm going to climb down and check the supports," Jack said suddenly. "If it looks okay we can take off, but I'll bet the sand's being washed away from them and the whole place'll tip over."

"Wh..what about the tow?" Joey asked.

"Yeah, Jack," Pam said, her voice still rippling as she turned her back on Donny. "We don't want you to float away."

"Oh God," Donny snapped in derision.

"Well, you're sure no hero about it, are you," Pam snapped back.

"I better get a rope," Jack said.

"No, and I'm not stupid either! I mean who cares whether the Creyton's place floats away or not," Donny said loudly. Then he added more softly, "C'mon Pam, let's get out of here."

"Sandy h..has a rope in her garage," Joey spoke up.

I was pulled reluctantly back into the circle of action. I grimaced, wishing I could have stayed removed by the darkness. But I was accustomed like Joey to follow Jack's decisions.

We jumped from the porch onto the bank of sand, then slogged through the night toward our garage. I could still hear the *slap, slap* of water, but now it was mingled with the sighing rustle of poplars we threaded our way through. Overtop it all I could hear Alison's shrilling voice rising and rising, punctuated by Pam's angry retorts. I wished they would be silent like the rest of the night, but there was so much hate between them. I didn't understand the hatred in their family. It made me angry. Everything made me angry.

We got the rope and house key and silently returned to the porch along the Creyton's cottage. Pam and Alison were at it tooth and nail.

"Just like the good old days," Jack said wryly, pausing for a moment to watch Alison grab Pam's hair in her fist, while Pam hurled obscenities at her sister, both shoving and grunting all the while. They had always fought like this, regardless of who was around, except maybe their parents. I had a feeling there was something in their home that kept a lid on most of their rage against each other.

Donny stomped over while Jack knotted the rope around the porch railing.

"Maybe we should throw them both in the lake," he growled. We grinned.

"And another thing," Alison shrieked as they fell apart finally, "I'm going to tell Dad what a tramp you are. I found everything!"

"You..." screamed Pam. "I wish you were dead!"

It was like a surrealistic movie. We saw Pam shove Alison, and then suddenly we all felt ourselves tip. The porch groaned, and slowly began to tilt. Alison skidded somehow, and with a yelp that ended suddenly, slipped under the railing into the sucking water.

We stood without moving.

"Alison!" Pam shrieked. She ran to the edge of the porch, looked over, then climbed up and jumped in after her sister. I watched frozen, unable and unwilling to move. We all knew about the undertow.

"Pam! *Pam!*" Donny yelled.

Our paralysis snapped and we leaned over the railing, desperately trying to spot them.

"*Donny!*"

We could see her gripping Alison under the chin as she struggled blindly in the surging, sucking water.

"The rope!" Joey snapped fiercely. I watched, still unable to act or think as he tried to tie it around his waist. "I'll go after th..them. Pu..ull me b..back!"

"No, you can't," Jack snapped and grabbed

the end of the rope from Joey's fumbling fingers. "You'd never make it."

Quickly, he knotted the rope around his waist. Donny stared frantically out into the dark water. I looked back and forth, at the water, at Pam's bobbing head as she fought her sister and the undertow. She was the best swimmer of us all. Surely she could stay above water...

"She's gone under! No, they're back, no..." Donny cried.

Jack climbed up to the railing, his shirt and shoes already tossed aside. He spotted them, then dove downward. The moonlight shone an instant over his flashing body. The tow caught him, pulled him under, then tossed him up again beyond Pam and Alison.

"Gr..ab the rope!" Joey ordered. We two grabbed the slack and pulled back, hauling Jack in from the sucking waves. He came close, was carried back, then on the second try caught hold of Pam's reaching hand. Alison was limp, floating in the waves, held afloat by Pam's tightly encircling arm.

"Pull!" Joey shouted, kicking Donny from his trance. We pulled, desperately fighting against the tow. It dragged them under, but we dragged them up again, straining until they were close to the porch, until we could reach them. We pulled up Alison's limp body and Pam's conscious but nearly immovable one. Jack, panting and gasping, pulled himself up.

"Alison, oh my God, Alison," Pam whimpered, trying to smooth her sister's hair.

Joey shoved her roughly aside. The strain was catching him and his shoulders were beginning to shudder with spasms, but somehow he kept his movements sure where it mattered. He tilted Alison's head back and began to breath into her.

"Doctor...Doctor Parker..." Jack panted.

Once again I ran for the doctor. Close by. At the Muller's having drinks. Everyone gasped and then everyone ran. Pam's mother had hysterics. Pam's father cradled Alison as she spluttered, gasped, and vomited, fighting to regain consciousness. Donny wrapped a blanket around Pam, gently pulling her dripping hair back from her face.

Then everyone moved away. Jack and Joey and I were alone in the shadows. Jack wearily untied the rope and looped it into a neat coil.

"Nobody said thank you," I spoke up suddenly. The twins looked at me. Joey shrugged and turned away. Jack grinned, a slow grin of amusement at my naiveté.

"Even Pam," I persisted.

"She'd rather have Donny for a hero," Jack

replied and shrugged. "We'd better check the furniture."

We opened the door and silently began inspecting the cottage for damage. Joey kept a little apart from us. Some of the furniture had slipped across the floor, but so slowly there was no real damage.

"I think I'd better take the china out," I said. I didn't know if the figurines, cups and saucers, and plates on display were antiques, but I was sure they'd be valuable and might smash if the cottage tipped any more. Jack nodded. Wordlessly we found towels, then wrapped each piece carefully. Finally we cleaned out the fridge and shut off the electricity. The twins helped me carry everything back to the summer house, then they disappeared into the night.

I fell asleep wondering what Daddy would think of the twins now.

Chapter 17

The hurricane died away, drifting off into the ocean somewhere, leaving only a slightly changed shoreline littered with refuse from the battered trees. But even that was soon covered by the shifting sand and sprawling undergrowth. Many of the cottagers returned and we resumed our delivery service. Len Creyton came out of intensive care at last. Building contractors righted the cottage and rebuilt the supports so that once again it stood rigid, dominating that strip of beach. Mrs. Creyton bustled up to the summer house one afternoon and shrewed at me for entering her cottage without permission. My mother put everything we had saved in a box, carried it to our porch, then coolly told Mrs. Creyton to leave. She had never stood up for herself or me before.

The days were hot and sticky, drifting one into another, July into August. Somehow the weather affected us so that my emotions too, seemed hot and sticky and vague. I felt as though I was waiting, restless, unable to decide anything. My mother seemed to understand, and she let me be. We no longer quarreled.

A letter came for me in the first week of August from the magazine that was sponsoring the young writers contest. They said they had had an unprecedented number of entries, but they were pleased to advise me that my story was among the twenty-five being given final consideration.

I showed the letter to my mother who flushed with pleasure.

"Oh Sandy, I knew you had talent when I read your story," she said breathlessly. "I'm so pleased. You should be so proud of yourself."

"Well, I haven't won anything," I replied, trying to achieve some modesty above my conviction that Hemmingway would be made to look an amateur beside me.

"No," my mother agreed. "Probably you won't either. But you've made a good showing."

I felt squashed by her return to her normal manner. Something must have shown in my face, or perhaps my mother was beginning the long, slow change that came after she became her own person again. She looked at me, her eyes widening a bit.

"But..." she said unsurely, "maybe it's good enough. Maybe you will win something Sandy. I hope so."

"Maybe," I agreed.

I carried the letter into my room and reread it. It was so noncommittal, but it was my own. Daddy laughed down at me, as always. Restless suddenly, I jumped up again and ran out of the room to the telephone. I dialed quickly.

"Hello Daddy! It's me Sandy!"

"Well Sandy. How are you Dream Girl? I was beginning to think you'd forgotten about your old man."

"Oh Daddy, as if I could. You'll never guess what's happened."

"Your mother's run off with the milkman?"

I giggled perfunctorily.

"No. Remember that writing contest I entered? Well I got a letter from them today telling me I'm one of twenty-five finalists."

"Out of how many?"

"They said they had eight hundred entries. Can you imagine that – eight hundred!"

"Well that's terrific, Dream Girl. Just terrific. You've really impressed your old man. And you know that takes some doing."

"Yes," I said softly. There was a pause. "Is there any chance you might come down soon? I really miss you, you know."

There was a pause. I tried to hold my stomach rigid so that it wouldn't cave in when he told me he was too busy.

"Well," he hesitated. *"I'd really like to see you Sandy."*

"It's okay Daddy. I know you're really busy these days. And...and it's a long drive too."

"Don't put words in my mouth Dream Girl. I was just looking at my calendar. How about I take a run up there on Saturday, day after tomorrow. We'll take a spin into Simcoe, go for lunch maybe."

"Oh, Daddy," I exclaimed. "That would be fantastic. I could try the sole at that restaurant if you wanted."

He laughed a warm, rich sound over the telephone.

"You could, Dream Girl. But I've remembered you hate seafood. I know a good restaurant along the highway that's just opened. They have terrific seafood – and Italian food, which I know you do love. See you Saturday around ten, Dream Girl. So long."

*   *   *

It was the best day I had ever had with my father. We didn't discuss his last trip up when I refused to go with him. He even seemed interested in our delivery service and in my efforts to earn my own tuition to East Lakes. I remember him glancing sideways as we drove, as I chatted about the difficulties of it and my growing amount of money. When I told him about Jack and Joey's struggle to earn enough for college he made no blighting remarks about them. I hardly noticed it then, but it was perhaps the first time he had not jibed a hot, stammering defense of my friends from me. He did not laugh at me. He did not laugh at my friends.

And he told me about his work, about what he was trying to do now.

"Phil Barnet, you know the fellow from New York? He's really interested in my work, and he brings a lot of influence with him. It's hard though, to keep growing – not to fall back on the things I've already done." He shifted restlessly, brought his hand to his hair, then let it drop again. "I need to develop new ideas."

"He really likes my picture," I offered. Daddy nodded but kept his eyes on the road.

We drove a while in silence. I felt comfortable and happy, just being with him like this.

"How's it going with your mother?" he asked abruptly.

I shrugged. "Pretty good. Okay, I guess. We don't fight much any more. She pretty much leaves me alone."

We remained silent for several more minutes.

"Daddy, why did you and Mom get a divorce?" I had blurted the question out almost before I realized it. What kind of simple answer did I expect to receive, I wonder. He looked at me an instant, shook his head slightly, but he answered.

"I don't know, Dream Girl. There were lots of logical reasons – your Mom wanted her own career, I was too absorbed in my work, that affair I had..."

I blushed slightly.

"You knew about that didn't you?"

I nodded.

"So many reasons..." he went on softly. "But none of them were the real reasons. I don't even know what they were, Sandy. We loved each other so much at one time, and slowly it was just eaten away, bit by bit." He heaved an exasperated sigh. "Romantic isn't it? Forget it Sandy. These things just happen. Your mother can be a damned exasperating person – never satisfied, you know? Well, we just got sick of each other. I got sick of trying to please her, that's all."

I nodded, wondering what was true, and what they really felt. It seemed very odd that my father, always so sure and headlong, didn't know either. I had never noticed before that he could be unsure and frightened too. I settled back into the cushions of the seat, faintly smug that I was becoming so perceptive and detached.

*   *   *

"When are you planning to go up to the university?" I asked idly. We had finished the day's delivery service and were lounging in the store, Joey and me at a table and Jack roving restlessly behind the counter.

"We're not," Jack said softly, fiercely.

"You're what?"

"We're no..ot," Joey repeated.

"But why? Jeez, I mean you've been working all summer. And you'll lose the scholarships. And," I added, suddenly seeing something clearly, "if you don't go this year, you probably won't go at all. You might end up staying here forever. You can't do that. You know you can't."

Joey rubbed his hands through his hair.

"The..ere's not enough money. The st.. storm screwed it. And D..dad..." He trailed off and stared at his crumb-covered plate, lost in himself.

"Is your dad that sick?" I looked from one to the other. They didn't answer, didn't acknowledge my question. I felt suddenly weighted down, almost beyond bearing. I had been ignoring their silence before, avoiding Joey's eyes because he needed me. I hadn't wanted to hurt for their sakes.

"Don't worry about it," Jack said harshly, his eyes hard, piercing me. I hated him for seeing me so clearly.

"You can't go at all?" I repeated.

"D..dad won't go to the hosp..ital," Joey said heavily, tilting back in the chair. "Th..there's maybe enough for one of us to..to go, but Jack has to b..be able to drive him, when...if he gets sick, or anything. I..it doesn't matter. W..we do alright here. M..maybe we'll fix up the store more...over the winter. M..maybe in a f..few years we'll make enough to get t..to college."

"Don't worry, Sandy," Jack said mockingly. "We do fine here. Just fine."

"Yeah, sure. Poor white trash!" I spat out. I was choking on my rage. Joey was jerking, twitching. I had not heard his speech so bad since we were little, since that summer they almost lost their father...I hated Jack! I felt suddenly like my story had leapt back into our lives. A rhythm was growing in my anger, and it was pounding on me, washing around the steel that was filling my spine.

"If you don't go, Jack, you'll never go. And you *will* be poor white trash."

"Goddamnit!" shouted Jack suddenly, "what are we suppose to do! Leave Dad? Let him fall into a coma or something all alone here? And there isn't enough for us to go anyway!" He turned from me and smashed his fist on the counter. "That bastard is going to screw our whole lives," he hissed. "Everything, just everything."

"You sure give up easy!" I shouted. "Lie down and die Jack!"

He spun toward me, his fists clenched, and then he turned aside again. I was trembling.

"Sh..shutup, S..sandy," Joey stuttered. "J.. jack's right. We'll lose the s..scholarships. J..jack can't earn en..nough for both of us t..to go."

I looked at them, not understanding, afraid of their feelings. But I tried to struggle into clear air again.

"But why couldn't Joey earn his own money? And why couldn't Joey go this year, if you have to stay and look after your father?"

"Joey, go by himself? Why don't you wake up Sandy! He's spastic. He can't survive without me!" Jack exclaimed. He stood scornful, towering strong and sure behind the lunch counter. Joey leaned forward staring down, unmoving but for the twitches and shudders.

I felt I was drowning. I couldn't think. I pushed violently away from the table and ran outside, letting the door bang behind me. I knew now why I hadn't wanted to share their hurt, their pain. It was twisting them, breaking them. I couldn't bear to be at the bottom of that sandy hole, staring upward at a round patch of sky. And the sand would cave inward on them and no one would care. No one would dig them out. They would kick and twitch together, and then they would suffocate and be broken.

*   *   *

The beach was still hot, but the breeze of evening was beginning to stir across it. I had wandered a long way along the shore to where the cottages were spaced far apart and the scrub poplars and brush screened them from the water.

I squatted on the sand, just beside the brush that I would have called a fort a few years ago. Part of me wanted to crawl into its shelter, to hide from the world, and so I squatted very near. But another part, a new, unshaped part refused, and so I stayed on the open beach.

I had no thoughts to think. My mind was kept blank as everything kept away my emotions. Rage and grief fought each other underneath the blankness. The water lapped on the shore, sucking back the sand, taking back to itself the pretty stones before losing interest and tossing them aside again. I still wanted to walk into the water, keep walking until it washed over me, caressing, powerful, consummate loving, as it carried me into its depth. But it would never hear my agony for air. My life would be nothing to it. When it was done with me, it would drop my body on the shore, indifferent to what I had wanted to give and what it had taken from me.

I had been so frightened when I ran home from the twins. I wanted to go to my room, to look at my picture of my Daddy, to feel the love he had for his Dream Girl, to be made safe again – protected from pain.

My mother was sitting on the porch steps, smoking furiously. She stood up as she saw me running up the driveway.

"Sandy," she said, her voice low, insistent. I pushed away her hand as it tried to catch mine.

"Not now! I want to be by myself. I need to see my picture."

I pushed past her into the house, and ran to my room, to my Daddy.

My picture was gone. My Daddy, his Dream Girl, and the little toad who had tried so hard to escape, they were all gone. I just stood there, emptied out in that moment of shock and disbelief. I felt an inward whistling of wind. Darkness and emptiness with a lifeless wind shrilling through me.

"Oh Sandy," my mother said behind me. I looked at her without comprehension.

"Where did he take it?" I asked at last.

"He sold it to that museum in New York. Mr. Barnet..."

I nodded, beginning to understand. The deal must have been transacted even before Daddy took me for our wonderful day together. I wondered if he had wanted to tell me and been unable to face it, or if he was just trying to give me the treat that usually followed his indifference. I had seen his fear, heard his worry about his career, but I hadn't understood after all.

I knew I would have to go back to the summer house soon. The sun was close to setting, and it would be a long walk down the beach in the dark. And my mother would be waiting. For perhaps the first time, that mattered to me. She had looked at me, she had tried to share my pain. I wondered how long she had been trying to share the pain that was twisting me. When had she seen the illusion of the Dream Girl sucking me away?

I knew I would begin to cry soon. Soon the grief would break away and I would begin to cry. I began running down the packed sand. I needed my mother.

*   *   *

We decided to end the delivery service in mid-August. The beach had remained half-empty, and the amount we could earn no longer made the work worthwhile. Jack and I barely spoke to each other. Joey didn't seem to talk to anyone. I spent a lot of time walking up and down the beach, floating almost unmoving in the lake, or sometimes swimming with Pam. She talked all the time about Donny and never about Jack.

On the day the delivery service ended, I received a letter from my father. It read:

Dear Sandy,

Well, how is my Dream Girl? Things have been really happening for me these last few weeks, all the things we talked about when we went out for lunch. I'm on my way to being a great man after all, Dream Girl! That picture that was in the cottage brought

*in a lot of money, and so your old
man can come through for you. I'm
enclosing a check that will cover your
tuition and expenses for the next year
at East Lakes. I've wanted to do this
for you because the Dream Girl has
done so much for me.*

Dad

I took the letter and went down to the
beach. There I sat, almost motionless in the
sun, watching the waves swinging into the
shore, swishing, lapping, an element I could
not be part of. I scooped handfuls of the hot,
white sand and sifted it through my fingers,
catching the washed pebbles and broken shells
that had been hidden in its depths. I stared at
the flies that rose and settled on the brilliant
green mounds of rotting seaweed that had
been washed ashore. I tried to understand
how the world I had been so sure of could
have been such a fairy tale.

I hated him. I hated the illusion he had
helped me build. I had been his mythical
muse, an illusion to be abandoned when
reality was more inviting. I felt he had
maimed me, crippled me, twisted me so that
I was only half alive. I understood now why

I had to be half illusion, why I was a Dream Girl. And I understood now why the little toad had scrambled so frantically to escape. But he had never really escaped and she had never completely caught him. Never completely. Never complete.

No wonder he had hated the twins. No wonder he had despised Joey's twitches and Jack's effortless indifference. They could not be twisted into his illusions because they had their own.

And when I was with them, chasing toads in the eternal summer dusk, some strange hidden part of me, a part that my father could never grasp hold of, had loved the twins. If Jack and Joey had not been here, what would have become of me? How could I have raced through my own aliveness in those summer dusks, if I was entirely alone?

I hugged my knees close and buried my head. My Daddy had almost killed me. Mr. Barnet, that powerful, influential art expert from New York had accidentally saved my life. I wondered if I should send him a polite note of thanks. My father had cast me ashore before I had quite run out of air, before I had quite drowned. And now he had sent me such a cheerful note inviting me back in for a swim, at his expense.

My fists clenched. I wanted to kill him. I wanted him dead and suffering as I had been half dead and suffering. I hated him.

"Sandy, dear," my mother said suddenly. I looked up. "I'm taking a run into town. Do you need anything?"

I need everything, I thought. I need... I need...

"I need something to read. Would you pick me up a book or two, please?"

"Sure," my mother hesitated, and looked at me. "Are you alright, Sandy?"

I opened my mouth to scream, to call her to comfort me, to make everything better. I wanted someone to run to, to shelter in.

"Mom," I started. "I...I guess the sun is too hot. Maybe I'll go have a nap."

"That must be it," she replied, fishing around in her bag for her keys. "Take it easy until dinner. You're a little pale. I'll stop by Mrs. Patterson's and see what she has left over today. I think we both need a treat."

I nodded and she left. I plodded up the beach, across the sand-covered patio stones, up the hot steps, and head lowered, into my room. I had not looked at the empty wall since I first saw the painting was gone. Now I lay on the bed and stared at the emptiness, felt the emptiness inside me.

There was a gigantic hole in my internal universe. I had wrenched out the festering illusion of the Dream Girl and I had nothing to put in its place. I felt as though a wind was blowing up through my belly-button and echoing and whistling about in the dead space inside me.

I knew it might start to hurt soon. I knew that the numbness, the absence of pain that was such a relief, was probably just a breather before the real hurting of that wrenching began. But I had the moment of resignation, of acceptance of what I was and what belonged to me. I knew suddenly that I would survive because I had survived hidden away all these years. I had survived the loneliness and the war against myself. And I had not begged my mother to fill my emptiness. But I was not staying empty. I could feel myself filling up now. I was filling with all the years of hidden anger that was turning and churning inside.

I hated him!

Chapter 18

It hadn't even been a decision. I dropped the coldly polite letter to my father into the mailbox, hoping he would be hurt by my refusal to accept his check. Then, unmindful of the traffic, I bounded across the highway to the general store.

"Joey! Hey Jack!" I yelled "Anybody home? I need a malted milkshake."

I grinned in anticipation, my hands behind my back as they slouched in from the back. And then my grin faded away as I finally saw the unhappiness they were carrying.

"Hi Sandy," Jack said.

Joey murmured something, but I could not make out what. The milkshake mixer whirred in the silence as Jack put together the shake I had asked for. It seemed suddenly hard to tell them why I had come. I had imagined how I would startle them, delight them with my magnificent gift, but that was a hangover from my days as the Dream Girl. It could not be done like that.

I sat down at a table beside Joey. Jack plunked the shake down in front of me, then straddled a chair opposite us, his elbows and chin resting on the back.

"So, how's it going Sandy?" Jack asked.

I looked at them, wondering if I could ever put into words how it had been going for me. And what about them?

"I have something for you," I said, my words hardly above a whisper. I put the envelope onto the table. Jack picked it up, opened it, and stared without moving. I saw the muscle in his jaw working as he clenched and unclenched his teeth. Then he tossed the envelope back on the table so the bills spilled out.

"No thanks," he said abruptly and jerked out of his chair. He leaned against the counter and stared at me. Joey picked up the money and counted it.

"It's your share for the summer," Joey observed.

"Yeah. Dad sent me a check for the tuition for East Lakes, and... and it doesn't matter any more. I'm not going after all. The delivery service was your idea and mostly your work. If I hadn't been thinking about getting money for East Lakes, I would have helped you anyway."

"We don't need any handouts, thanks," Jack snapped.

"Good! Because you're not getting any, Jack. Believe it or not you guys helped me when...when I was having a bad time. It's the only way I can help you. That's all. Fair's fair."

"Yeah, sure," Jack said.

I turned away and watched Joey counting the money over and over again. His hands trembled with spasms. I rubbed my forehead remembering the dream toad that had twitched and trembled as the sand caved in on him. The sand was caving in on me too, but I was digging for the sun, clawing upward away from the darkness. Joey and Jack were my friends. I wouldn't leave them in the hole to smother. I was afraid and my palms were sweating.

"Take the money, Joey," I urged, unable to fight with Jack any more. "Maybe things will work out. If they don't you can always give it back to me."

He looked at me, but said nothing. I think perhaps words were becoming too hard for him again. I hated seeing him close into himself, away from all of us, even Jack. I felt as though even the air was painted grey and weighted down. I wanted clean air. I needed the sunshine. I left them unmoving where they were.

*   *   *

The next couple of weeks were sharp and clear to me, but only as a series of still photographs, not a movie with expressions and actions to focus on. I spent a lot of time with Jack and Joey. But we were like very small children who don't know how to play with each other. We were aware of each other, we stayed physically close, we watched each other. But our words were simple and inadequate, our actions without awareness of each other's rhythms, and our eyes would lock occasionally as we looked helplessly for each other.

I don't know how I forced myself each day to go to the general store, to sit beside Joey's agony of tremors, to speak casual nothings to Roy. Perhaps it was because I knew the Dream Girl would never have lasted, and the Dream Girl represented everything I hated, everything I needed to escape from, everything that had nearly suffocated me.

Joey was being slowly sucked away. Jack was fighting the undertow, but he fought blindly, in panic and without much hope. Roy meandered in and out, drifting further and further away from all of us. And I sat with them. I had no words. I had no strength. I just existed with them. It was all I could do.

And still the sun shone, and my friend Melany wrote ecstatic letters about the French boys she met, and Mom wrote stories, and I made hot dogs for lunch when we drifted to the summer house. And Roy had some sort of seizure and had to be taken to the hospital, but he checked himself out again. And one evening Jack began to cry silently on the beach, but he turned away from us. And my Daddy wrote me a letter, but I didn't open it.

The lake was calm, clear reflecting blue, rippling slightly in its gentle *wash, wash* over the sand. We struggled with cold, grey spray and black waves that beat over us, sucking us into the cold warmth of its depths. We struggled toward a shore that was bleak and hidden, a memory, no longer a certainty. We tried to grab each other's hands but could not. The waves pulled us apart and threw us together, roaring and ringing through the silence.

The spasms began to reach Joey's legs, and sometimes he would stagger a little as he walked. Once, while we walked along the hot, dusty back road, Joey grabbed Jack's arm for support. Jack jumped away, frantic, revolted.

"Don't touch me!" he screamed. "I can't stand it! Let go of me, Joey. You're killing me. You're dragging me under and I can't carry you any more. I'm not the hero in the fairy tale, and you're not the old man. I can't carry you any more! Let go of me before you kill me!"

He ran from us, down the road, behind the screen of trees, perhaps to the beach. I opened and shut my mouth several time, trying to find words. Joey just stood there, his face white and chiseled in lonely marble. He began to twitch but would not come near me. He leaned against a pine, his face against the harsh bark, scraping his skin as he twitched against it. I glimpsed the red blood against his white cheek, but he turned from me still.

After a while he began walking along the road away from the direction Jack had gone. I tried to follow but he stared me away.

"I...I...I..." he stammered and looked at me. I left then. We had never needed a lot of words, Joey and I. If I went with him, I knew he would be even more alone than if he was by himself. I went back to the summer house. He was still walking along the road when I went between the trees.

*　　*　　*

I was sprawled on the lounge chair on our sand-covered patio, trying to read my story about the twins and the summer of toad catching. The sun had just set, so I held my story so it caught the stray beams of electric light spilling from the window. The words were dark and grey, the letters swimming into each other, but I knew them so well I could read them anyway. Jack appeared out of the dusk and thumped down into the chair beside me.

We looked at each other silently.

"Joey's not here," he stated flatly at last. I shook my head.

His sigh was hard, short and sharp. He leaned forward, his elbows on his knees, his fingers combing roughly into his hair.

"I should never have gone with Pam. I shouldn't have laid her. I didn't know then that Joey couldn't...I mean..." He twisted violently in his chair. "I just wanted to show that smart ass Donny – pay him back for all those cracks he's made. He's got no right to look down on us!"

"Pore white trash," I echoed softly, vindictively.

Jack stared at me, then laughed viciously.

"That's us, isn't it Sandy? And then there's Joey. Pam thinks he's some kind of freak or something. You know that? She's known us all these years, and she still thinks he's mentally defective. Like father like son, maybe. *'You're really lucky, Jack, that you didn't inherit that...that – you know – from your father',*" he mimicked Pam harshly. "And...and I began to think maybe she was right. You don't know what it's like, Sandy, to have a father everyone knows is crazy."

"He's not crazy, I don't think anyways," I said angrily. I was afraid.

"Sure, and you're the expert. But then Pam was making me think Joey was weird too. And I've been riding him, Sandy. I've been trying to make him go away or something. And he has!"

His voice was panicked. I had never known Jack to be afraid before. He had always been the tough guy, the one that could take anything.

And I had always been the Dream Girl. I'd always been so afraid, envying them their close love. Joey always had Jack to turn to. And Jack always had Joey to make him feel strong and needed. No one had needed me. No one had ever been there for me to turn to.

"He can't manage without me," Jack hurried on. "Especially now. He can't do anything by himself..."

I had been angry for so long. I had been angry for years. But there hadn't been words before. I wanted to kill Jack the way I'd wanted to kill my father.

"He can!" I shouted, throwing myself out of the chair. "You didn't want him to. You made him weird, Jack. You made him helpless. It's your fault because all you ever wanted to do was be a big shot. You've practically killed him, the way my father nearly killed me! You've told yourself that you love him, but not when he needs you. Not then. You only wanted someone to make you feel important! You're killing him! You're killing your brother!"

I was screaming, hysterical. I tried to hit him, but he caught my arms. I struggled with him wildly, but he held me away, his face without emotion as too many emotions churned him inside.

"They're killing me. They're killing me!" Jack repeated, his voice empty and his face desperate. I began to cry and I collapsed suddenly. He seemed to go limp too, and we stood close together, maybe for the first time. He rubbed his arm along his forehead and eyes.

"I'm so scared, Sandy," he whispered. I may have nodded. It didn't matter.

"Sandy! What's going on!" my mother called angrily from the doorway. I hadn't noticed that the background noise of her typewriter had disappeared.

"Nothing. We...Jack and I were just fooling around. That's all. We're going for a walk down the beach."

We moved off together in the deepening dark along the water's edge. The moon broke away from some clouds, lightening the dark into gradations of shadow.

"Where is Joey?" I asked finally.

Jack shrugged. "I don't know. I don't know where he's gone. There isn't anyone around other than you that he'd go to. And how could he manage by himself?"

"He'll manage fine, same as you would," I replied, infusing all the scorn I felt and all the certainty I knew I should feel, into my words. "He's not a baby, and if he's supposed to be so smart, he can survive being away from his father and big brother for just a while."

"He can survive leaving his father alright."

"At least your father cares about you," I muttered.

"Yeah, sure. He cares so much he's doing everything he can to drop dead."

"Well, maybe you're not the only one who can't stand living in this dead end any more," I snapped.

Jack looked at me sharply. "But that's not the way out. I mean, it's...it's..."

The feeling that I knew all the answers evaporated.

"I don't know," I muttered. "I don't know anything except that people are never what you think they are, and that any time you try to make them what you think they should be, everything gets screwed up. Just like us."

Abruptly, Jack started to laugh.

"Have you ever met anybody who wasn't screwed up?" he demanded.

And suddenly I began to laugh too. I don't know why it seemed so funny, but it did. Then our laughter trailed off and we were silent again. But we were together for a bit, instead of alone. It wasn't so terrible that way.

"Guess I'd better head back and see if Joey's showed up yet," Jack said at last, breaking the quiet rhythm of the lapping waves.

I nodded and he walked slowly away down the beach, I looked up the shore, in the direction the moon shone, the way Joey had walked that afternoon. Could he walk all the way to the end of the Point, to the wild part we had always tried to get to and never succeeded in reaching? Joey had always wanted to go there more than any of us. Maybe he was a little like Roy, needing a freedom from all of us just to exist with himself.

I wished I had gone with him after all.

*　　*　　*

"I'm sorry, Bryce," my mother said into the telephone, "but it was entirely Sandy's decision. In fact she didn't even tell me you had been so magnanimous."

I twisted in exasperation in the chair. Dad

had obviously gotten my returned check and decided to blame my mother again. For once, she was not being intimidated by him, but I was sick of their personalities constantly intruding on my life.

"Sarcastic? Me?" Mom laughed. "You hurt the child, Bryce. You hurt her terribly and you know it." There was a pause. "Now don't you pull that misunderstood genius act with me! I know every in and out of you, and unfortunately Sandy does now too. You saw an advantage to yourself and you took the painting – exactly the way you gave it to her I might add." Another pause. "Well, you're entitled to your opinion, Bryce, but unless you want Sandy to turn against you the way Joanie did you had better start thinking of her for a change." Pause. "Maybe you're right Bryce, it is the same old thing – your career or your family. Sandy's the only one left who gives a damn about you, so stick that in your paint brush." Pause. Laughter. "Listen, you son of a bitch, it's too late to charm me. I know you too well." She laughed again wryly, then hung up.

I put the magazine up over my face, but Mom pulled it down, perching on the arm of the sofa.

"You didn't tell me about the check, Sandy," she commented.

"It didn't seem to be any of your business," I said. "It was between Dad and me. And I just didn't want to go to East Lakes after all."

I stared at her, a little defiant, mostly wishing I could explain that I knew I couldn't depend on Dad, that I couldn't bear being poor white trash while the other girls' fathers automatically kept them in funds. And I knew Mom wouldn't bail me out when she didn't approve of what I was doing in the first place.

"I'm sick of playing games," I added as Mom walked into the kitchen. She turned around quickly, but I put the magazine up to my face again, and didn't see her expression.

*   *   *

I wanted to write. For weeks I had been fighting the urge to make a unity of my universe by enclosing it in words, but now the uncertainty, work, and pain were worth the beauty of a unified rhythm.

Before I wrote the story of the twins and the summer of toad catching, I had only known writing as a finished product or an assignment on an impersonal subject in my English classes. But this need was different. I was anxious, excited, wondering. The story in my head was drawing me into its twists and turns and I needed to let it come to existence. And I felt presumptuous, foolish and embarrassed.

I didn't want Mom to know anything about it, so I took my notebook and pens and slipped unseen out back. I ran to the road, feeling like a little kid on an adventure. Without thinking I turned in the direction of the secret place Joey had shown me earlier in the summer.

Three days had passed, and Joey had not yet come back. Jack was white-faced and grim. I was scared. Roy smiled as if he was pleased about the whole thing. Jack had called the police, but they refused to do anything. Sixteen-year-old boys apparently took off too frequently for the authorities to list them as missing persons after only a couple of days.

I wanted to write about Joey. I wanted to somehow make sense of my feelings for my friend – the one who was so sure and safe and gentle. The one who had simply walked out on us all because we took too much and wouldn't let him be.

Turning off the road, I darted between the bushes, and awkwardly scaled the dune. Joey was lying in the sand at the bottom. I thought he was dead.

I let out a strangled yelp, and suddenly Joey opened his eyes, stared up at me sleepily, then grinned.

"Hey Sandy," he said and yawned.

I slid down the dune, dropping my notebook and pens, and pounced on him. He grabbed my arms and laughed.

"Where have you been?" I demanded. "Jack thinks you must be dead or something."

Joey's face hardened slightly. It struck me that he looked a little like Jack after all.

"I went up t..to the end of the Point. Always w..wanted to, but before I was afraid t..to." He looked at me, his eyes suddenly soft and warm as they had always been.

"Were the deer there?"

He nodded.

"I s..slept in a meadow. Jeez, it was cold and wet in the m..morning. But the d..deer were grazing just a few f..feet from me. Like Dad said they did."

We sat in silence for a minute while I looked at him. He was dirty and tired looking. He smelled and there was a smear on his shirt where mustard or something had spilled and been wiped off. I wanted to sit close to him.

"I m..managed really well," he said, his voice proud. "Th..there's a campground at the end, with a s..snackbar. I ordered what I wanted and I didn't spill the change. You know, I have nightmares about m..money falling out of my hands, into the s..sand. Th..they didn't laugh at me. One guy m..made fun of me – g..got mad when I had trouble ordering. But I told him to go to hell – didn't s..stutter either. The owner waited on me, then reamed that g..guy out when he thought I w..was out of earshot. I've never f..fought for myself that way before," he said simply. "Jack always l..looked after me."

I had always envied him Jack. Maybe that was why I had loved Joey so much, wanting a closeness from him that he gave to Jack. Now I saw that it had been all wrong – like Daddy and his Dream Girl.

"Do you hate him?"

Joey looked at me, his eyes wide.

"Jack? How could I h..hate Jack?"

"But he used you! He used you to make himself feel important. He took your love and he used you!" My fists had clenched themselves, and my shoulders began to shake. I didn't care. "He said he loved you and he hurt you. How can you not hate someone who hurts you like that?"

Joey bit his lips and stared at me, frowning.

"How can you not be hurt wh..when you love someone?" he asked. The sun was so warm and bright in our secret place. I felt so cold and grey. "I used J..Jack too. If someone uses you, and y..you stick around for it, then you've g..got to be using them too. If you're that c..close to someone, that involved with th..them, then probably some of it will hurt. N..nothing stays easy or perfect. I..it got too much f..for me wh..when Jack was laying P..Pam. Everything ch..changed. I held him d..down, because I c..can't...I couldn't. Maybe it w..will be alright after a wh..while, do you think Sandy?"

His voice had changed, become frightened and reaching. I pulled myself from the greyness. He needed me, and I didn't want to leave him alone again. I didn't want to hurt my special friend any more.

Everything was quiet and hot and still. His face was white and strong somehow. He was better at facing the things that hurt than I was. He had never tried to become a Dream Girl. I wanted to be strong like he was. I wanted to help him, to accept the hurt that came with love, and not pretend any more. And I didn't know if I could, so I became angry.

"I don't know anything about it," I said harshly, my head down. But when I looked at him, his eyes seemed strong and steady, even when they were afraid. "Are you sure there's something wrong with you?"

"I..I couldn't with P..Pam."

"Well, are you so damn sure that you really wanted to!" I snapped. "I mean, she's not that great, and besides, you'd end up at least third in line after Donny and Jack. And aren't you sick of always coming in second after Jack? I'll bet you weren't offered first crack at her."

Joey stared at me, and then suddenly he laughed aloud, strong and sure again.

"Sandy," he said, grabbing my arms again. "Y..you are such a bitch, and," he said, his voice soft, his head near mine, "I l..love you, you know. Y..you're right. I didn't want P..Pam. But I really love you."

"I know," I sighed. "You're the only one who likes me, even when I'm a bitch."

He grinned and pulled me closer, hard against him. His arm went around my shoulder, and his hands began sliding over me.

"And you l..love me?"

"Yeah," I snapped. "You know I do."

I really did. I really do.

Chapter 19

The twins were sauntering down the road toward me when I went to the mailbox, and I was relieved and jealous to see them laughing together. Absently I took the letters out of the box while I tried to make sense of what I felt. Maybe this was the hurt part of loving Joey – there would always be something special between him and Jack. But then I thought suddenly, if we tried to absorb each other, it would be the same as Daddy and his Dream Girl, or Jack dominating Joey the way he used to. I didn't know and I didn't especially care. I was just suddenly afraid of trying to own Joey, or selfishly trying to twist him into something I wanted. Just like Daddy and me.

"Hey Sandy," Jack greeted me cheerfully.

I was afraid Joey would put his arm around me, or try to kiss me or something. I didn't want a teen romance like Donny and Pam. But he didn't – he just smiled at me.

We had talked for a long while afterwards, a long, slow, lazy talk of coming to terms with ourselves – our old selves that had become new but stayed old just the same. I told him about my father and mother. He listened and said nothing. He told me about Jack and his father. I listened but threw my two cents worth in. I guess I don't change that much. Then we both went home.

"Hey S..Sandy," Joey said, "Jack and I talked it over. If I c..can get the money together, I'm going to college this fall."

"Yeah," Jack grimaced. "I'm going to keep the home fires burning. We only need about three hundred more. We might be able to get a loan or something for the rest. We can't count on Joey earning anything."

"Well, maybe he'll surprise you," I snapped.

Jack rolled his eyes.

"Don't you ever back off?" he demanded. I stuck out my tongue at him.

"I'm going to t..try to earn some money," Joey grinned. "B..but who knows if I can. W..we're not counting on it, that's all."

I wanted to ask Joey if he was scared, but I knew he was anyway. When the first delight in grabbing his life away from Jack had worn off, he would be scared again. Just like me.

I looked at them, wondering if I'd know when they were scared. I felt I had a new awareness of how they felt, but I didn't have any confidence in it lasting or even emerging when it was needed. I don't know if I'll ever be the person I want to be, the person I like to imagine myself as. My thoughts and actions don't fly with the people I care about. They bump and collide, avoid and interfere with theirs. But at least now I knew it and could try.

"Got any hot dogs for a couple of starving friends?" Jack interrupted my thoughts.

"Come back, Sandy." Joey laughed and took my arm. "You're t..treating us to a celebration lunch."

"Gee that's nice of me," I said as they guided me forcefully up to the summer house.

"We thought so," Jack grinned.

I liked the feel of them on either side of me. I wondered how they felt, or if Joey and I felt different after yesterday. I liked watching them lounge on our shabby furniture while I made lunch. My mother came in with a pie from Mrs. Patterson, and was appropriately greeted with cheers from the twins.

"What was in the mail?" she asked, setting the pie on the table and picking up the letters I'd dropped.

I frowned, trying to remember.

"I don't think I looked."

"Well, there's one here for you Sandy – from the magazine you entered your story in."

She passed it to me, and I looked at it for

a long time. It was so crisp and neat looking with my name typed on the front.

"Well?" My mother was biting her lip. I grinned foolishly, shrugged, and opened the letter.

"Well?" my mother demanded again.

I looked at her, bewildered.

"They picked ten. Mine was third." I pulled out a blue, imprinted check. "They sent me three hundred dollars and the story will be printed in the Christmas issue."

I grinned foolishly while Joey and Jack whooped and thumped me on the back. Mom hugged me and started to cry. I flopped into the big easy chair and tried to get my breathing back to normal.

"I knew you had talent! I knew it," Mom repeated fiercely to herself, as if that was the question that had mattered. "Why don't you phone your father right now?"

And suddenly everything was hollow again, and my victory turned in on me, hurting me, making me small and vulnerable to them. I shook my head, letting it drop so the hair would hide my eyes.

"All this excitement," I murmured. "I need to get some fresh air or something."

I no longer wanted to walk into the water, to lose myself and my hurts within it. But I loved its swishing, lapping, and sliding eternal rhythm. I dug my toes into the soft, cool sand and watched the small waves slide over them, covering and smoothing. Now I knew why Roy loved the Point so much. Because you were so small, it made you big after a while. It was like the water, you could give yourself to it and be absorbed, slowly, caressingly. You could pull yourself away from the pain and live in a limbo of skies and water and drifting sand. You could become as empty as last year's dun-colored stalks that still stood upright, hidden amid the green offspring that crowded energetically around them.

Joey came and stood beside me in the sand. I was glad that he had followed me, known that I was too alone.

We sat on the beach in the sun, and were quiet together. I was beyond thinking, finding a reason to be only in the fact that I did exist.

After awhile Jack came down to the water's edge.

"Just as well you didn't try to phone your old man," Jack said dispassionately. "He just showed up at the door, Sandy. Your mom wants you to go up to the house."

I looked at Joey, tried to smile then shrugged. I stared at the sand all the way up to the house. It wasn't solid. It was beautiful and I liked to play in it and feel the sun, but it wasn't solid. The sand fairies weren't real. My mother and father were.

They were together. I hadn't seen them together for years. None of us had been very good at surviving. We'd all been brangling too much to be together.

I stared at them, not having any words. My mother slumped on the sofa. My father sat on the arm, his elbow resting on the back of the sofa, his stiff-fingered hand supporting the back of his head.

They stared at me. They had no words either.

"Well! This is stupid," my father exploded. Then his words trickled away again. "I'm sorry, Sandy," he said finally.

I nodded.

"You should have asked me for the picture," I stated flatly, feeling no emotion.

My father smiled wryly. "What would you have said, Dream Girl?"

I laughed suddenly, seeing the farce we were now embarked on.

"I would have told you to stop calling me Dream Girl. She's something you made up, Dad – your vision of perfection and innocence. And then..." He looked at me, his eyebrows raised, questioning. "And then I would have told you to go to hell because it was my picture!"

He threw back his head and laughed, and I grinned at him. I had missed my Daddy, my father. His laugh was loud and his absorbing gaze was charming and seductive, especially for me.

"And then you know what?" I went on, drawing him back with my clear vision of him. "And then, you would have taken it anyway, you son of a bitch!"

My father's laughter stopped and he stared at me, his eyes challenging and somehow delighted and alive. I could see him, and I knew that he could see me. I knew that I existed for him.

I looked then at my mother. She had watched us, listened, understood what we said to each other. But she had no words to say. She could never compete with my father. There was no charm of joy and mischief in her. Yet she loved me. You can't measure someone else's love, but I knew it was there, that it was deep, probably deeper than my father's would ever be. She still wanted my father's love and looked for it in me. But she claimed me for herself, almost as though I had sprung from her only.

"Did you tell Dad that I've dredged some talent up after all?" I said, dropping down on the sofa beside her. She grabbed my hand and squeezed it, even as she turned eagerly to my father, forgetting me.

*   *   *

Summer drifted into autumn. I gave my prize money to Joey. Jack insisted it was only a loan until they finished their education and could pay me back. Joey just smiled. But the day Mrs. Creyton closed the gift shop for the last time, Joey took me into the cluttered store, bought the little porcelain toad and put it in my hands.

The next day, white-faced and stern looking, Joey got on the bus in Simcoe and left for university. Jack and I shouted goodbye until we were hoarse, then drove silently back to the Point.

All through the fall I traveled the school bus to the regional high school. Every day after school, I would drop by the store and visit with Jack.

Roy Cilento died three weeks after Christmas. He was buried beside his wife behind the tiny, white frame church. I wonder if his spirit rests, or if it still roams, dreaming and alone across the marshes and the sands.

A month later Jack and Joey sold the store and the old pick-up and went back to the city together. We wrote to each other often with the grim faithfulness of people who are scared and need each other.

When my mother told me the next spring that she had decided we were ready to face the city again, we bought an old house near the university. Jack and Joey helped us repair and paint it. My mother picked up with her old friends, made new ones, and secured a job with one of the top radio stations. He life became full and bustling and for the first time since I could remember, she was happy. She had many men friends, which seemed to infuriate my father, but she became close to none of them.

My father was back in my life again. Once or twice a week, I would drop by the studio, make tea, and watch him work for a while. Sometimes I was alone with him. Sometimes I was one of several adoring students that he had taken a fancy to. But I was special to him after all. I learned that he cared that I admired his paintings, and trusted me to always believe in him. He would take me out for dinner, introduce me to his friends as his Dream Girl, and forget me when he became absorbed in his work.

The painting, *Dream Girl Catching Toads*, still hangs in one of the New York art galleries.

Joey won a big award for research he's doing at the university last year, and with the prize money he took me to New York for a week. It was very strange to see my picture again, hung amid hundreds of other works of art where the people softly wandered by. No one knew it had been me and mine.

Sometimes I still dream that I'm chasing toads in the velvet evening, but it's me, Sandy, who catches those golden-eyed creatures. I left the Dream Girl in New York, posed between the ugly toad and her Daddy on that beach so long ago.

Thank you for reading
Catching Toads

If you enjoyed this, please leave a review on
Amazon.com (even a sentence helps!) so that other
readers can more easily find *Catching Toads*.

You can find more exciting books by
Susan Brown at www.susanbrownwrites.com

And keep reading for excerpts from
other books by Susan Brown.

Enjoy!

And now a Sneak Peek at

Twelve

Another city, another run-down hotel. Jared longs for a normal life, but he is haunted by the Song that no one else hears and lured by the Stones that no one else sees. As Jared and his twin, Meghan, are dragged into the ancient battle, they are mercilessly stalked by the Titan, Kronos, risen from his prison to challenge the millennia of human dominance.

Frantic to save his family, Jared dares to learn the truth about his heritage. He wants to run, but the rocks show him what is at stake. Somehow, he will have to protect the Twelve Stones and defeat Kronos. Nothing else can save humanity.

Dip into this thrilling story that weaves the world's mythology with a heart-pounding tale of what it means to be human.

First Place Winner in Chanticleer's International Book Awards Competition.

Not Yet Summer

Shuttled from one foster home to another, Marylee has never belonged anywhere. When she finds an abandoned baby, she is determined not to ever let April feel as unloved as she has. In desperation, she cons Petey, another neglected kid, into helping her raise the baby.

But what kind of life can she give April really? And what is happening to Petey? Marylee never knew that loving could hurt so much.

A new edition of the best-selling book from Scholastic Canada.

Find these and other books at
www.susanbrownwrites.com

Twelve

by

Susan Brown

Bodhhgaya, India

Transformation

At first Deirdre grips the six-year-old twins' hands tightly, and at first Jared and Meghan are happy to press close. Jared twists to look back at the hotel sign, and stares at the letters: Hotel Bodhgaya Ashok. He doesn't know what the last two words are. He doesn't know where he is, except this place is called India. Most of the buildings have signs, but the words are written in the curly-cues and slants that his mother says is Indian writing.

Jared can't make it out.

This city makes him afraid, with its hot, hot air. Dust rises in the streets, so that when the wind blows he can see nothing but a reddish cloud. The crowded, smelly train had frightened him. Everyone shouted and laughed and talked in words he couldn't understand. The bus after that was worse – more crowded and smellier.

When Deirdre pauses for a moment, Jared shuts his eyes and tries again to imagine the place that is green and safe with a pattern of pink flowers on the floor. But with a jab of fear, he remembers that even in the dream, there are shadows lurking in cupboards and behind stone walls. He opens his eyes again and looks at his twin, but she is busy staring at everything.

Meghan isn't afraid at all. Ever. She loves this hot, strange place and is determined to meet all the people and try all the food sold from roadside tents. She tugs her hand loose, and before Deirdre can stop her, darts away, disappearing into the crowd.

"Oh, drat her!" Deirdre exclaims. She stands Jared by a tree. "Don't move. Not one step!"

She runs in search of her daughter.

Jared looks in every direction. Kronos, The Man Who Watches is staring at them again. Jared can feel it. His mother won't notice him while she chases Meghan.

There. At the edge of the streaming crowd...Jared sees the burning eyes in the pale face. Despite the still air, Kronos' black hair looks like it has been thrashed by a storm. Jared knows that no one else in the pushing crowd sees Kronos. If they did, their shadowed eyes would open wide with fear and their muttering voices would rise into screams. Kronos raises a hand to Jared, beckoning, commanding. Sunlight glimmers on his golden mark.

Jared squeezes his eyes shut, breathing hard, fighting the urge to follow the beckoning hand. His Mama told him to stay put.

"Jared!" Deirdre grabs his hand. He opens his eyes with relief. "At least one of you will stand still." She glares at Meghan who laughs and tosses her fire-red hair.

"The grandpa was nice." Meghan holds up a small orange that a toothless old man has given her.

Jared looks back to Kronos. He is gone now. With his mother and sister, Jared joins the mass of people walking down the road to the temple.

"This is the holiest place in India," Deirdre tells them. "The monks know things we don't understand. I hope..." She bites her lip. "I think they might help us..."

The temple rises like a pointed ant hill. Low walls of carved pinky-red rock direct the flow of the crowd. Most people swarm along a walkway. It looks like a parade with all the flowers and fluttering silk scarves. Deirdre pulls them forward, down stone steps and past another stream of people walking round and round the temple. Jared nearly falls over a man lying on his stomach with his arms stretched out.

"Is he hurt?" He clutches his mother's hand more tightly.

"No, he's praying." She steers them past more people lying on their stomachs and over to a wall, out of the press of people. "Shoes off, kids. We can't wear them in the temple."

His mom puts their shoes in her bag, and then in sock feet, they rejoin the crowd.

People pour through the gate and towards a huge open door. Jared, Meghan and Deirdre are swept along with them into a cool, dim room. Everyone sits on the floor.

An old man in baggy yellow clothes with a red shawl over one shoulder is speaking to the seated people. Deirdre leans forward, hands twisting in her lap. Jared's eyes fix on a huge gold statue of a seated man. Buddha. Many of the people are bowing to the statue. Meghan elbows her twin and points around the room. Every wall and even the ceiling are decorated with vast pictures. While the old man talks and talks, Jared stares open-mouthed at the paintings of scenery, people, gods and demons. Some are happy; some are crying; some are writhing their many arms and showing fangs.

One picture draws his eyes. It is The Man Who Watches, riding a horse breathing fire from its mouth and striking flames from its hooves. Jared hears the hoof beats, smells the acrid smoke...

"No!" he whispers. The sounds and smells fade. He thinks the smiling statue of Buddha may have chased Kronos away.

The old man at the front stops talking. Their mother surges up from the pillows and taking each of them by hand, approaches a yellow-robed monk.

"Excuse me," she says, "I have an appointment to see His Holiness Lama Choedak Jamyang." She drops the twins' hands to pull a letter from her bag. Her voice trembles. "I was told he can help me."

The monk nods. "He expects you. Also, his Holiness Lama Satya asks permission to visit with your children."

Deirdre looks at them doubtfully. "I don't know..."

"I'm not going," Meghan grips her mother's hand. "I want to come with you, Mama, and give our presents to the llama."

The monk looks calmly at Jared.

"I'll go," Jared says. Why did he say that?

The monk bows, hands pressed together. Another young monk appears at his side. Deirdre and Meghan go with him. Nervously, Jared follows the older one along narrow corridors filled with weird smells and quiet footsteps.

"It is custom to bow three times when entering the presence of His Holiness," the monk whispers and opens a door. Jared steps into a room ablaze with color. Red walls are highlighted by yellow cloth that hangs like curtains or drapes across the furniture. A soccer ball lies under a table. On a raised platform, a boy about ten, sits cross-legged. He is dressed like the monks.

Jared stares, then says, "Hi." Behind him, the monk is bowing.

The boy smiles. "Hi, Jared," he replies. "Didn't Meghan come?"

Jared shakes his head. "She's with my mother."

The boy's expression becomes serious again and he jumps down from the platform. "I am sorry she is not here. I have something important to show you."

He heads out of the room and down the hallway. Not knowing what else to do, Jared follows. They walk down several more narrow corridors, all scented like smoky flowers, then come into the sunlight in an open courtyard. A large twisted tree grows in the center. Bits of gold glimmer on its trunk. Masses of flowers are strewn on the ground and white scarves tied to the branches lift and fall in the breeze.

Jared thinks the place should be full of people, but he and the boy are alone.

"It is under the ancestor of this fig tree that Buddha received enlightenment," the boy says. "And here," he leads Jared to a slab of brick-red stone, "is the stone on which he sat. It is the only stone strong enough to have held the world together when the transformation came. It is the center of the universe."

As though he had been told to do it, Jared steps forward and stands on the stone. Heat gathers in a pool, rises through his feet and floats up into his body, lifting him into the air.

"I'm flying!" he cries. "Can Meghan come and do this?"

The boy shakes his head. "There is only this one moment when the flow of time has stilled and she did not come. You alone are chosen."

Jared flaps his arms trying to rise higher.

The boy takes something from inside his robe – a stone, the same reddish color as the one Jared hovers over. He offers it. "I have guarded this for you through all my lifetimes. It is carved with the eyes of Buddha and holds the key to transformation and enlightenment."

"What's that?" Jared's hands close on the rock and his mind glows.

"The ancient gods cannot change. They are what they are. Neither love nor death nor suffering can transform their hearts and spirits. Only humans can become more than they were. One day people may become greater than the gods. They fear this."

"Jared!" Deirdre's voice pierces the air. Startled, Jared's feet touch the ground and he jumps off the stone. Like ghosts melting back into reality, people and chatter fill the courtyard. The stone is now covered in bright cloth, with oranges, money, and bowls of rice heaped over it. The boy smiles, then walks back into the temple.

Deirdre and Meghan run to Jared. "Thank goodness!" Deirdre hugs him. "None of the other monks spoke English. I thought I'd lost you."

"There wasn't a llama," Meghan complains as they put their shoes back on. "Just an old man with glasses. Did you see a llama?"

Jared shakes his head. "Just a boy. He gave me a stone."

For the first time Jared really looks at it. The eyes of Buddha look back. More of the curly writing he can't read has been carved into the stone.

"The old man gave me a handkerchief." Meghan displays a small square of white silk with a faded picture and the same curly writing.

"Well, at least you two got something out of this trip." Deirdre takes their hands and hauls them toward the gate. "Come on kids, we have hurry. If we're lucky, we can still make it to New York by next Friday. Pat has an audition set up for me."

"I thought we were staying," Jared protests.

"No," Deirdre says. "The Lama says he can't protect me from my demons. We have to keep going."

Part I

Seattle, Washington

Chapter 1

The Song

March rain splattered down, cold and insistent, as fifteen-year-old Jared stepped off the San Francisco to Seattle bus and looked around. Another city, another bus station. He hefted his backpack onto his shoulders and took a couple of quick steps to catch up to his mom and Meghan. It had seemed like a miracle when this job came through – they'd been down to their last hundred dollars. If the job worked out, if they didn't have to run, the family might get a few dollars into a savings account again.

If they didn't have to run. Head down, eyelids slightly lowered, Jared scanned the milling crowds. A grandmother here, a homeless man there, a few kids running wild while their harassed parents groped through bags. Nothing to set the short hairs on his neck prickling. No hint of the hunters who never gave up, never seemed to rest.

Meghan and his mom had paused in front of a snack bar, Meghan clearly arguing to immediately make up for their missed lunch; his mom just as clearly urging for her to wait, to conserve their few remaining dollars. Jared swept his eyes over the crowd again. Everything ordinary. He let out his pent-up breath and eased through the jostling crowd of travelers.

And then...*the Song*. Jared stopped cold. He could feel sweat forming on his forehead and upper lip. He could hear it – the singing had started again.

He lifted his head like a dog to a scent. The singing was clear, very clear. This time... surely this time, he would be able to make out the words. Jared shook his head, tried to separate the unearthly melody from noises surrounding him – the growl of traffic, shouting passengers, and drumming rain. But there was too much confusion.

Over there...the singing came from the end of the station. He ran through the crowd, dodging bags, boxes and people. At an empty loading platform, he stopped and shut his eyes tightly. This time he would arrow himself to the source of the singing – finally hear all the words.

A picture crowded into his mind. He could hear everything in the bus terminal, but behind it, like a brightening movie screen, the thrumming began...

Noise of a heart beating too fast...beating in terror....
Fist clutching....

Behind...red eyes...the red-eared dogs of night... howling...closer...closer....hunting through the woods... baying for blood...

Heart throbbing...

But the last Guardian will follow the lines of power and sing the Song of Light...He begins the chanting melody...it lifts into the wind.

Jared can hear it now...it fills him again...he can sing with the old man...

A hard hand tugged his sleeve. "Hey kid, spare some change?"

The Song shattered. Jared blinked, confused. A raggedy teenager, only a couple of years older than himself, held out her hand. Her eyes were grey nuggets in a white face.

"What?"

"Change," the girl whined. "I got nowhere to sleep. Nothing to eat...you got some money? Something in your pack to help me out?"

Her hand inserted itself under the flap, fingers searching.

"No way," Jared twisted away. "Hey! What do you think you're doing?"

"I could trade," the girl whispered. "I got this to trade..."

She held up her fist, so close to Jared's face that he could scarcely make out the twisted shape of a tattoo above the knuckle of her middle finger. It seemed to be a distorted spider...shimmering in front of his eyes.

"Hey! Get away!" the girl shrieked.

A black and white dog pushed between Jared and the girl, growling deep in its throat. The girl faltered back, made shooing motions with her hands, then with a hoarse sob turned and ran. The dog's growling stopped, his head raised and with an air of all business taken care of, scratched his ear with a hind foot. Without a glance at Jared, he turned and trotted through the crowds.

"Now, that was weird," Jared muttered. Almost as weird, he thought, as trying to learn a Song that no one else could hear. Or as weird as carrying ten heavy rocks in his backpack and one more stone in his pocket as his family gypsied around the world. The Song was silent again. Slowly, he wove back through the thinning crowd to his mom and sister.

"Jared," his mom's voice rose over the hubbub. "Get the bags, hon."

His small family had not paid any attention to his dash through the crowd. Jared wasn't really surprised – he had long since become aware that the Song sometimes suppressed time, or memory, or just plain noticing. With a nod to his mom, he picked up two suitcases; Meghan dropped the bag she'd held to push back her long red hair with both hands.

"The rain's turning me into a frizzball." She pulled an elastic from her pocket and caught her hair into a fat ponytail. Like her brother, she carried a bulging, frayed backpack over her shoulders. Hers was weighted down with books, music and a flute; Jared's shoulders ached with the weight of his fist-sized rocks.

"Now, if you just turn left, Mrs. Singer," the ticket agent was telling their mother, "and go along Stewart about two blocks, there's the Regency Inn right there." He beamed at her. "It's a nice place. Better than that Carmen Hotel you were talking about."

"Thank you, so much." Deirdre smiled charmingly and turned back to her children.

"Another guy?" Meghan teased softly. She hoisted her bag higher on her shoulders.

"Oh, don't be silly," her mom shushed her. "He's just a nice person trying to be helpful." She picked up her own suitcase and led them toward the street.

Outside the station, an old man with a curling white beard sat with a sign:

Real Change, Seattle's Homeless Newspaper.
Help the Homeless Help Themselves.

Jared eyed at the man's tattered clothes and turned his head away. His stomach knotted. Homeless came after broke. His family was awfully close to broke....

Meghan's gaze slid past the dirt and rips, up to the man's face. She smiled. "Wet today," she said.

His clear eyes sparkled. "Not so bad as yesterday. It'll come onto sun in a bit. Have a good afternoon."

"Thank you," she called back.

"Why'd you talk to him?" Jared hissed.

"Why didn't you?" she retorted. "He's broke. That's hard enough without being invisible, too."

Jared flushed and glanced back. The black and white dog stood with its front paws propped on the old man's knees. His master was talking to him and gently rubbing his ears.

The family trudged down Stewart Street, giving the Regency Inn only a brief look of regret. The Seattle Space Needle, built for the '62 World's Fair, towered in the distance.

Above, city crows wheeled and squawked. At Sixth Avenue they turned left, away from the Space Needle, and kept on walking. Expensive shops gave way to shabby stores. To his right, down a steep hill, Jared could see the rippling glint of Puget Sound.

"How far is it?" Meghan grunted.

"Another couple of blocks. It's very central – close to Pike Place Market and the historic part of town," Deirdre Singer said.

Jared and Meghan exchanged depressed glances. Historic always meant old and run-down when it came to their rooms.

Rain fell more heavily. Jared's dark hair slicked down and hung in his eyes. Despite the ponytail, Meghan's writhed into tight corkscrews. Finally, they cut through a parking lot to a grey hotel crouched behind an office building.

"Sweet," Meghan muttered.

The door squealed. Light barely penetrated the lobby. Behind the counter, a young man put down his phone, and stood to greet them with a wide smile.

Jared dropped the bags. An air of mildew and dust drifted upward from the threadbare carpet. An ancient elevator clanked open. No one got out.

"Ghosts," Meghan whispered.

Their mom headed to the desk.

"Welcome to The Carmen," the clerk said. "Marquis is my name, and I'm here to make your stay as comfortable as your favorite dream. Your name, please, Ma'am?"

"Deirdre Singer. My children and I have a reservation."

Marquis typed something into a computer.

"Yes, Ma'am, here it is." Marquis smiled widely again. "Six weeks. That's a long time to be sightseeing."

"I'll be working. I have a role in *The Phantom of the Opera* revival."

"No way!" Marquis exclaimed. "I thought they all was staying at the Warwick."

"The main players are. I have a small part a friend arranged for me."

"You sing then?"

"Whenever I can."

"Well, well!" Marquis rubbed his hands together. "A star staying at our hotel. I'll give you the best efficiency suite in the house. Big and at the back. None of that traffic noise. Fully equipped with a range top, fridge and dishes. And no extra charge!"

"Thank you." Mrs. Singer smiled. "We appreciate it."

"Yes, Ma'am. Comfortable as a dream. Take the elevator to sixth floor then turn right.

Corner room on your left."

The twins picked up the bags and followed their mom into the elevator.

"I think this dream's going to be a nightmare," Meghan said. The doors crashed shut, opened a couple of inches, and then banged shut again.

"At least there's a nice desk clerk," Mrs. Singer pointed out. "That makes it more pleasant."

"And the hotel's in a business area," Jared added. "We can go sightseeing without getting mugged."

Over the last few years, the hotels had gotten worse and worse as their mom struggled harder and harder for bit parts in the operas and traveling musical productions that supported them. Most big cities had their own opera companies and regular theater players. Deirdre picked up the leavings – this time taking a part in the chorus. The contracted actor had broken her leg.

That was the way it always was now. Sometimes a singer would get sick, or take time off for a baby, or quarrel with the director. The production company would frantically call the agents, and Pat, their mom's agent would call Deirdre, telling her what city she had to get to – right away.

"I fill in for disaster," Deirdre had said wryly.

The elevator clanged to a stop. The doors

squealed open.

A young man, unshaven with greasy hair, eyed them from the hall.

"Up or down?" he demanded.

"Up," Deirdre said.

He grunted. Deirdre pushed the "Close Door" button. Nothing happened. They stared at the man in the hall and he stared at them. His eyes slid over to Meghan and his expression changed. Jared stepped in front of his sister. She elbowed him.

"What floor..." Deirdre began to ask. The doors clanged shut.

"I know I'm going to just love this place," Meghan said.

"Only six weeks, sweetie. Seattle's a great city. When the weather clears we can rent a car and drive to the ocean beaches. They're spectacular."

A sudden memory of sound...pounding waves...pounding footsteps. Jared stiffened. The call was from a place by the ocean. But, how could his whole family have been maneuvered here from hundreds of miles away? Did the magic in the rocks completely control their lives?

Automatically, Jared closed his fingers around the rock in his pocket...remembering.

Not Yet Summer

by

Susan Brown

Prologue

For almost seven years the warehouse had been empty. Once the town had made a profit leasing it to a succession of companies, but now it was too small for modern business needs, and so it stood abandoned and unnoticed among the squat, grey buildings that lined the cemented-up banks of the town's dying stream. As winter turned to summer and then to winter again, the building became rundown, its windows broken, the locks on the doors smashed. There was no money available either to tear down or to modernize the warehouse; so it stood as it was, empty, except for occasional strays that took refuge before looking elsewhere for a home.

Chapter One

Marylee

When the alarm clock went off, Marylee slapped it with her hand, then lay back, trying to recapture the haven of sleep. There had been a dream – a rare thing of happiness and warmth. It lingered in her consciousness like beads of sunlight strung out in a haze, warming and drawing her. If she could just sleep awhile longer....

"Marylee!" Mrs. Watson rapped sharply on the door to her bedroom. "Get up. I heard that alarm, so there's no use pretending you didn't. You'd better not be late for school again!"

Marylee heard her walking briskly down the hall and pictured her squat form, her small-featured face. Her foster mother's face was routinely kind, but somehow it never warmed to affection.

Reluctantly Marylee opened her eyes. She stared at the blue wall with the framed magazine picture of a boy hauling in a fish from a foaming stream.

It was one of the two things in the room she really cared for – in spite of the grinning boy. The rest of the room was like the intent of the picture – square, dull and boyish. The Watsons had always had boys as foster children before, and the room was still impersonally geared to the male gender. The only concession to her sex was the bouquet of artificial flowers hastily stuck in one corner.

Except for the boy's intrusion into the scene, the picture evoked a wild freedom that Marylee longed for. There were old trees, some bent, some upright, all crowding down to the stream. The water gurgled and rushed over the rocks, foaming around the jagged edges. Way off in the background were mountains, misty blue and solitary.

Once, between foster homes, Marylee had been sent to a camp in country like that – a magic time. Her raging soul had emptied into the laughing water, and the twisting hurt and loneliness had drifted away into a haze. The silent trees had crowded close, feeling warm and loving when she stretched her childish arms around them. She had never cared for the lifelessness of her doll after that – after she had hugged the cool, living warmth of the great trees.

And the counselor had not told Marylee she was odd when she had whispered that she imagined the trees as people who would love her and sweep down their leaves to hug her. The gentle woman had smiled, and three days later had given her a book about four children who had found a country where trees walked and animals talked. She still had the book, ragged now from her love of it, carefully placed in the locked box where she kept her few treasures.

But the camp had been almost six years ago, when she was only eight – when her short, weak leg had simply made her feel miserably different from the other people who drifted into and out of her life. She had been too young then to realize that her lameness was a curse, the reason she was always alone, always alone and hated.

"Marylee!" Mrs. Watson called sharply. "For heaven's sake, are you going to get up?"

Marylee's lips pursed as familiar hatred drove the old memories away. Resentfully she pulled herself up and finally lurched out of bed. She was hungry. Might as well get up and eat.

But first she paused to examine the pale green flower shoots in the plastic pot balanced on the narrow window ledge. Marylee had filled the pot with earth from the garden as soon as the ground had thawed, almost a month ago. Before long the small shoots would bud and then flower.

A slight smile, stiff because it so rarely appeared, hovered on her lips. She loved small, growing things, things she could care for and make blossom. Once someone had said that she had "a way" with her. Marylee still cherished that stray compliment.

The kitchen smelled good when she finally limped downstairs. Pancakes and sausages, she noted with a tinge of pleasure. Mrs. Watson was a good cook, and as people went, she wasn't too bad. She talked too much about Marylee's limp, but at least she didn't look away or drip sickening pity over her, as most people did.

Once Marylee had thought the people cared and had been merely embarrassed by their reactions. But as little incident had piled on little incident over the years, her naive hopes about people had been worn away, leaving only a cynical hatred of them all.

"Good morning," Mrs. Watson said, too brightly.

Marylee sat down wordlessly and helped herself from the heaped plates on the table.

"There's something I have to talk to you about, dear," Mrs. Watson began after an uncomfortable pause.

Marylee looked up at her for a moment and clenched her jaw slightly. She hated that false word, "dear." When people called her that, they never meant it.

Nervously Mrs. Watson wiped her hands on a towel.

"Mr. Watson and I have talked about this a lot lately, so I don't want you to think it's a hasty decision. Or a personal one either," she added, with an embarrassed titter that was foreign to her normal manner. "But we feel we're really too old to continue parenting as we have in the past. We want to live our lives more for our own enjoyment now – travel a bit, get prepared for our retirement. So I'm afraid we'll have to give you up. We've already told Mrs. Wojansky of our decision, and the Children's Aid are trying hard to find a new home for you. I hope you understand our position, dear...."

There was a long, cold pause as, fork suspended halfway to her mouth, Marylee stared at her foster mother.

"Yeah, sure. Why not?" she said loudly, indifferently.

Deliberately she resumed eating, trying to ignore the sick feeling of fear churning in her stomach. Another home – another set of people to discover how much they really didn't like her.

I hate them. I hate them.... The words ground through her mind. But she had to seem normal. She had to go upstairs, brush her teeth, collect her books and sweater.

She found herself counting everything – the number of times the toothbrush slid over her teeth, the number of steps she took to cross the hall and enter her room, the number of papers she flipped through to find her homework page.

One, two, three, four, five... one, two, three... one... one...

Fiercely she bit her lip and forced her mind away from the monotonous drone of the number counting – her instinctive refuge from the searing hurt that was boiling up in her throat.

Oh, how she hated them....

"Time to go to school," Mrs. Watson called up the stairs. "Don't forget to take a sweater. It's not summer yet."

Numbly Marylee picked up her sweater and backpack and left for school.

The spring sun shone at an angle through the broken window of the warehouse, making Marylee's shadow strangely long and distorted on the debris-strewn floor. She didn't notice, however. Her eyes were shut, her body hugged to herself as she tried to raise memories of that beautiful warm forest and stream.

Aspens shiver, red maples wave,
While I and my enemies lie
Still
In the grave.

She shivered with melancholy pleasure at the poem she had made up. But she would have to go soon. They would all be looking for her.

"So who cares!" she whispered, tossing her head so the straight strands of brown hair slid over her shoulders for a moment before they drooped back around her face. She hugged herself tighter, relishing the feelings of hate that had soared through her that morning at school.

The sun, unusually hot and bright for the last day of March, was beating down on the asphalt of the school yard. Marylee leaned back against the wall of the school so that the shadows shrouded her slightly.

A group of girls had organized a game of skipping. Normally they would have felt themselves too mature to indulge in such a childish game, but the sunshine and the fresh air had raised their spirits. A hint of wistfulness grew in Marylee's mind as she watched them. Angela had a new outfit – another of the many things her parents showered on her curly blonde head. She was in the center of the girls now, laughing merrily.

As usual, they ignored Marylee.

She wondered what it would be like to be included in everything the gang did. Well, maybe she'd give it a try. A week or two more – a month at the most – and she'd be gone anyway.

She pulled herself upright and stared at the other girls. Taking a deep breath, she limped toward them, chin lifted. In a moment Marylee stood beside her giggling classmates, waiting stiffly for someone to acknowledge her presence. No one said anything.

"I want to play," she announced loudly.

The other girls looked at her in embarrassment. One of the gushy ones regarded Marylee's leg with obvious pity. "Do you think you should?"

"I want to play!" Marylee repeated in staccato tones.

"You can't just barge in where you haven't been invited. Jeez, are you rude!" Angela remarked, placing her hands on her hips and glaring at Marylee.

"It's a free country," Marylee said defiantly, breathlessly. "If I want to play, I can."

There was a cold pause. Miserably, Marylee realized she had done it all wrong – but there was no way to back down or to smooth over her presence.

"All right, if you want to play," Angela snapped, "then play!" She threw one end of the long skipping rope to another girl, so that Marylee was in the center. Then she began turning the rope.

Desperately Marylee hopped, trying to keep her balance despite her bad leg. Once, twice she managed to jump the rope. But Angela twisted it faster and faster and the rope began slapping Marylee's ankles as it turned first one way and then another.

"You wanted to play," Angela taunted. "Well, play then!"

Marylee stood still, frozen, as the rope snapped painfully across her skin. The circle of giggling girls closed in on her, snickering louder and louder. Marylee's hate churned up, pounded in her head, and finally broke loose.

She grabbed the swinging rope, jerking it out of the girls' hands. Then she shoved Angela, hard. Angela staggered slightly and Marylee pounced on her, pushing and shoving, finally tripping her.

"I'll show you!" Marylee shouted wildly, bouncing heavily onto Angela's stomach. "Have some dirt! It suits you!"

Gleefully she rubbed handfuls of dirt and gravel into Angela's clothes, all the while jabbing at her with her knees.

"Stop it! Stop it!" Angela shrieked. Her eyes were streaming with tears. The other girls stood in a circle, openmouthed and unmoving.

"Bitch! Bitch! Bitch!" Marylee screamed in glorious, roaring hate.

Then suddenly she felt someone pulling on her arms. The roaring died slightly. A teacher yanked Marylee roughly to her feet.

"What's going on here?" she demanded furiously, shaking Marylee's arm. "Who started this?"

"Marylee did!"

"Marylee started it! She shoved Angela down!" "She called her a bitch!"

"She rubbed dirt all over Angela and we couldn't stop her!"

"Marylee!"

The sun was low now, the shadows almost melted. Marylee's shorter, weaker leg had begun to feel numb. Cautiously she flexed her toes, waiting for the pins-and-needles feeling of returning circulation.

I'll take another look at my garden, she told herself. No way she would run home for them.

The garden was a patch of sandy soil where the concrete had broken up. Marylee had spent long, painful hours carrying the heavy chunks of cement to where she could dump them into the sluggish green water of the stream. Her limp had become worse from the strain.

But she had a garden all her own. No one else knew the feel of that coarse sand-dirt, or the rich smell of good peat moss and fertilizer worked into the soil. In her mind she could smell and feel every particle of the ground she was making come alive. Soon there would be flowers – something beautiful left behind even after they sent her to a new foster home.

Well, she could spend lots of time nursing the ragged patch of earth now – the principal had suspended her. There was a lot of talk which had floated by her exhausted indifference. Telephone calls, too. Everyone was informed – Mrs. Wojansky, her case manager, and the Watsons, her soon-not-to-be foster parents.

There were many solemn words, heavy pauses, and meaningful noises from the principal's mouth. Marylee paid no attention;

it didn't matter. Then he told her to go get her things and wait on the bench in the outer office.

She just shrugged at him and tried to saunter casually out of the office. But instead, she limped, her weak leg making the harsh *shuuing* sound she hated. She limped down the empty halls, hearing lonely echoes of other kids in their classes. Once she had retrieved her backpack and sweater, she had slipped out a back entrance and walked to the warehouse – her warehouse. No one knew she came here.

"Who would care anyhow?" she muttered defiantly as she limped across the floor toward the small window. Who cares about *anything*, she thought as she put her head out the square, glassless hole. She folded her elbows on the sill, peered down at the worked soil of her garden below and then out at the smelly stream only a few yards away.

Maybe once you were a real brook, she thought, not all poisoned and crippled by the cement. A real brook....

A shrill bark pierced the quiet. A dog! A dog had trotted up and was digging at her garden, ripping out her seeds!

"Stop! Get away!" Marylee shrieked. She beat her arms, trying desperately to slap the dog away. But the window was too high.

Frantically, she looked around for help. A boy with a lean face and uncombed hair was standing a short distance away, grinning and sipping on a carton of milk.

"Stop him! Please!" she pleaded.

But he just shrugged and stood by indifferently while the dog tore into her seeds.

You can find *Twelve* and *Not Yet Summer*
and Susan's other great books on Amazon.com or at
www.susanbrownwrites.com

About Award-Winning Author, Susan Brown

What if? What if the extraordinary erupts into an ordinary life? Adventure, mystery, and magic fuel Susan Brown's imagination and writing, propelling her towards more and more stories for book-lovers who also live in wonder.

Susan lives with her border collie rescue dogs amid wild woods and overgrown gardens in Snohomish, Washington. From there she supervises her three daughters, assorted sons-in-law and two grandsons. It's a great way to be a writer!

Find more information, free stories, and news about upcoming books at:
http://www.susanbrownwrites.com

Susan Brown is also a founding member of the Writers Cooperative of the Pacific Northwest.
http://www.writers-coop.com

Made in the USA
Monee, IL
11 October 2024

67071144R00203